Selected Stories of Lu Hsun

Selected Stories of Lu Hsun

Lu Hsun

*Translated by
Yang Hsien-yi
and Gladys Yang*

WILDSIDE PRESS
Doylestown, Pennsylvania

Selected Stories of Lu Hsun
A publication of
WILDSIDE PRESS
P.O. Box 301
Holicong, PA 18928–0301

www.wildsidepress.com

Table of Contents

Preface. 7

A Madman's Diary 13

Kung I-Chi. 27

Medicine. 33

Tomorrow 43

An Incident 51

Storm in a Teacup 55

My Old Home 65

The True Story of Ah Q 75

Village Opera. 123

The New Year's Sacrifice. 135

In the Wine Shop. 155

A Happy Family. 167

Soap 175

The Misanthrope 187

Regret for the Past 209

The Divorce. 229

The Flight to the Moon 239

Forging the Swords. 251

Preface

TO THE FIRST COLLECTION OF SHORT STORIES, "CALL TO ARMS"

*W*hen I was young I, too, had many dreams. Most of them came to be forgotten, but I see nothing in this to regret. For although recalling the past may make you happy, it may sometimes also make you lonely, and there is no point in clinging in spirit to lonely bygone days. However, my trouble is that I cannot forget completely, and these stories have resulted from what I have been unable to erase from my memory.

For more than four years I used to go, almost daily, to a pawnbroker's and to a medicine shop. I cannot remember how old I was then; but the counter in the medicine shop was the same height as I, and that in the pawnbroker's twice my height. I used to hand clothes and trinkets up to the counter twice my height, take the money proffered with contempt, then go to the counter the same height as I to buy medicine for my father who had long been ill. On my return home I had other things to keep me busy, for since the physician who made out the prescriptions was very well-known, he used unusual drugs: aloe root dug up in winter, sugar-cane that had been three years exposed to frost, twin crickets, and *ardisia* . . . all of which were difficult to procure. But my father's illness went from bad to worse until he died.

I believe those who sink from prosperity to poverty will probably come, in the process, to understand what the world is really like. I wanted to go to the K—— school* in N—— perhaps because I was in search of a change of scene and faces. There was nothing for my mother to do but to raise eight dollars for my traveling expenses, and say I might do as I pleased. That she cried was only natural, for at that time the proper thing was to study the classics and take the official examinations. Anyone who studied "foreign subjects" was looked down upon as a fellow good for nothing, who, out of desperation, was forced to sell his soul to foreign devils.

Besides, she was sorry to part with me. But in spite of that, I went to N—— and entered the K—— school; and it was there that I heard for the first time the names of such subjects as natural science, arithmetic, geography, history, drawing and physical training. They had no physiology course, but we saw woodblock editions of such works as *A New Course on the Human Body* and *Essays on Chemistry and Hygiene.* Recalling the talk and prescriptions of physicians I had known and comparing them with what I now knew, I came to the conclusion those physicians must be either unwitting or deliberate charlatans; and I began to sympathize with the invalids and families who suffered at their hands. From translated histories I also learned that the Japanese Reformation had originated, to a great extent, with the introduction of Western medical science to Japan.

These inklings took me to a provincial medical college in Japan. I dreamed a beautiful dream that on my return to China I would cure patients like my father, who had been wrongly treated, while if war broke out I would serve as an army doctor, at the same time strengthening my countrymen's faith in reformation.

I do not know what advanced methods are now used to reach microbiology, but at that time lantern slides were used to show the microbes; and if the lecture ended early, the instructor might show slides of natural scenery or news to fill up the time. This was during the Russo-Japanese War, so there were many war films, and I had to join in the clapping

---

* The Kiangnan Naval Academy in Nanking.

and cheering in the lecture hall along with the other students. It was a long time since I had seen any compatriots, but one day I saw a film showing some Chinese, one of whom was bound, while many others stood around him. They were all strong fellows but appeared completely apathetic. According to the commentary, the one with his hands bound was a spy working for the Russians, who was to have his head cut off by the Japanese military as a warning to others, while the Chinese beside him had come to enjoy the spectacle.

Before the term was over I had left for Tokyo, because after this film I felt that medical science was not so important after all. The people of a weak and backward country, however strong and healthy they may be, can only serve to be made examples of, or to witness such futile spectacles; and it doesn't really matter how many of them die of illness. The most important thing, therefore, was to change their spirit, and since at that time I felt that literature was the best means to this end, I determined to promote a literary movement. There were many Chinese students in Tokyo studying law, political science, physics and chemistry, even police work and engineering, but not one studying literature or art. However, even in this uncongenial atmosphere I was fortunate enough to find some kindred spirits. We gathered the few others we needed, and after discussion our first step, of course, was to publish a magazine, the title of which denoted that this was a new birth. As we were then rather classically inclined, we called it *Xin Sheng* (*New Life*).

When the time for publication drew near, some of our contributors dropped out, and then our funds were withdrawn, until finally there were only three of us left, and we were penniless. Since we had started our magazine at an unlucky hour, there was naturally no one to whom we could complain when we failed; but later even we three were destined to part, and our discussions of a dream future had to cease. So ended this abortive *New Life*.

Only later did I feel the futility of it all; at that time I did not really understand anything. Later I felt if a man's proposals met with approval, it should encourage him; if they met with opposition, it should make him fight back; but the real tragedy for him was to lift up his voice among the living and meet with no response, neither approval nor opposition, just as if he were left helpless in a boundless desert. So I began to feel lonely.

And this feeling of loneliness grew day by day, coiling about my soul like a huge poisonous snake. Yet in spite of my unaccountable sadness, I felt no indignation; for this experience had made me reflect and see that I was definitely not the heroic type who could rally multitudes at his call.

However, my loneliness had to be dispelled, for it was causing me agony. So I used various means to dull my senses, both by conforming to the spirit of the time and turning to the past. Later I experienced or witnessed even greater loneliness and sadness, which I do not like to recall, preferring that it should perish with me. Still my attempt to deaden my senses was not unsuccessful — I had lost the enthusiasm and fervor of my youth.

*I*n S———* Hostel there were three rooms where it was said a woman had lived who hanged herself on the locust tree in the courtyard. Although the tree had grown so tall that its branches could no longer be reached, the rooms remained deserted. For some years I stayed here, copying ancient inscriptions. I had few visitors, there were no political problems or issues in those inscriptions, and my only desire was that my life should slip quietly away like this. On summer nights, when there were too many mosquitoes, I would sit under the locust tree, waving my fan and looking at the specks of sky through the thick leaves, while the caterpillars which came out in the evening would fall, icy-cold, on to my neck.

The only visitor to come for an occasional talk was my old friend Chin Hsin-yi. He would put his big portfolio down on the broken table, take off his long gown, and sit facing me, looking as if his heart was still beating fast after braving the dogs.

"What is the use of copying these?" he demanded inquisitively one night, after looking through the inscriptions I had copied.

---

* Shaohsing.

"No use at all."

"Then why copy them?"

"For no particular reason."

"I think you might write something. . . ."

I understood. They were editing the magazine *New Youth*,* but hitherto there seemed to have been no reaction, favorable or otherwise, and I guessed they must be feeling lonely. However I said:

"Imagine an iron house without windows, absolutely indestructible, with many people fast asleep inside who will soon die of suffocation. But you know since they will die in their sleep, they will not feel the pain of death. Now if you cry aloud to wake a few of the lighter sleepers, making those unfortunate few suffer the agony of irrevocable death, do you think you are doing them a good turn?"

"But if a few awake, you can't say there is no hope of destroying the iron house."

True, in spite of my own conviction, I could not blot out hope, for hope lies in the future. I could not use my own evidence to refute his assertion that it might exist. So I agreed to write, and the result was my first story, *A Madman's Diary*. From that time onwards, I could not stop writing, and would write some sort of short story from time to time at the request of friends, until I had more than a dozen of them.

As for myself, I no longer feel any great urge to express myself; yet, perhaps because I have not entirely forgotten the grief of my past loneliness. I sometimes call out, to encourage those fighters who are galloping on in loneliness, so that they do not lose heart. Whether my cry is brave or sad, repellent or ridiculous, I do not care. However, since it is a call to arms, I must naturally obey my general's orders. This is why I often resort to innuendoes, as when I made a wreath appear from nowhere at the son's grave in *Medicine*, while in *Tomorrow* I did not say that Fourth Shan's Wife had no dreams of her little boy. For our chiefs then were against pessimism. And I, for my part, did not want to infect with the loneliness I had found so bitter those young people who were still dreaming pleasant dreams, just as I had done when young.

---

* The most influential magazine in the cultural revolution of that time.

It is clear, then, that my short stories fall far short of being works of art; hence I count myself fortunate that they are still known as stories, and are even being compiled in one book. Although such good fortune makes me uneasy, I am nevertheless pleased to think they have readers in the world of men, for the time being at least.

Since these short stories of mine are being reprinted in one collection, owing to the reasons given above, I have chosen the title *Na Han (Call to Arms)*.

December 3, 1922, Peking

A Madman's Diary

*T*wo brothers, whose names I need not mention here, were both good friends of mine in high school; but after a separation of many years we gradually lost touch. Some time ago I happened to hear that one of them was seriously ill, and since I was going back to my old home I broke my journey to call on them, I saw only one, however, who told me that the invalid was his younger brother.

"I appreciate your coming such a long way to see us," he said, "but my brother recovered some time ago and has gone elsewhere to take up an official post." Then, laughing, he produced two volumes of his brother's diary, saying that from these the nature of his past illness could be seen, and that there was no harm in showing them to an old friend. I took the diary away, read it through, and found that he had suffered from a form of persecution complex. The writing was most confused and incoherent, and he had made many wild statements; moreover he had omitted to give any dates, so that only by the color of the ink and the differences in the writing could one tell that it was not written at one time. Certain sections, however, were not altogether disconnected, and I have copied out a part to serve as a subject for medical research. I have not altered a single illogicality in the diary and have changed only the names, even though the people referred to are all country folk, unknown to the world and of no consequence. As for the title, it was chosen by the diarist himself after his recovery, and I did not change it.

I

*T*onight the moon is very bright.

I have not seen it for over thirty years, so today when I saw it I felt in unusually high spirits. I begin to realize that during the past thirty-odd years I have been in the dark; but now I must be extremely careful. Otherwise why should that dog at the Chao house have looked at me twice?

I have reason for my fear.

II

*T*onight there is no moon at all, I know that this bodes ill. This morning when I went out cautiously, Mr. Chao had a strange look in his eyes, as if he were afraid of me, as if he wanted to murder me. There were seven or eight others, who discussed me in a whisper. And they were afraid of my seeing them. All the people I passed were like that. The fiercest among them grinned at me; whereupon I shivered from head to foot, knowing that their preparations were complete.

I was not afraid, however, but continued on my way. A group of children in front were also discussing me, and the look in their eyes was just like that in Mr. Chao's while their faces too were ghastly pale. I wondered what grudge these children could have against me to make them behave like this. I could not help calling out: "Tell me!" But then they ran away.

I wonder what grudge Mr. Chao can have against me, what grudge the people on the road can have against me. I can think of nothing except that twenty years ago I trod on Mr. Ku Chiu's* account sheets for many years past, and Mr. Ku was very displeased. Although Mr. Chao does not know him, he must have heard talk of this and decided to avenge him, so he is conspiring against me with the people on the road, But then what of the children? At that time they were not yet born, so why should they eye me so strangely today, as if they were afraid of me, as if they wanted to murder me? This really frightens me, it is so bewildering and upsetting.

I know. They must have learned this from their parents!

III

I can't sleep at night. Everything requires careful consideration if one is to understand it.

Those people, some of whom have been pilloried by the magistrate, slapped in the face by the local gentry, had their wives taken away by bailiffs, or their parents driven to suicide by creditors, never looked as frightened and as fierce then as they did yesterday.

The most extraordinary thing was that woman on the street yesterday who spanked her son and said, "Little devil! I'd like to bite several mouthfuls out of you to work off my feelings!" Yet all the time she looked at me. I gave a start, unable to control myself; then all those green-faced, long-toothed people began to laugh derisively. Old Chen hurried forward and dragged me home.

He dragged me home. The folk at home all pretended not to know me; they had the same look in their eyes as all the others. When I went into the study, they locked the door outside as if cooping up a chicken or a duck. This incident left me even more bewildered.

A few days ago a tenant of ours from Wolf Cub Village came to report the failure of the crops, and told my elder brother that a notorious character in their village had been

---

† Ku Chiu means "Ancient Times." Lu Hsun had in mind the long history of feudal oppression in China.

beaten to death; then some people had taken out his heart and liver, fried them in oil and eaten them, as a means of increasing their courage. When I interrupted, the tenant and my brother both stared at me. Only today have I realized that they had exactly the same look in their eyes as those people outside.

Just to think of it sets me shivering from the crown of my head to the soles of my feet.

They eat human beings, so they may eat me.

I see that woman's "bite several mouthfuls out of you," the laughter of those green-faced, long-toothed people and the tenant's story the other day are obviously secret signs. I realize all the poison in their speech, all the daggers in their laughter. Their teeth are white and glistening: they are all man-eaters.

It seems to me, although I am not a bad man, ever since I trod on Mr. Ku's accounts it has been touch-and-go. They seem to have secrets which I cannot guess, and once they are angry they will call anyone a bad character. I remember when my elder brother taught me to write compositions, no matter how good a man was, if I produced arguments to the contrary he would mark that passage to show his approval; while if I excused evil-doers, he would say: "Good for you, that shows originality." How can I possibly guess their secret thoughts — especially when they are ready to eat people?

Everything requires careful consideration if one is to understand it. In ancient times, as I recollect, people often ate human beings, but I am rather hazy about it. I tried to look this up, but my history has no chronology, and scrawled all over each page are the words: "Virtue and Morality." Since I could not sleep anyway, I read intently half the night, until I began to see words between the lines, the whole book being filled with the two words — "Eat people."

All these words written in the book, all the words spoken by our tenant, gaze at me strangely with an enigmatic smile.

I too am a man, and they want to eat me!

IV

*I*n the morning I sat quietly for some time. Old Chen brought lunch in: one bowl of vegetables, one bowl of steamed fish. The eyes of the fish were white and hard, and its mouth was open just like those people who want to eat human beings. After a few mouthfuls I could not tell whether the slippery morsels were fish or human flesh, so I brought it all up.

I said, "Old Chen, tell my brother that I feel quite suffocated, and want to have a stroll in the garden." Old Chen said nothing but went out, and presently he came back and opened the gate.

I did not move, but watched to see how they would treat me, feeling certain that they would not let me go. Sure enough! My elder brother came slowly out, leading an old man. There was a murderous gleam in his eyes, and fearing that I would see it he lowered his head, stealing glances at me from the side of his spectacles.

"You seem to be very well today," said my brother.

"Yes," said I.

"I have invited Mr. Ho here today," said my brother, "to examine you."

"All right," said I. Actually I knew quite well that this old man was the executioner in disguise! He simply used the pretext of feeling my pulse to see how fat I was; for by so doing he would receive a share of my flesh. Still I was not afraid. Although I do not eat men, my courage is greater than theirs. I held out my two fists, to see what he would do. The old man sat down, closed his eyes, fumbled for some time and remained still for some time; then he opened his shifty eyes and said, "Don't let your imagination run away with you. Rest quietly for a few days, and you will be all right."

Don't let your imagination run away with you! Rest quietly for a few days! When I have grown fat, naturally they will have more to eat; but what good will it do me, or how can it be "all right?" All these people wanting to eat human flesh and at the same time stealthily trying to keep up appearances, not daring to act promptly, really made me nearly die of laughter. I could not help roaring with laughter, I was so amused. I knew that in this laughter were courage and integrity. Both the old man and my brother turned pale, awed by my courage and integrity.

But just because I am brave they are the more eager to eat me, in order to acquire some of my courage. The old man went out of the gate, but before he had gone far he said to my brother in a low voice, "To be eaten at once!" And my brother nodded. So you are in it too! This stupendous discovery, although it came as a shock, is yet no more than I had expected: the accomplice in eating me is my elder brother!

The eater of human flesh is my elder brother!

I am the younger brother of an eater of human flesh!

I myself will be eaten by others, but nonetheless I am the younger brother of an eater of human flesh!

V

*T*hese few days I have been thinking again: suppose that old man were not an executioner in disguise, but a real doctor; he would be nonetheless an eater of human flesh. In that book on herbs, written by his predecessor Li Shih-chen,* it is clearly stated that men's flesh can he boiled and eaten; so can he still say that he does not eat men?

As for my elder brother, I have also good reason to suspect him. When he was teaching me, he said with his own lips, "People exchange their sons to eat." And once in discussing a bad man, he said that not only did he deserve to be killed, he should "have his flesh eaten and his hide slept on. . . .† I

---

* A famous pharmacologist (1518-1593), author of *Ben-cao-gang-mu*, the *Materia Medica*.

was still young then, and my heart beat faster for some time, he was not at all surprised by the story that our tenant from Wolf Cub Village told us the other day about eating a man's heart and liver, but kept nodding his head. He is evidently just as cruel as before. Since it is possible to "exchange sons to eat," then anything can be exchanged, anyone can be eaten. In the past I simply listened to his explanations, and let it go at that; now I know that when he explained it to me, not only was there human fat at the corner of his lips, but his whole heart was set on eating men.

VI

*P*itch dark. I don't know whether it is day or night. The Chao family dog has started barking again.

The fierceness of a lion, the timidity of a rabbit, the craftiness of a fox. . . .

VII

I know their way; they are not willing to kill anyone outright, nor do they dare, for fear of the consequences. Instead they have banded together and set traps everywhere, to force me to kill myself. The behavior of the men and women in the street a few days ago, and my elder brother's attitude these last few days, make it quite obvious. What they like best is for a man to take off his belt, and hang himself from a beam; for then they can enjoy their heart's desire without being blamed for murder. Naturally that sets them roaring with

‡ These are quotations from the old classic *Zuo Zhuan.*

delighted laughter. On the other hand, if a man is frightened or worried to death, although that makes him rather thin, they still nod in approval.

They only eat dead flesh! I remember reading somewhere of a hideous beast, with an ugly look in its eye, called "hyena" which often eats dead flesh. Even the largest bones it grinds into fragments and swallows: the mere thought of this is enough to terrify one. Hyenas are related to wolves, and wolves belong to the canine species. The other day the dog in the Chao house looked at me several times; obviously it is in the plot too and has become their accomplice. The old man's eyes were cast down, but that did not deceive me!

The most deplorable is my elder brother. He is also a man, so why is he not afraid, why is he plotting with others to eat me? Is it that when one is used to it he no longer thinks it a crime? Or is it that he has hardened his heart to do something he knows is wrong?

In cursing man-eaters, I shall start with my brother, and in dissuading man-eaters, I shall start with him too.

VIII

*A*ctually, such arguments should have convinced them long ago. . . .

Suddenly someone came in. He was only about twenty years old and I did not see his features very clearly. His face was wreathed in smiles, but when he nodded to me his smile did not seem genuine. I asked him "Is it right to eat human beings?"

Still smiling, he replied, "When there is no famine how can one eat human beings?"

I realized at once, he was one of them; but still I summoned up courage to repeat my question:

"Is it right?"

"What makes you ask such a thing? You really are . . fond of a joke. . . . It is very fine today."

"It is fine, and the moon is very bright. But I want to ask you: Is it right?"

He looked disconcerted, and muttered: "No. . . ."

"No? Then why do they still do it?"

"What are you talking about?"

"What am I talking about? They are eating men now in Wolf Cub Village, and you can see it written all over the books, in fresh red ink."

His expression changed, and he grew ghastly pale. "It may be so," he said, staring at me. "It has always been like that. . . ."

"Is it right because it has always been like that?"

"I refuse to discuss these things with you. Anyway, you shouldn't talk about it. Whoever talks about it is in the wrong!"

I leaped up and opened my eyes wide, but the man had vanished. I was soaked with perspiration. He was much younger than my elder brother, but even so he was in it. He must have been taught by his parents. And I am afraid he has already taught his son: that is why even the children look at me so fiercely.

IX

*W*anting to eat men, at the same time afraid of being eaten themselves, they all look at each other with the deepest suspicion. . . .

How comfortable life would be for them if they could rid themselves of such obsessions and go to work, walk, eat and sleep at ease. They have only this one step to take. Yet fathers and sons, husbands and wives, brothers, friends, teachers and students, sworn enemies and even strangers, have all joined

in this conspiracy, discouraging and preventing each other
from taking this step.

X

*E*arly this morning I went to look for my elder brother. He
was standing outside the hall door looking at the sky, when
I walked up behind him, stood between him and the door,
and with exceptional poise and politeness said to him:

"Brother, I have something to say to you."

"Well, what is it?" he asked, quickly turning towards me
and nodding.

"It is very little, but I find it difficult to say. Brother,
probably all primitive people ate a little human flesh to begin
with. Later, because their outlook changed, some of them
stopped, and because they tried to be good they changed into
men, changed into real men. But some are still eating — just
like reptiles. Some have changed into fish, birds, monkeys
and finally men; but some do not try to be good and remain
reptiles still. When those who eat men compare themselves
with those who do not, how ashamed they must be. Probably
much more ashamed than the reptiles are before monkeys.

"In ancient times Yi Ya boiled his son for Chieh and Chou
to eat; that is the old story.* But actually since the creation
of heaven and earth by Pan Ku men have been eating each
other, from the time of Yi Ya's son to the time of Hsu Hsi-lin,†
and from the time of Hsu Hsi-lin down to the man caught
in Wolf Cub Village. Last year they executed a criminal in the

---

* According to ancient records, Yi Ya cooked his son and presented him
  to Duke Huan of Chi who reigned from 685 to 643 B.C. Chieh and
  Chou were tyrants of an earlier age. The madman has made a mistake
  here.

† A revolutionary at the end of the Ching dynasty (1644-1911), Hsu
  Hsi-lin was executed in 1907 for assassinating a Ching official. His
  heart and liver were eaten.

city, and a consumptive soaked a piece of bread in his blood and sucked it.

"They want to eat me, and of course you can do nothing about it single-handed; but why should you join them? As man-eaters they are capable of anything. If they eat me, they can eat you as well; members of the same group can still eat each other. But if you will just change your ways immediately, then everyone will have peace. Although this has been going on since time immemorial, today we could make a special effort to be good, and say this is not to be done! I'm sure you can say so, brother. The other day when the tenant wanted the rent reduced, you said it couldn't be done."

At first he only smiled cynically, then a murderous gleam came into his eyes, and when I spoke of their secret his face turned pale. Outside the gate stood a group of people, including Mr. Chao and his dog, all craning their necks to peer in. I could not see all their faces, for they seemed to be masked in cloths; some of them looked pale and ghastly still, concealing their laughter. I knew they were one band, all eaters of human flesh. But I also knew that they did not all think alike by any means. Some of them thought that since it had always been so, men should be eaten. Some of them knew that they should not eat men, but still wanted to; and they were afraid people might discover their secret; thus when they heard me they became angry, but they still smiled their. cynical, tight-lipped smile.

Suddenly my brother looked furious, and shouted in a loud voice:

"Get out of here, all of you! What is the point of looking at a madman?"

Then I realized part of their cunning. They would never be willing to change their stand, and their plans were all laid; they had stigmatized me as a madman. In future when I was eaten, not only would there be no trouble, but people would probably be grateful to them. When our tenant spoke of the villagers eating a bad character, it was exactly the same device. This is their old trick.

Old Chen came in too, in a great temper, but they could not stop my mouth, I had to speak to those people:

"You should change, change from the bottom of your hearts!" I said. "You most know that in future there will be no place for man-eaters in the world.

"If you don't change, you may all be eaten by each other. Although so many are born, they will be wiped out by the real men, just like wolves killed by hunters. Just like reptiles!"

Old Chen drove everybody away. My brother had disappeared. Old Chen advised me to go back to my room. The room was pitch dark. The beams and rafters shook above my head. After shaking for some time they grew larger. They piled on top of me.

The weight was so great, I could not move. They meant that I should die. I knew that the weight was false, so I struggled out, covered in perspiration. But I had to say:

"You should change at once, change from the bottom of your hearts! You must know that in future there will be no place for man-eaters in the world. . . ."

XI

*T*he sun does not shine, the door is not opened, everyday two meals.

I took up my chopsticks, then thought of my elder brother; I know now how my little sister died: it was all through him. My sister was only five at the time. I can still remember how lovable and pathetic she looked. Mother cried and cried, but he begged her not to cry, probably because he had eaten her himself, and so her crying made him feel ashamed. If he had any sense of shame. . . .

My sister was eaten by my brother, but I don't know whether mother realized it or not.

I think mother must have known, but when she cried she did not say so outright, probably because she thought it proper too. I remember when I was four or five years old, sitting in the cool of the hall, my brother told me that if a man's parents were ill, he should cut off a piece of his flesh and boil it for them if he wanted to be considered a good son; and mother did not contradict him. If one piece could be eaten, obviously so could the whole. And yet just to think of the mourning then still makes my heart bleed; that is the extraordinary thing about it!

XII

I can't bear to think of it.

I have only just realized that I have been living all these years in a place where for four thousand years they have been eating human flesh. My brother had just taken over the charge of the house when our sister died, and he may well have used her flesh in our rice and dishes, making us eat it unwittingly.

It is possible that I ate several pieces of my sister's flesh unwittingly, and now it is my turn, . . .

How can a man like myself, after four thousand years of man-caring history — even though I knew nothing about it at first — ever hope to face real men?

XIII

*P*erhaps there are still children who have not eaten men? Save the children. . . .

April 1918

Kung I-Chi

The wine shops in Luchen are not like those in other parts of China. They all have a right-angled counter facing the street, where hot water is kept ready for warming wine. When men come off work at midday and in the evening they buy a bowl of wine; it cost four coppers twenty years ago, but now it costs ten. Standing beside the counter, they drink it warm, and relax. Another copper will buy a plate of salted bamboo shoots or peas flavored with aniseed, to go with the wine; while for a dozen coppers you can buy a meat dish. But most of these customers belong to the short-coated class, few of whom can afford this. Only those in long gowns enter the adjacent room to order wine and dishes, and sit and drink at leisure.

At the age of twelve I started work as a waiter in Prosperity Tavern, at the entrance to the town. The tavern keeper said I looked too foolish to serve the long-gowned customers, so I was given work in the outer room. Although the short-coated customers there were more easily pleased, there were quite a few trouble-makers among them too. They would insist on watching with their own eyes as the yellow wine was ladled from the keg, looking to see if there were any water at the bottom of the wine pot, and inspecting for themselves the immersion of the pot in hot water. Under such keen scrutiny, it was very difficult to dilute the wine. So after a few days my employer decided I was not suited for this work. Fortunately I had been recommended by someone influential, so he could not dismiss me, and I was transferred to the dull work of warming wine.

Thenceforward I stood all day behind the counter, fully engaged with my duties. Although I gave satisfaction at this work, I found it monotonous and futile. Our employer was a fierce-looking individual, and the customers were a morose lot, so that it was impossible to be gay. Only when Kung I-chi came to the tavern could I laugh a little. That is why I still remember him.

Kung was the only long-gowned customer to drink his wine standing. He was a big man, strangely pallid, with scars that often showed among the wrinkles of his face. He had a large, unkempt beard, streaked with white. Although he wore a long gown, it was dirty and tattered, and looked as if it had not been washed or mended for over ten years. He used so many archaisms in his speech, it was impossible to understand half he said. As his surname was Kung, he was nicknamed "Kung I-chi," the first three characters in a children's copybook. Whenever he came into the shop, everyone would look at him and chuckle. And someone would call out:

"Kung I-chi! There are some fresh scars on your face!"

Ignoring this remark, Kung would come to the counter to order two bowls of heated wine and a dish of peas flavored with aniseed. For this he produced nine coppers. Someone else would call out, in deliberately loud tones:

"You must have been stealing again!"

"Why ruin a man's good name groundlessly?" he would ask, opening his eyes wide.

"Pooh, good name indeed! The day before yesterday I saw you with my own eyes being hung up and beaten for stealing books from the Ho family!"

Then Kung would flush, the veins on his forehead standing out as he remonstrated: "Taking a book can't be considered stealing, . . . Taking a book, the affair of a scholar, can't be considered stealing!" Then followed quotations from the classics, like "A gentleman keeps his integrity even in poverty,"* and a jumble of archaic expressions till everybody was roaring with laughter and the whole tavern was gay.

From gossip I heard, Kung I-chi had studied the classics but had never passed the official examination. With no way

---

* From *The Analects of Confucius.*

of making a living, he grew poorer and poorer, until be was practically reduced to beggary. Happily, he was a good calligrapher, and could get enough copying work to support himself. Unfortunately he had failings: he liked drinking and was lazy. So after a few days he would invariably disappear, taking books, paper, brushes and inkstone with him. After this had happened several times, nobody wanted to employ him as a copyist again. Then there was no alternative for him but to take to occasional pilfering. In our tavern his behavior was exemplary. He never failed to pay up, although sometimes, when he had no ready money, his name would appear on the board where we listed debtors. However, in less than a month he would always settle, and his name would be wiped off the board again.

After drinking half a howl of wine, Kung would regain his composure. But then someone would ask:

"Kung I-chi, do you really know how to read?"

When Kung looked as if such a question were beneath contempt, they would continue: "How is it you never passed even the lowest official examination?"

At that Kung would look disconsolate and ill at ease. His face would turn pale and his lips move, but only to utter those unintelligible classical expressions. Then everybody would laugh heartily again, and the whole tavern would be merry.

At such times, I could join in the laughter without being scolded by my master. In fact he often put such questions to Kung himself, to evoke laughter. Knowing it was no use talking to them, Kung would chat to us children. Once he asked me:

"Have you had any schooling?"

When I nodded, he said, "Well then, I'll test you. How do you write the character *hui* in *hui-xiang* (aniseed — *Translator*) peas?"

I thought, "I'm not going to be tested by a beggar!" So I turned away and ignored him. After waiting for some time, he said very earnestly:

"You can't write it? I'll show you how. Mind you remember! You ought to remember such characters, because later when you have a shop of your own, you'll need them to make up your accounts."

It seemed to me I was still very far from owning a shop; besides, our employer never entered *hui-xiang* peas in the account book. Amused yet exasperated, I answered listlessly: "Who wants you as a teacher? Isn't it the character hui with the grass radical?"

Kung was delighted, and tapped two long fingernails on the counter. "Right, right!" he said, nodding. "Only there are four different ways of writing *hui*. Do you know them?" My patience exhausted, I scowled and made off. Kung I-chi had dipped his finger in wine, in order to trace the characters on the counter; but when he saw how indifferent I was, he sighed and looked most disappointed.

Sometimes children in the neighborhood, hearing laughter, came to join in the fun, and surrounded Kung I-chi Then he would give them peas flavored with aniseed, one apiece. After eating the peas, the children would still hang round, their eyes on the dish. Flustered, he would cover the dish with his hand and, bending forward from the waist, would say: "There isn't much. I haven't much as it is." Then straightening up to look at the peas again, he would shake his head. "Not much! Verily, not much, forsooth!" Then the children would scamper off, with shouts of laughter.

Kung I-chi was very good company, but we got along all right without him too.

One day, a few days before the Mid-Autumn Festival, the tavern keeper was laboriously making out his accounts. Taking down the board from the wall, he suddenly said: "Kung I-chi hasn't been in for a long time. He still owes nineteen coppers!" That made me realize how long it was since we had seen him.

"How could he come?" one of the customers said. "His legs were broken in that last beating."

"Ah!"

"He was stealing again. This time he was fool enough to steal from Mr. Ting, the provincial scholar! As if anybody could get away with that!"

"What then?"

"What then? First he had to write a confession, then he was beaten. The beating lasted nearly all night, until his legs were broken."

"And then?"

"Well, his legs were broken."

"Yes, but after that?"

"After. . . ? Who knows? He may be dead."

The tavern keeper did not pursue his questions, but went on slowly making up his accounts.

After the Mid-Autumn Festival the wind grew colder every day, as winter came on. Even though I spent all my time by the stove, I had to wear my padded jacket. One afternoon, when the shop was empty, I was sitting with my eyes closed when I heard a voice:

"Warm a bowl of wine."

The voice was very low, yet familiar. But when I looked up, there was no one in sight. I stood up and looked towards the door, and there, facing the threshold, beneath the counter, sat Kung I-chi. His face was haggard and lean, and he looked in a terrible condition. He had on a ragged lined jacket, and was sitting cross-legged on a mat which was attached to his shoulders by a straw rope. When he saw me, he repeated:

"Warm a bowl of wine."

At this point my employer leaned over the counter and said: "Is that Kung I-chi? You still owe nineteen coppers!"

"That . . . I'll settle next time," replied Kung, looking up disconsolately. "Here's ready money; the wine must be good."

The tavern keeper, just as in the past, chuckled and said:

"Kung I-chi, you've been stealing again!"

But instead of protesting vigorously, the other simply said:

"You like your joke."

"Joke? If you didn't steal, why did they break your legs?"

"I fell," said Kung in a low voice. "I broke them in a fall." His eyes pleaded with the tavern keeper to let the matter drop. By now several people had gathered round, and they all laughed. I warmed the wine, carried it over, and set it on the threshold. He produced four coppers from his ragged coat pocket, and placed them in my hand. As he did so I saw that his hands were covered with mud — he must have crawled here on them. Presently he finished the wine and, amid the laughter and comments of the others, slowly dragged himself off by his hands.

A long time went by after that without our seeing Kung again. At the end of the year, when the tavern keeper took down the board, he said, "Kung I-chi still owes nineteen coppers!" At the Dragon Boat Festival the next year, he said the same thing again. But when the Mid-Autumn Festival came, he did not mention it. And another New Year came round without our seeing anymore of him.

Nor have I ever seen him since — probably Kung I-chi is really dead.

March 1919

Medicine

I

*I*t was autumn, in the small hours of the morning. The moon had gone down, but the sun had not yet risen, and the sky appeared a sheet of darkling blue. Apart from night-prowlers, all was asleep. Old Chuan suddenly sat up in bed. He struck a match and lit the grease-covered oil lamp, which shed a ghostly light over the two rooms of the tea-house.

"Are you going now, dad?" queried an old woman's voice. And from the small inner room a fit of coughing was heard.

"H'm."

Old Chuan listened as he fastened his clothes, then stretching out his hand said, "Let's have it."

After some fumbling under the pillow his wife produced a packet of silver dollars which she handed over. Old Chuan pocketed it nervously, patted his pocket twice, then lighting a paper lantern and blowing out the lamp went into the inner room. A rustling was heard, and then more coughing. When all was quiet again, Old Chuan called softly: "Son. . . ! Don't you get up. . . ! Your mother will see to the shop."

Receiving no answer, Old Chuan assumed his son must be sound asleep again; so he went out into the street. In the darkness nothing could be seen but the grey roadway. The lantern light fell on his pacing feet. Here and there he came across dogs, but none of them barked. It was much colder than indoors, yet Old Chuan's spirits rose, as if he had grown suddenly younger and possessed some miraculous life-giving power. He lengthened his stride. And the road became increasingly clear, the sky increasingly bright.

Absorbed in his walking, Old Chuan was startled when he saw distinctly the cross-road ahead of him. He walked back a few steps to stand under the eaves of a shop, in front of its closed door. After some time he began to feel chilly.

"Uh, an old chap."

"Seems rather cheerful. . . ."

Old Chuan started again and, opening his eyes, saw several men passing. One of them even turned back to look at him, and although he could not see him clearly, the man's eyes shone with a lustful light, like a famished person's at the sight of food. Looking at his lantern, Old Chuan saw it had gone out. He patted his pocket — the hard packet was still there. Then he looked round and saw many strange people, in twos and threes, wandering about like lost souls. However, when he gazed steadily at them, he could not see anything else strange about them.

Presently he saw some soldiers strolling around. The large white circles on their uniforms, both in front and behind, were clear even at a distance; and as they drew nearer, he saw the dark red border too. The next second, with a trampling of feet, a crowd rushed past. Thereupon the small groups which had arrived earlier suddenly converged and surged forward. Just before the cross-road, they came to a sudden stop and grouped themselves in a semi-circle.

Old Chuan looked in that direction too, but could only see people's backs. Craning their necks as far as they would go, they looked like so many ducks held and lifted by some invisible hand. For a moment all was still; then a sound was heard, and a stir swept through the on-lookers. There was a rumble as they pushed back, sweeping past Old Chuan and nearly knocking him down.

"Hey! Give me the cash, and I'll give you the goods!" A man clad entirely in black stood before him, his eyes like daggers, making Old Chuan shrink to half his normal size. This man thrust one huge extended hand towards him, while in the other he held a roll of steamed bread, from which crimson drops were dripping to the ground.

Hurriedly Old Chuan fumbled for his dollars, and trembling he was about to hand them over, but he dared not take the object. The other grew impatient and shouted: "What are you afraid of? Why not take it?" When Old Chuan still hesitated, the man in black snatched his lantern and tore off its paper shade to wrap up the roll. This package he thrust into Old Chuan's hand, at the same time seizing the silver and giving it a cursory feel. Then he turned away, muttering, "Old fool. . . ."

"Whose sickness is this for?" Old Chuan seemed to hear someone ask; but he made no reply. His whole mind was on the package, which he carried as carefully as if it were the sole heir to an ancient house. Nothing else mattered now. He was about to transplant this new life to his own home, and reap much happiness. The sun had risen, lighting up the broad highway before him, which led straight home, and the worn tablet behind him at the cross-road with its faded gold inscription: "Ancient Pavilion."

II

*W*hen Old Chuan reached home, the shop had been cleaned, and the rows of tea-tables shone brightly; but no customers had arrived. Only his son sat eating at a table by the wall. Beads of sweat stood out on his forehead, his lined jacket clung to his spine, and his shoulder blades stuck out so sharply, an inverted V seemed stamped there. At this sight, Old Chuan's brow, which had been clear, contracted again. His wife hurried in from the kitchen, with expectant eyes and a tremor to her lips:

"Get it?"

"Yes."

They went together into the kitchen, and conferred for a time. Then the old woman went out, to return shortly with a dried lotus leaf which she spread on the table. Old Chuan unwrapped the crimson-stained roll from the lantern paper and transferred it to the lotus leaf. Little Chuan had finished his meal, but his mother exclaimed hastily:

"Sit still, Little Chuan! Don't come over here."

Mending the fire in the stove, Old Chuan put the green package and the red and white lantern paper into the stove together. A red-black flame flared up, and a strange odor permeated the shop.

"Smells good! What are you eating?" The hunchback had arrived. He was one of those who spend all their time in tea-shops, the first to come in the morning and the last to leave. Now he had just stumbled to a corner table facing the street, and sat down. But no one answered his question.

"Puffed rice gruel?"

Still no reply. Old Chuan hurried out to brew tea for him.

"Come here, Little Chuan!" His mother called him into the inner room, set a stool in the middle, and sat the child down. Then, bringing him a round black object on a plate, she said gently:

"Eat it up . . . then you'll be better."

Little Chuan picked up the black object and looked at it. He had the oddest feeling, as if he were holding his own life in his hands. Presently he split it carefully open. From within the charred crust a jet of white vapor escaped, then scattered, leaving only two halves of a steamed white flour roll. Soon it was all eaten, the flavor completely forgotten, only the empty plate being left. His father and mother were standing one on each side of him, their eyes apparently pouring something into him and at the same time extracting something. His small heart began to beat faster, and, putting his hands to his chest, he began to cough again.

"Have a sleep; then you'll be all right," said his mother.

Obediently, Little Chuan coughed himself to sleep. The woman waited till his breathing was regular, then covered him lightly with a much patched quilt.

III

*T*he shop was crowded, and Old Chuan was busy, carrying a big copper kettle to make tea for one customer after another. There were dark circles under his eyes.

"Aren't you well, Old Chuan. . . ? What's wrong with you?" asked one greybeard.

"Nothing."

"Nothing. . . ? No, I suppose from your smile, there couldn't be . . ." the old man corrected himself.

"It's just that Old Chuan's busy," said the hunchback. "If his son. . . ." But before he could finish, a heavy-jowled man burst in. Over his shoulders he had a dark brown shirt, unbuttoned and fastened carelessly by a broad dark brown girdle at his waist. As soon as he entered, he shouted to Old Chuan:

"Has he eaten it? Any better? Luck's with you, Old Chuan. What luck! If not for my hearing of things so quickly. . . ."

Holding the kettle in one hand, the other straight by his side in an attitude of respect, Old Chuan listened with a smile. In fact, all present were listening respectfully. The old woman, dark circles under her eyes too, came out smiling with a bowl containing tea leaves and an added olive, over which Old Chuan poured boiling water for the newcomer.

"This is a guaranteed cure! Not like other things!" declared the heavy-jowled man. "Just think, brought back warm, and eaten warm!"

"Yes indeed, we couldn't have managed it without Uncle Kang's help." The old woman thanked him very warmly.

"A guaranteed cure! Eaten warm like this. A roll dipped in human blood like this can cure any consumption!"

The old woman seemed a little disconcerted by the word "consumption," and turned a shade paler; however, she forced a smile again at once and found some pretext to leave. Meanwhile the man in brown was indiscreet enough to go on talking at the top of his voice until the child in the inner room was woken and started coughing.

"So you've had a great stroke of luck for your Little Chuan! Of course his sickness will be cured completely. No wonder Old Chuan keeps smiling." As he spoke, the greybeard walked up to the man in brown, and lowered his voice to ask:

"Mr. Kang, I heard the criminal executed today came from the Hsia family. Who was it? And why was he executed?"

"Who? Son of Widow Hsia, of course! Young rascal!"

Seeing how they all hung on his words, Mr. Kang's spirits rose even higher. His jowls quivered, and he made his voice as loud as he could.

"The rogue didn't want to live, simply didn't want to! There was nothing in it for me this time. Even the clothes stripped from him were taken by Red-eye, the jailer. Our Old Chuan was luckiest, and after him Third Uncle Hsia. He pocketed the whole reward — twenty-five taels of bright silver — and didn't have to spend a cent!"

Little Chuan walked slowly out of the inner room, his hands to his chest, coughing repeatedly. He went to the kitchen, filled a bowl with cold rice, added hot water to it, and sitting down started to eat. His mother, hovering over him, asked softly:

"Do you feel better, son? Still as hungry as ever?"

"A guaranteed cure!" Kang glanced at the child, then turned back to address the company. "Third Uncle Hsia is really smart. If he hadn't informed, even *his* family would have been executed, and their property confiscated. But instead? Silver! That young rogue was a real scoundrel! He even tried to incite the jailer to revolt!"

"No! The idea of it!" A man in his twenties, sitting in the back row, expressed indignation.

"You know, Red-eye went to sound him out, but he started chatting with him. He said the great Ching empire belongs to us. Just think: is that kind of talk rational? Red-eye knew he had only an old mother at home, but had never imagined he was so poor. He couldn't squeeze anything out of him; he was already good and angry, and then the young fool would 'scratch the tiger's head,' so he gave him a couple of slaps."

"Red-eye is a good boxer. Those slaps must have hurt!" The hunchback in the corner by the wall exulted.

"The rotter was not afraid of being beaten. He even said how sorry he was."

"Nothing to be sorry about in beating a wretch like that," said Greybeard.

Kang looked at him superciliously and said disdainfully: "You misunderstood. The way he said it, he was sorry for Red-eye."

His listeners' eyes took on a glazed look, and no one spoke. Little Chuan had finished his rice and was perspiring profusely, his head steaming.

"Sorry for Red-eye — crazy! He must have been crazy!" said Greybeard, as if suddenly he saw light.

"He must have been crazy!" echoed the man in his twenties.

Once more the customers began to show animation, and conversation was resumed. Under cover of the noise, the child was seized by a paroxysm of coughing. Kang went up to him, clapped him on the shoulder, and said:

"A guaranteed cure! Don't cough like that, Little Chuan! A guaranteed cure!"

"Crazy!" agreed the hunchback, nodding his head.

IV

*O*riginally, the land adjacent to the city wall outside the West Gate had been public land. The zigzag path running across it, trodden out by passers-by seeking a short cut, had become a natural boundary line. Left of the path were buried executed criminals or those who had died of neglect in prison. Right of the path were paupers' graves. The serried ranks of grave mounds on both sides looked like the rolls laid out for a rich man's birthday.

The Ching Ming Festival that year was unusually cold. Willows were only just beginning to put forth shoots no larger than grains. Shortly after daybreak, Old Chuan's wife brought four dishes and a bowl of rice to set before a new grave in the right section, and wailed before it. When she had burned paper money she sat on the ground in a stupor as if waiting for something; but for what, she herself did not know. A breeze sprang up and stirred her short hair, which was certainly whiter than the previous year.

Another woman came down the path, grey-haired and in rags. Carrying an old, round, red-lacquered basket with a string of paper money hanging from it, she walked haltingly. When she saw Old Chuan's wife sitting on the ground watching her, she hesitated, and a flush of shame spread over her pale face. However, she summoned up courage to cross over to a grave in the left section. where she set down her basket.

That grave was directly opposite Little Chuan's, separated only by the path. As Old Chuan's wife watched the other woman set Out four dishes of food and a bowl of rice, then stand up to wail and burn paper money, she thought: "It must be her son in that grave too." The older woman took a few aimless steps and stared vacantly around, then suddenly she began to tremble and stagger backwards, as though giddy.

Fearing sorrow might send her out of her mind, Old Chuan's wife got up and stepped across the path, to say quietly: "Don't grieve, let's go home."

The other nodded, but she was still staring fixedly, and she muttered: "Look! What's that?"

Looking where she pointed, Old Chuan's wife saw that the grave in front had not yet been overgrown with grass. Ugly patches of soil still showed. But when she looked carefully, she was surprised to see at the top of the mound a wreath of red and white flowers.

Both of them suffered from failing eyesight, yet they could see these red and white flowers clearly. There were not many, but they were placed in a circle; and although not very fresh, were neatly set out. Little Chuan's mother looked round and found her own son's grave, like most of the rest, dotted with only a few little, pale flowers shivering in the cold. Suddenly she had a sense of futility and stopped feeling curious about the wreath.

In the meantime the old woman had gone up to the grave to look more closely. "They have no roots," she said to herself. "They can't have grown here. Who could have been here? Children don't come here to play, and none of our relatives ever come. What could have happened?" She puzzled over it, until suddenly her tears began to fall, and she cried aloud:

"Son, they all wronged you, and you do not forget. Is your grief still so great that today you worked this wonder to let me know?"

She looked all around, but could see only a crow perched on a leafless bough. "I know," she continued. "They murdered you. But a day of reckoning will come, Heaven will see to it. Close your eyes in peace. . . . If you are really here, and can hear me, make that crow fly on to your grave as a sign."

The breeze had long since dropped, and the dry grass stood stiff and straight as copper wires. A faint, tremulous sound vibrated in the air, then faded and died away. All around was deathly still. They stood in the dry grass, looking up at the crow; and the crow, on the rigid bough of the tree, its head drawn in, perched immobile as iron.

Time passed. More people, young and old, came to visit the graves.

Old Chuan's wife felt somehow as if a load had been lifted from her mind and, wanting to leave, she urged the other:

"Let's go."

The old woman sighed, and listlessly picked up the rice and dishes. After a moment's hesitation she started off slowly, still muttering to herself:

"What does it mean?"

They had not gone thirty paces when they heard a loud caw behind them. Startled, they looked round and saw the crow stretch its wings, brace itself to take off, then fly like an arrow towards the far horizon.

April 1919

Tomorrow

"Not a sound — what's wrong with the kid?"

A bowl of yellow wine in his hands, Red-nosed Kung jerked his head towards the next house as he spoke. Blue-skinned Ah-wu set down his own bowl and punched the other hard in the back.

"Bah . . ." he growled thickly. "Going sentimental again!"

Being so out-of-the-way, Luchen was rather old-fashioned. Folk closed their doors and went to bed before the first watch sounded. By midnight there were only two households awake. Prosperity Tavern where a few gluttons guzzled merrily round the bar, and the house next door where Fourth Shan's Wife lived. Left a widow two years earlier, she had nothing but the cotton-yarn she spun to support herself and her three-year-old boy; this is why she also slept late.

It was a fact that for several days now there had been no sound of spinning. But since only two households were awake at midnight, Old Kung and the others were naturally the only ones who would notice if there were any sound from Fourth Shan's Wife's house, and the only ones to notice if there were no sound.

After being punched, Old Kung — looking quite at his ease — took a great swig at his wine and piped up a folk tune.

Meanwhile Fourth Shan's Wife was sitting on the edge of her bed, Pao-erh — her treasure — in her arms, while her loom stood silent on the floor. The murky lamplight fell on Pao-erh's face, which showed livid beneath a feverish flush.

"I've drawn lots before the shrine," she was thinking. "I've made a vow to the gods, he's taken the guaranteed cure. If he still doesn't get better, what can I do? I shall have to take him to Dr. Ho Hsiao-hsien. But maybe Pao-erh's only bad at night; when the sun comes out tomorrow his fever may go and he may breathe more easily again. A lot of illnesses are like that."

Fourth Shan's Wife was a simple woman, who did not know what a fearful word "but" is. Thanks to this "but," many bad things turn out well, many good things turn out badly. A summer night is short. Soon after Old Kung and the others stopped singing the sky grew bright in the east; and presently through the cracks in the window filtered the silvery light of dawn.

*W*aiting for the dawn was not such a simple matter for Fourth Shan's Wife as for other people. The time dragged terribly slowly: each breath Pao-erh took seemed to last at least a year. But now at last it was bright. Clear daylight swallowed up the lamplight. Pao-erh's nostrils quivered as he gasped for breath.

Fourth Shan's Wife smothered a cry, for she knew that this boded ill. But what could she do? she wondered. Her only hope was to take him to Dr. Ho. She might be a simple woman, but she had a will of her own. She stood up, went to the cupboard, and took out her entire savings — thirteen small silver dollars and a hundred and eighty coppers in all. Having put the whole lot in her pocket, she locked the door and carried Pao-erh as fast as she could to Dr. Ho's house.

Early as it was, there were already four patients sitting there. She produced forty silver cents for a registration slip, and Pao-erh was the fifth to be seen. Dr. Ho stretched out two fingers to feel the child's pulses. His nails were a good four inches long, and Fourth Shan's Wife marveled inwardly, thinking: "Surely my Pao-erh must be fated to live!" She could not help feeling anxious all the same, and could not stop herself asking nervously:

"What's wrong with my Pao-erh, doctor?"

"An obstruction of the digestive tract."

"Is it serious? Will he . . .?"

"Take these two prescriptions to start with."

"He can't breathe, his nostrils are twitching."

"The element* of fire overpowers that of metal. . . ."

Leaving this sentence unfinished, Dr. Ho closed his eyes; and Fourth Shan's Wife did not like to say anymore. Opposite the doctor sat a man in his thirties, who had now finished making out the prescription.

"The first is Infant Preserver Pills," he told her, pointing to the characters in one corner of the paper. "You can get those only at the Chin family's Salvation Shop."

Fourth Shan's Wife took the paper, and walked out thinking as she went. She might be a simple woman, but she knew Dr. Ho's house, Salvation Shop and her own home formed a triangle; so of course it would be simpler to buy the medicine first before going back. She hurried as fast as she could to Salvation Shop. The assistant raised his long fingernails too as he slowly read the prescription, then slowly wrapped up the medicine. With Pao-erh in her arms, Fourth Shan's Wife waited. Suddenly Pao-erh stretched up a little hand and tugged at his loose tuft of hair. He had never done this before, and his mother was terrified.

The sun was fairly high now. With the child in her arms and the package of medicine to carry, the further she walked the heavier she found her load. The child kept struggling too, which made the way seem even longer. She had to sit down on the doorstep of a big house by the roadside to rest for a while; and presently her clothes lay so clammy against her skin that she realized she had been sweating. But Pao-erh seemed fast asleep. When she stood up again to walk slowly on, she still found him too heavy. A voice beside her said:

"Let me take him for you, Fourth Shan's Wife!" It sounded like Blue-skinned Ah-wu.

When she looked up, sure enough it was Ah-wu, who was following her with eyes still heavy from sleep.

Though Fourth Shan's Wife had been longing for an angel to come to her rescue, she had not wanted her champion to

---

* The ancient Chinese believed that there were five elements: fire, wood, earth, metal and water. Fire could conquer metal. The traditional Chinese doctors also considered that the heart, lungs, liver, spleen and kidney corresponded to the five elements. Here, Dr. Ho is saying that heart trouble had affected the lungs.

be Ah-wu. But there was something of the gallant about
Ah-wu, for he absolutely insisted on helping her; and at last,
after several refusals, she gave way. As he stretched his arm
between her breast and the child, then thrust it down to take
over Pao-erh, she felt a wave of heat along her breast. She
flushed right up to her ears.

They walked along, two and a half feet apart. Ah-wu made
some remarks, most of which Fourth Shan's Wife left unanswered. They had not gone far when he gave the child back
to her, saying he had arranged yesterday to have a meal at this
time with a friend. Fourth Shan's Wife took Pao-erh back.
Luckily it wasn't far now: already she could see Ninth Aunt
Wang sitting at the side of the street. She called out:

"Fourth Shan's Wife, how's the child? Did you get to see
the doctor?"

"We saw him . . . Ninth Aunt Wang, you're old and you've
seen a lot. Will you look him over for me, and say what you
think?"

"Um."

"Well. . .?"

"Ummm. . . ."

When Ninth Aunt Wang had examined Pao-erh, she nodded her head twice, then shook it twice.

By the time Pao-erh had taken his medicine it was after
noon. Fourth Shan's Wife watched him closely, and he did
seem a good deal quieter. In the afternoon he suddenly
opened his eyes and called: "Ma!" Then he closed his eyes
again and seemed to be sleeping. He had not slept long before
his forehead and the tip of his nose were beaded with sweat,
which, when his mother felt it, stuck to her fingers like glue.
In a panic she felt his chest, then burst out sobbing.

After quieting down, his breathing had stopped completely. After sobbing, she started wailing. Soon groups of
people gathered: inside the room Ninth Aunt Wang, Blue-
skinned Ah-wu and the like; outside others like the landlord
of Prosperity Tavern and Red-nosed Kong. Ninth Aunt Wang
decreed that a string of paper coins should be burned; then,
taking two stools and five articles of clothing as security, she
borrowed two dollars for Fourth Shan's Wife to prepare a
meal for all those who were helping.

The first problem was the coffin. Fourth Shan's Wife still had a pair of silver earrings and a silver hair-pin plated with gold, which she gave to the landlord of Prosperity Tavern so that he would go surety for her and buy a coffin half for cash, half on credit. Blue-skinned Ah-wu raised his hand to volunteer to help, but Ninth Aunt Wang would not hear of it. All she would let him do was carry the coffin the next day. "Old bitch!" he cursed, and stood there grumpily pursing his lips. The landlord left, coming back that evening to report that the coffin would have to be specially made, and would not be ready till nearly morning.

By the time the landlord came back the other helpers had finished their meal. And Luchen being rather old-fashioned, they all went home to sleep before the first watch. Only Ah-wu leaned on the bar of Prosperity Tavern drinking, while Old Kong croaked a song.

Meanwhile Fourth Shan's Wife sat on the edge of the bed crying. Pao-erh lay on the bed, and the loom stood silent on the floor. After a long time, when Fourth Shan's Wife had no more tears to shed, she opened her eyes wide, and looked around in amazement. All this was impossible! "This is only a dream," she thought. "It's all a dream. I shall wake up tomorrow lying snug in bed, with Pao-erh sleeping snugly beside me. Then he'll wake and call: 'Ma!' and jump down like a young tiger to play."

Old Kong had long since stopped singing, and the light had gone Out in Prosperity Tavern. Fourth Shan's Wife sat staring, but could not believe all that had happened. A cock crowed, the sky grew bright in the east, and through the cracks in the window filtered the silvery light of dawn.

By degrees the silvery light of dawn turned copper, and the sun shone on the roof. Fourth Shan's Wife sat there staring till someone knocked, when she gave a start and ran to open the door. A stranger was there with something on his back, and behind him stood Ninth Aunt Wang.

Oh, it was the coffin he'd brought!

*N*ot till that afternoon was the lid of the coffin put on, because Fourth Shan's Wife kept crying, then taking a look, and could nor bear to have the lid closed down. Luckily, Ninth Aunt Wang grew tired of waiting, hurried forward indignantly and pulled her aside. Then they hastily closed it.

Fourth Shan's Wife had really done all she could for her Pao-erh — nothing had been forgotten. The previous day she had burned a string of paper coins, this morning she had burned the forty-nine books of the *Incantation of Great Mercy,** and before putting him in the coffin she had dressed him in his newest clothes and set by his pillow all the toys he liked best — a little clay figure, two small wooden bowls, two glass bottles. Though Ninth Aunt Wang reckoned carefully on her fingers, even then she could not think of anything they had forgotten.

Since Blue-skinned Ah-wu did not turn up all day, the landlord of Prosperity Tavern hired two porters for Fourth Shan's Wife at 210 large coppers each, who carried the coffin to the public graveyard and dug a grave. Ninth Aunt Wang helped her prepare a meal to which everyone who had lifted a finger or opened his mouth was invited. Soon the sun made it clear that it was about to set, and the guests unwittingly made it clear that they were about to leave — home they all went.

Fourth Shan's Wife felt dizzy at first, but after a little rest she quietened down. At once, though, she had the impression that things were rather strange. Something which had never happened to her before, and which she had thought never could happen, *had* happened. The more she thought, the more surprised she felt, and another thing that struck her as rather strange was the fact that the room had suddenly grown too silent.

After she stood up and lit the lamp, the room seemed even more silent. She groped her way over to close the door, came back and sat on the bed, while the loom stood silent on the floor. She pulled herself together and looked around, feeling unable either to sit or stand. The room was not only too

---

* A Buddhist chant.

silent, it was far too big as well, and the things in it were far too empty. This overlarge room hemmed her in, and the emptiness all around bore hard on her, till she could hardly breathe.

She knew now her Pao-erh was really dead; and, nor wanting to see this room, she blew out the light and lay down to cry and think. She remembered how Pao-erh had sat by her side when she spun, eating peas flavored with aniseed. He had watched her intently with his small black eyes and thought. "Ma!" he suddenly said. "Dad sold *hun tun*.* When I'm big I'll sell *hun tun* too, and make lots and lots of money — and I'll give it all to you."

At such times even every inch of yarn she spun seemed worthwhile and alive. But what now? Fourth Shan's Wife had not considered the present at all — as I have said, she was only a simple woman. What solution could she think of? All she knew was that this room was too silent, too large, too empty.

But even though Fourth Shan's Wife was a simple woman, she knew the dead cannot come to life again, and she would never see her Pao-erh anymore. She sighed and said: "Pao-erh, you must still be here. Let me see you in my dreams." Then she closed her eyes, hoping to fall asleep at once so that she could see Pao-erh. She heard her own hard breathing clearly in the silence, the vastness and emptiness.

At last Fourth Shan's Wife dozed off, and the whole room was very still. Red-nosed Kung's folk song had long since ended, and he had staggered out of Prosperity Tavern to sing in a falsetto:

"I pity you — my darling — all alone. . . ."

Blue-skinned Ah-wu grabbed Old Kung's shoulder, and laughing tipsily they reeled away together.

Fourth Shan's Wife was asleep, Old Kung and the others had gone, the door of Prosperity Tavern was closed. Luchen was sunk in utter silence. Only the night, eager to change into the morrow, was journeying on in the silence; and, hidden in the darkness, a few dogs were barking.

June 1920

---

* Dumplings stuffed with meat and boiled in soup.

An Incident

Six years have slipped by since I came from the country to the capital. During that time I have seen and heard quite enough of so-called affairs of state; but none of them made much impression on me. If asked to define their influence, I can only say they aggravated my ill temper and made me, frankly speaking, more and more misanthropic.

One incident, however, struck me as significant, and aroused me from my ill temper, so that even now I cannot forget it.

It happened during the winter of 1917. A bitter north wind was blowing, but, to make a living, I had to be up and out early. I met scarcely a soul on the road, and had great difficulty in hiring a rickshaw to take me to S—— Gate. Presently the wind dropped a little. By now the loose dust had all been blown away, leaving the roadway clean, and the rickshaw man quickened his pace. We were just approaching S—— Gate when someone crossing the road was entangled in our rickshaw and slowly fell.

It was a woman, with streaks of white in her hair, wearing ragged clothes. She had left the pavement without warning to cut across in front of us, and although the rickshaw man had made way, her tattered jacket, unbuttoned and fluttering in the wind, had caught on the shaft. Luckily the rickshaw man pulled up quickly, otherwise she would certainly have had a bad fall and been seriously injured.

She lay there on the ground, and the rickshaw man stopped. I did not think the old woman was hurt, and there had been no witnesses to what had happened, so I resented this off viciousness which might land him in trouble and hold me up.

"It's all right," I said. "Go on."

He paid no attention, however — perhaps he had not heard — for he set down the shafts, and gently helped the old woman to get up. Supporting her by one arm, he asked:

"Are you all right?"

"I'm hurt."

I had seen how slowly she fell, and was sure she could not be hurt. She must be pretending, which was disgusting. The rickshaw man had asked for trouble, and now he had it. He would have to find his own way out.

But the rickshaw man did not hesitate for a minute after the old woman said she was injured. Still holding her arm, he helped her slowly forward. I was surprised. When I looked ahead, I saw a police station. Because of the high wind, there was no one outside, so the rickshaw man helped the old woman towards the gate.

Suddenly I had a strange feeling. His dusty, retreating figure seemed larger at that instant. Indeed, the further he walked the larger he loomed, until I had to look up to him. At the same time he seemed gradually to be exerting a pressure on me, which threatened to overpower the small self under my fur-lined gown.

My vitality seemed sapped as I sat there motionless, my mind a blank, until a policeman came out. Then I got down from the rickshaw.

The policeman came up to me, and said, "Get another rickshaw. He can't pull you anymore."

Without thinking, I pulled a handful of coppers from my coat pocket and handed them to the policeman. "Please give him these," I said.

The wind had dropped completely, but the road was still quiet. I walked along thinking, but I was almost afraid to turn my thoughts on myself. Setting aside what had happened earlier, what had I meant by that handful of coppers? Was it a reward? Who was I to judge the rickshaw man? I could not answer myself.

Even now, this remains fresh in my memory. It often causes me distress, and makes me try to think about myself. The military and political affairs of those years I have forgotten as completely as the classics I read in my childhood. Yet this incident keeps coming back to me, often more vivid than in actual life, teaching me shame, urging me to reform, and giving me fresh courage and hope.

July 1920

Storm in a Teacup

The sun's bright yellow rays had gradually faded on the mud flat by the river. The leaves of the tallow trees beside the river were at last able to draw a parched breath, while a few striped mosquitoes danced, humming, beneath them. Less smoke was coming from the kitchen chimneys of the peasants' houses along the river, as women and children sprinkled water on the ground before their doors and brought out little tables and stools. You could tell it was time for the evening meal.

The old folk and the men sat on the low stools, fanning themselves with plantain-leaf fans as they chatted. The children raced about or squatted under the tallow trees playing games with pebbles. The women brought out steaming hot, black, dried vegetables and yellow rice. Some scholars, who were passing in a pleasure boat, waxed quite lyrical at the sight. "So free from care!" they exclaimed. "Here's real idyllic happiness."

The scholars were rather wide of the mark, however. That was because they had not heard what Old Mrs. Ninepounder was saying. Old Mrs. Ninepounder, who was in a towering temper, whacked the legs of her stool with a tattered plantain fan.

"I've lived to seventy-nine, that's long enough," she declared. "I don't like watching everything going to the dogs — I'd rather die. We're going to have supper right away, yet they're still eating roast beans, eating us out of house and home!"

Her great-granddaughter, Sixpounder, had just come running towards her holding a handful of beans; but when she sized up the situation she flew straight to the riverbank and hid herself behind a tallow tree. Then, sticking out her small head with its twin tufts, she called loudly: "Old Never-dying!"

Though Old Mrs. Ninepounder had lived to a great age, she was by no means deaf; she did nor, however, hear what the child said, and went on muttering to herself, "Yes, indeed! Each generation is worse than the last!"

It was the somewhat unusual custom in this village for mothers to weigh their children when they were born, and then use as a name the number of pounds they weighed. Since Old Mrs. Ninepounder's celebration of her fiftieth birthday, she had gradually become a fault-finder, who was always saying that in her young days the summer had not been so hot nor the beans so tough as now. In brief, there was something radically wrong with the present-day world. Otherwise, why should Sixpounder have weighed three pounds less than her great-grandfather and one pound less than her father, Sevenpounder? This was really irrefutable evidence. So she repeated emphatically: "Yes, indeed! Each generation is worse than the last."

Her granddaughter-in-law, Mrs. Sevenpounder, had just come up to the table with a basket of rice. Planking it down on the table, she said angrily: "There you go again! Sixpounder weighed six pounds five ounces when she was born, didn't she? Your family uses private scales which weigh light, eighteen ounces to the pound. With proper sixteenounce scales, Sixpounder ought to have been over seven pounds. I don't believe grandfather and father really weighed a full nine or eight pounds either. Perhaps they used fourteenounce scales in those days. . . ."

"Each generation is worse than the last!"

Before Mrs. Sevenpounder could answer, she saw her husband coming out from the top of the lane, and shifted her attack to shout at him: "Why are you so late back, you slacker! Where have you been all this time? You don't care how long you keep us waiting to start supper!"

Although Sevenpounder lived in the village, he had always wanted to better himself. From his grandfather to himself, not a man in his family for three generations had handled a hoe. Like his father before him he worked on a boat which went every morning from Luchen to town, and came back in the evening. As a result, he knew pretty well all that was going on. He knew, for instance, where the thunder god had struck dead a centipede spirit, or where a virgin had given birth to a demon. Though he had made a name for himself in the village, his family abided by country customs and did not light a lamp for supper in the summer; hence, if he came home late, he would be in for a scolding.

In one hand Sevenpounder held a speckled bamboo pipe, over six feet long, which had an ivory mouth-piece and a pewter bowl. He walked over slowly, hanging his head, and sat on one of the low stools. Sixpounder seized this chance to slip out and sit down beside him. She spoke to him, but he made no answer.

"Each generation is worse than the last!" grumbled Old Mrs. Ninepounder.

Sevenpounder raised his head slowly, and said with a sigh: "The emperor has ascended the throne again."

For a moment, Mrs. Sevenpounder was struck dumb. Then, suddenly taking in the news, she exclaimed: "Good! That means the emperor will declare another amnesty, doesn't it?"

"I've no queue," Sevenpounder sighed again.

"Does the emperor insist on queues?"

"He does."

Mrs. Sevenpounder was rather upset. "How do you know?" she demanded hastily.

"Everybody in Prosperity Tavern says so."

At that Mrs. Sevenpounder realized instinctively that things were in a bad way, because Prosperity Tavern was where you could pick up all the news. She looked angrily at Sevenpounder's shaved head, with a feeling of hatred and resentment; then fatalistically filled a bowl with rice and slapped it down before him, saying: "Hurry up and eat! Crying won't grow a queue for you, will it?"

*T*he sun had withdrawn its last rays, and the darkling water was gradually cooling off. There was a clatter of bowls and chopsticks on the mud flat, and sweat stood our on the backs of the people there. Mrs. Sevenpounder had finished three bowls of rice when, happening to look up, she saw something that set her heart pounding. Through the tallow leaves, Mr. Chao's short plump figure could be seen approaching from the one-plank bridge. And he was wearing his long sapphire-blue cotton gown. Mr. Chao was the owner of Abundance Tavern in a neighboring village, and the only notable within a radius of ten miles who was also something of a scholar. His learning gave him a little of the musty air of a departed age. He had a dozen volumes of the *Romance of the Three Kingdoms* annotated by Chin Sheng-tan,* which he would sit reading and re-reading, character by character. He could tell you not only the names of the five tiger generals,† but even that Huang Chung was also known as Han-sheng, and Ma Chao as Meng-chi. After the Revolution he had coiled his queue on the top of his head like a Taoist priest, and often remarked with a sigh that if Chao Yun were still alive the empire would not be in such a bad way. Mrs. Sevenpounder's eyesight was good, and she had noticed at once that Mr. Chao was not wearing his hair like a Taoist priest today. The front of his head was shaved, and he had let his queue down. She knew that an emperor must have ascended the throne, that queues must be essential again, and that Sevenpounder must be in great danger too. For Mr. Chao did not wear this long cotton gown for nothing — in fact, during the last three years he had only worn it twice. Once when his enemy Pockmarked Ah-szu fell ill, once when Mr. Lu who had smashed up his wine shop died. This was the third time, and it must mean that something had happened to rejoice his heart and bode ill for his enemies.

Two years ago, Mrs. Sevenpounder remembered, her husband when drunk had cursed Mr. Chao as a "bastard."

---

* A commentator of literature (1609-1661).

† During the Three Kingdoms period there were five famous generals in the Kingdom of Shu (221-263): Kuan Yu, Chang Fei, Chao Yun, Huang Chung and Ma Chao.

Immediately she realized instinctively the danger her husband was in, and her heart started thumping furiously.

The folk sitting at supper stood up when Mr. Chao passed by, and pointed their chopsticks at their rice bowls as they said: "Please join us, Mr. Chao."

Mr. Chao nodded greetings to all whom he passed, saying, "Go on with your meal, please!" He made straight for Sevenpounder's table. Everybody rose hastily to greet him, and Mr. Chao said with a smile, "Go on with your meal, please!" At the same time he took a good look at the food on the table.

"Those dried vegetables smell good — have you heard the news?" Mr. Chao was standing behind Sevenpounder, opposite Mrs. Sevenpounder.

"The emperor's ascended the throne," said Sevenpounder.

Watching Mr. Chao's expression, Mrs. Sevenpounder forced herself to smile. "Now that the emperor's ascended the throne, when will there be a general amnesty?" she asked.

"A general amnesty? — There'll be an amnesty all in good time." Then Mr. Chao's voice grew sterner. "But what about Sevenpounder's queue, eh? That's the important thing. You know how it was in the time of the Long Hairs:* keep your hair and lose your head; keep your head and lose your hair. . ."

Sevenpounder and his wife had never read any books, so this classical lore was lost on them; but they supposed that since the learned Mr. Chao said this, the situation must be extremely serious, irrevocable in fact. They felt as if they had received their death sentence. There was a buzzing in their ears, and they were unable to utter another word.

"Each generation is worse than the last." Old Mrs. Ninepounder, quite put out again, seized this chance to speak to Mr. Chao. "The rebels nowadays just cut people's queues off, so that they look neither Buddhist nor Taoist. Were the rebels before like that too? I've lived seventy-nine years, and that's enough. The rebels in the old days wrapped their heads in lengths of red satin that hung all the way down to their heels.

---

* The Taiping army of the peasant revolt (1851-1864). After the establishment of the Ching dynasty, Chinese men were forced to shave the hair above their foreheads and wear queues. Since the Taipings kept all their hair, they were called Long Hairs.

The prince wore yellow satin that hung down . . . yellow satin; red satin and yellow satin — I've lived long enough at seventy-nine."

"What's to be done?" muttered Mrs. Sevenpounder, standing up. "We've such a big family, young and old, and all depend on him."

"There's nothing you can do," said Mr. Chao. "The punishment for being without a queue is written down quite distinctly, sentence by sentence in a book. Makes no difference how big your family is."

When Mrs. Sevenpounder heard that it was written down in a book, she really gave up all hope. Beside herself with anxiety, she suddenly hated Sevenpounder. Pointing her chopsticks at the tip of his nose, she cried: "You've made your bed, and now you can lie on it! I said during the revolt, better not go out on the boat, better not go to town! But he would go. He rolled off to town, and they cut his queue off. He used to have a glossy black queue, but now he doesn't look like Buddhist or Taoist. He's made his own bed, he'll have to lie on it. What right has he to drag us into it? Living corpse of a jail-bird. . . ."

Since Mr. Chao had arrived, the villagers finished their meal quickly and gathered round Sevenpounder's table. Sevenpounder knew how unseemly it was for a prominent citizen to be cursed by his wife in public. So he raised his head to say slowly:

"You've plenty to say today, but at the time. . . ."

"Living corpse of a jail-bird!"

Widow Pa Yi had the kindest heart of all the onlookers there. Carrying her two-year-old baby, born after her husband's death, she was standing next to Mrs. Sevenpounder watching the fun. Now she felt things had gone too far, and hurriedly tried to make peace, saying: "Never mind, Mrs. Sevenpounder. People aren't spirits, how can they foretell the future? Didn't Mrs. Sevenpounder say at the time there was nothing to be ashamed of in having no queue? Besides, the great official in the government office hasn't issued any order yet. . . ."

Before she had finished, Mrs. Sevenpounder's ears were scarlet, and she swept her chopsticks round to point at the widow's nose. "Well, I never!" she protested. "What a thing to say, Mrs. Pa Yi! I'm still a human being, aren't I — how could I have said anything so ridiculous? I cried for three whole days when it happened, everybody saw me. Even that imp Sixpounder cried. . . ." Sixpounder had just finished a big bowl of rice, and was holding out her bowl clamoring to have it refilled. Mrs. Sevenpounder was in a temper, and brought her chopsticks down between the twin tufts on the child's head. "Stop that noise! Little slut!"

There was a crack as the empty bowl in Sixpounder's hand fell to the ground. It struck the corner of a brick and a big piece was knocked off. Sevenpounder jumped up to pick up the bowl and examine it as he fitted the pieces together. "Damn you!" he shouted, and gave Sixpounder a slap on the face that knocked her over. Sixpounder lay there crying until Old Mrs. Ninepounder took her by the hand and walked off with her, muttering, "Each generation is worse than the last."

It was Widow Pa Yi's turn to be angry. "Hitting a child, Mrs. Sevenpounder!" she shouted.

Mr. Chao had been looking on with a smile, but when Widow Pa Yi said that the great official in the government office had not issued any order yet, he began to grow angry. Now coming right up to the table, he said: "What does it matter hitting a child? The imperial army will be here anytime now. You know, the protector of the empire is General Chang, who's descended from Chang Fei of the period of the Three Kingdoms. He has a huge lance eighteen feet long, and dares take on ten thousand men. Nobody can stand against him." Raising his empty hands, as if grasping a huge invisible lance, he took a few paces towards Widow Pa Yi, saying, "Are you a match for him?"

Widow Pa Yi was trembling with rage as she held her child. But the sudden sight of Mr. Chao bearing down on her with perspiring face and staring eyes gave her the fright of her life. Without finishing what she had to say, she turned and fled. Mr. Chao left too. As they made way, the villagers blamed Widow Pa Yi for interfering, and a few men who had cut their queues and started growing them again hid hastily behind the crowd for fear Mr. Chao should see them. However, Mr. Chao passed through the group without making a careful inspection. Suddenly he dived behind the tallow trees, and with a parting "Think you're a match for him!" strode on to the one-plank bridge and was off.

The villagers stood there blankly, turning things over in their minds. They realized they really were no match for Chang Fei; hence Sevenpounder's life was as good as lost. And since Sevenpounder had broken the imperial law, they felt he should never have adopted that lordly air as he smoked that long pipe of his and told them the news in town. So the fact that he was in trouble gave them a certain pleasure. They would have liked to discuss the matter, but did not know what to say. Buzzing mosquitoes brushed past their bare arms, then zoomed back to swarm beneath the tallow trees. The villagers scattered to their homes, shut their doors and went to sleep. Grumbling to herself, Mrs. Sevenpounder cleared away the dishes, table and stools and went inside too, to close the door and go to sleep.

Sevenpounder took the broken bowl inside, and sat on the doorsill smoking; but he was still so worried he forgot to pull on the pipe, and the light in the pewter bowl of his sixfoot speckled bamboo pipe with the ivory mouthpiece gradually turned black. Matters seemed to have reached a very dangerous state, and he tried to think of a way out or some plan of action. But his thoughts were in a whirl, and he could not straighten them out. "Queues, eh, queues? A huge eighteen-foot lance. Each generation is worse than the last! The emperor's ascended his throne. The broken bowl will have to be taken to town to be riveted. Who's a match for him? It's written in a book. Damn. . . !"

*T*he next morning Sevenpounder went to town with the boat as usual. Towards evening he came back to Luchen, with his six-foot speckled bamboo pipe and the rice bowl. At supper he told Old Mrs. Ninepounder he had had the bowl riveted in town. Because it was such a large break, sixteen copper clamps had been needed, and they cost three cash each — making a total of forty-eight cash altogether.

"Each generation is worse than the last," said Old Mrs. Ninepounder crossly. "I've lived long enough. Three cash for a clamp. These aren't like the clamps we used to have. In the old days . . . ah. . . . I've lived seventy-nine years. . . ."

Though Sevenpounder went into town every day as before, his house seemed to be under a cloud. Most of the villagers kept out of his way, no longer coming to ask him what the news was in town. Mrs. Sevenpounder was always in a bad temper too, and constantly addressed him as "Gaol-bird."

About a fortnight later, when Sevenpounder came back from town, he found his wife in a rare good humor. "Heard anything in town?" she asked him.

"No, nothing."

"Has the emperor ascended his throne?"

"They didn't say."

"Did no one in Prosperity Tavern say anything?"

"No, nothing."

"I don't think the emperor will ascend the throne. I passed Mr. Chao's wine shop today, and he was sitting there reading again, with his queue coiled on the top of his head. He wasn't wearing his long gown either."

". . . . ."

"Do you think maybe he won't ascend the throne?"

"I think probably not."

*T*oday Sevenpounder is again respected and well treated by his wife and the villagers. In the summer his family still sit down to eat on the mud flat outside their door, and passers-by greet them with smiles. Old Mrs. Ninepounder celebrated her eightieth birthday some time ago, and is as hale and hearty as ever, and as full of complaints. Sixpounder's twin tufts of hair have changed into a thick braid. Although they started to bind her feet recently, she can still help Mrs. Sevenpounder with odd jobs, and limps about the mud flat carrying the rice bowl with its sixteen copper rivets.

October 1920

My Old Home

*B*raving the bitter cold, I traveled more than seven hundred miles back to the old home I had left over twenty years before.

It was late winter. As we drew near my former home the day became overcast and a cold wind blew into the cabin of our boat, while all one could see through the chinks in our bamboo awning were a few desolate villages, void of any sign of life, scattered far and near under the somber yellow sky. I could not help feeling depressed.

Ah! Surely this was not the old home I had remembered for the past twenty years?

The old home I remembered was nor in the least like this. My old home was much better. But if you asked me to recall its peculiar charm or describe its beauties, I had no clear impression, no words to describe it. And now it seemed this was all there was to it. Then I rationalized the matter to myself, saying: Home was always like this, and although it has not improved, still it is not so depressing as I imagine; it is only my mood that has changed, because I am coming back to the country this time with no illusions.

This time I had come with the sole object of saying goodbye. The old house our clan had lived in for so many years had already been sold to another family, and was to change hands before the end of the year. I had to hurry there before New Year's Day to say goodbye forever to the familiar old house, and to move my family to another place where I was working, far from my old home town.

At dawn on the second day I reached the gateway of my home. Broken stems of withered grass on the roof, trembling in the wind, made very clear the reason why this old house could not avoid changing hands. Several branches of our clan had probably already moved away, so it was unusually quiet. By the time I reached the house my mother was already at the door to welcome me, and my eight-year-old nephew, Hung-erh, rushed out after her.

Though mother was delighted, she was also trying to hide a certain feeling of sadness. She told me to sit down and rest and have some tea, letting the removal wait for the time being. Hung-erh, who had never seen me before, stood watching me at a distance.

But finally we had to talk about the removal. I said that rooms had already been rented elsewhere, and I had bought a little furniture; in addition it would be necessary to sell all the furniture in the house in order to buy more things. Mother agreed, saying that the luggage was nearly all packed, and about half the furniture that could not easily be moved had already been sold. Only it was difficult to get people to pay up.

"You must rest for a day or two, and call on our relatives, and then we can go," said mother.

"Yes."

"Then there is Jun-tu. Each time he comes here he always asks after you, and wants very much to see you again. I told him the probable date of your return home, and he may be coming anytime."

At this point a strange picture suddenly flashed into my mind: a golden moon suspended in a deep blue sky and beneath it the seashore, planted as far as the eye could see with jade-green watermelons, while in their midst a boy of eleven or twelve, wearing a silver necklet and grasping a steel pitchfork in his hand, was thrusting with all his might at a *zha* which dodged the blow and escaped between his legs.

This boy was Jun-tu. When I first met him he was just over ten — that was thirty years ago, and at that time my father was still alive and the family well off, so I was really a spoilt child. That year it was our family's turn to take charge of a big ancestral sacrifice, which came round only once in thirty years, and hence was an important one. In the first month the ancestral images were presented and offerings made, and since the sacrificial vessels were very fine and there was such a crowd of worshippers, it was necessary to guard against theft. Our family had only one part-time laborer. (In our district we divide laborers into three classes: those who work all the year for one family are called full-timers; those who are hired by the day are called dailies; and those who farm their own land and only work for one family at New Year, during festivals or when rents are being collected are called part-timers.) And since there was so much to be done, he told my father that he would send for his son Jun-tu to look after the sacrificial vessels.

When my father gave his consent I was overjoyed, because I had long since heard of Jun-tu and knew that he was about my own age, born in the intercalary month,* and when his horoscope was told it was found that of the five elements that of earth was lacking, so his father called him Jun-tu (Intercalary Earth). He could set traps and catch small birds.

I looked forward every day to New Year, for New Year would bring Jun-tu. At last, when the end of the year came, one day mother told me that Jun-tu had come, and I flew to see him. He was standing in the kitchen. He had a round, crimson face and wore a small felt cap on his head and a gleaming silver necklet round his neck, showing that his father doted on him and, fearing he might die, had made a pledge with the gods and buddhas, using the necklet as a talisman. He was very shy, and I was the only person he was not afraid of. When there was no one else there, he would talk with me, so in a few hours we were fast friends.

I don't know what we talked of then, but I remember that Jun-tu was in high spirits, saying that since he had come to town he had seen many new things.

The next day I wanted him to catch birds.

"Can't be done," he said. "It's only possible after a heavy snowfall. On our sands, after it snows, I sweep clear a patch of ground, prop up a big threshing basket with a short stick, and scatter husks of grain beneath. When the birds come there to eat, I tug a string tied to the stick, and the birds are caught

---

* The Chinese lunar calendar reckons 360 days to a year, and each month comprises 29 or 30 days, never 31. Hence every few years a 13th, or intercalary, month is inserted in the calendar.

in the basket. There are all kinds: wild pheasants,. woodcocks, wood-pigeons, 'blue-backs'. . . ."

Accordingly I looked forward very eagerly to snow.

"Just now it is too cold," said Jun-tu another time, "but you must come to our place in summer. In the daytime we'll go to the seashore to look for shells, there are green ones and red ones, besides 'scare-devil' shells and 'buddha's hands.' In the evening when dad and I go to see to the watermelons, you shall come too."

"Is it to look out for thieves?"

"No. If passers-by are thirsty and pick a watermelon, folk down our way don't consider it as stealing. What we have to look out for are badgers, hedgehogs and *zha*. When under the moonlight you hear the crunching sound made by the *zha* when it bites the melons, then you take your pitchfork and creep stealthily over. . . ."

I had no idea then what this thing called *zha* was — and I am not much clearer now for that matter — but somehow I felt it was something like a small dog, and very fierce.

"Don't they bite people?"

"You have a pitchfork. You go across, and when you see it you strike. It's a very cunning creature and will rush towards you and get away between your legs. Its fur is as slippery as oil. . . ."

I had never known that all these strange things existed: at the seashore there were shells all colors of the rainbow; watermelons were exposed to such danger, yet all I had known of them before was that they were sold in the greengrocer's.

"On our shore, when the tide comes in, there are lots of jumping fish, each with two legs like a frog. . . ."

Jun-tu's mind was a treasure-house of such strange lore, all of it outside the ken of my former friends. They were ignorant of all these things and, while Jun-tu lived by the sea, they like me could see only the four corners of the sky above the high courtyard wall.

Unfortunately, a month after New Year Jun-tu had to go home. I burst into teats and he took refuge in the kitchen, crying and refusing to come out, until finally his father carried him off. Later he sent me by his father a packet of shells and a few very beautiful feathers, and I sent him presents once or twice, but we never saw each other again.

Now that my mother mentioned him, this childhood memory sprang into life like a flash of lightning, and I seemed to see my beautiful old home. So I answered:

"Fine! And he — how is he?"

"He's not at all well off either," said mother. And then, looking out of the door: "Here come those people again. They say they want to buy our furniture; but actually they just want to see what they can pick up. I must go and watch them."

Mother stood up and went out. The voices of several women could he heard outside. I called Hung-erh to me and started talking to him, asking him whether he could write, and whether he would be glad to leave.

"Shall we be going by train?"

"Yes, we shall go by train."

"And boat?"

"We shall take a boat first."

"Oh! Like this! With such a long moustache!" A strange shrill voice suddenly rang out.

I looked up with a start, and saw a woman of about fifty with prominent cheekbones and thin lips. With her hands on her hips, not wearing a skirt but with her trousered legs apart, she stood in front of me just like the compass in a box of geometrical instruments.

I was flabbergasted.

"Don't you know me? Why, I have held you in my arms!"

I felt even more flabbergasted. Fortunately my mother came in just then and said:

"He has been away so long, you must excuse him for forgetting. You should remember," she said to me, "this is Mrs. Yang from across the road. . . . She has a bean curd shop."

Then, to be sure, I remembered. When I was a child there was a Mrs. Yang who used to sit nearly all day long in the bean curd shop across the road, and everybody used to call her Bean curd Beauty. She used to powder herself, and her cheekbones were not so prominent then nor her lips so thin; moreover she remained seated all the time, so that I had never noticed this resemblance to a compass. In those days people said that, thanks to her, that bean curd shop did very good business. But, probably on account of my age, she had made no impression on me, so that later I forgot her entirely. However, the Compass was extremely indignant and looked at me most contemptuously, just as one might look at a Frenchman who had never heard of Napoleon or an American who had never heard of Washington, and smiling sarcastically she said:

"You had forgotten? Naturally I am beneath your notice. . . ."

"Certainly not . . . I . . ." I answered nervously, getting to my feet.

"Then you listen to me, Master Hsun. You have grown rich, and they are too heavy to move, so you can't possibly want these old pieces of furniture anymore. You had better let me take them away. Poor people like us can do with them."

"I haven't grown rich. I must sell these in order to buy. . . ."

"Oh, come now, you have been made the intendant of a circuit, how can you still say you're not rich? You have three concubines now, and whenever you go out it is in a big sedan-chair with eight bearers. Do you still say you're not rich? Hah! You can't hide anything from me."

Knowing there was nothing I could say, I remained silent.

"Come now, really, the more money people have the more miserly they get, and the more miserly they are the more money they get . . ." remarked the Compass, turning indignantly away and walking slowly off, casually picking up a pair of mother's gloves and stuffing them into her pocket as she went out.

After this a number of relatives in the neighborhood came to call. In the intervals between entertaining them I did some packing, and so three or four days passed.

One very cold afternoon, I sat drinking tea after lunch when I was aware of someone coming in, and turned my head to see who it was. At the first glance I gave an involuntary start, hastily stood up and went over to welcome him.

The newcomer was Jun-tu. But although I knew at a glance that this was Jun-tu, it was not the Jun-tu I remembered. He had grown to twice his former size. His round face, once crimson, had become sallow, and acquired deep lines and wrinkles; his eyes too had become like his father's, the rims swollen and red, a feature common to most peasants who work by the sea and are exposed all day to the wind from the ocean. He wore a shabby felt cap and just one very thin padded jacket, with the result that he was shivering from head to foot. He carried a paper package and a long pipe, nor was his hand the plump red hand I remembered, but coarse and clumsy and chapped, like the bark of a pine tree.

Delighted as I was, I did not know how to express myself, and could only say:

"Oh! Jun-tu — so it's you. . . ?"

After this there were so many things I wanted to talk about, they should have poured out like a string of beads: wood-cocks, jumping fish, shells, *zha*. . . . But I was tongue-tied, unable to put all I was thinking into words.

He stood there, mixed joy and sadness showing on his face. His lips moved, but not a sound did he utter. Finally, assuming a respectful attitude, he said clearly:

"Master. . . !"

I felt a shiver run through me; for I knew then what a lamentably thick wall had grown up between us. Yet I could not say anything.

He turned his head to call:

"Shui-sheng, bow to the master." Then he pulled forward a boy who had been hiding behind his back, and this was just the Jun-tu of twenty years before, only a little paler and thinner, and he had no silver necklet.

"This is my fifth," he said. "He's not used to company, so he's shy and awkward."

Mother came downstairs with Hung-erh, probably after hearing our voices.

"I got your letter some time ago, madam," said Jun-tu. "I was really so pleased to know the master was coming back. . . ."

"Now, why are you so polite? Weren't you playmates to-gether in the past?" said mother gaily. "You had better still call him Brother Hsun as before."

"Oh, you are really too. . . . What bad manners that would be. I was a child then and didn't understand." As he was speaking Jun-tu motioned Shui-sheng to come and bow, but the child was shy, and stood stock-still behind his father.

"So he is Shui-sheng? Your fifth?" asked mother. "We are all strangers, you can't blame him for feeling shy. Hung-erh had better take him Out to play."

When Hung-eth heard this he went over to Shui-sheng, and Shui-sheng went out with him, entirely at his ease. Mother asked Jun-tu to sir down, and after a little hesitation he did so; then leaning his long pipe against the table he handed over the paper package, saying:

"In winter there is nothing worth bringing; but these few beans we dried ourselves, if you will excuse the liberty, sir."

When I asked him how things were with him, he just shook his head.

"In a very bad way. Even my sixth can do a little work, but still we haven't enough to eat . . . and then there is no security . . . all sorts of people want money, there is no fixed rule . . . and the harvests are bad. You grow things, and when you take them to sell you always have to pay several taxes and lose money, while if you don't try to sell, the things may go bad. . ."

He kept shaking his head; yet, although his face was lined with wrinkles, not one of them moved, just as if he were a stone statue. No doubt he felt intensely bitter, but could not express himself. After a pause he took up his pipe and began to smoke in silence.

From her chat with him, mother learned that he was busy at home and had to go back the next day; and since he had had no lunch, she told him to go to the kitchen and fry some rice for himself.

After he had gone out, mother and I both shook our heads over his hard life: many children, famines, taxes, soldiers, bandits, officials and landed gentry, all had squeezed him as dry as a mummy. Mother said that we should offer him all the things we were not going to take away, letting him choose for himself.

That afternoon he picked out a number of things: two long tables, four chairs, an incense burner and candlesticks, and one balance. He also asked for all the ashes from the stove (in our part we cook over straw, and the ashes can be used to fertilize sandy soil), saying that when we left he would come to take them away by boat.

That night we talked again, but not of anything serious; and the next morning he went away with Shui-sheng.

After another nine days it was time for us to leave. Jun-tu came in the morning. Shui-sheng did not come with him — he had just brought a little girl of five to watch the boat. We were very busy all day, and had no time to talk. We also had quite a number of visitors, some to see us off, some to fetch things, and some to do both. It was nearly evening when we left by boat, and by that time everything in the house, however old or shabby, large or small, fine or coarse, had been cleared away.

As we set off, in the dusk, the green mountains on either side of the river became deep blue, receding towards the stern of the boat.

Hung-erh and I, leaning against the cabin window, were looking out together at the indistinct scene outside, when suddenly he asked:

"Uncle, when shall we go back?"

"Go back? Do you mean that before you've left you want to go back?"

"Well, Shui-sheng has invited me to his home. . ."

He opened wide his black eyes in anxious thought.

Mother and I both felt rather sad, and so Jun-tu's name came up again. Mother said that ever since our family started packing up, Mrs. Yang from the bean curd shop had come over every day, and the day before in the ash-heap she had unearthed a dozen bowls and plates, which after some discussion she insisted must have been buried there by Jun-tu, so that when he came to remove the ashes he could take them home at the same rime. After making this discovery Mrs. Yang was very pleased with herself, and flew off raking the dog-teaser with her. (The dog-teaser is used by poultry keepers in our parts. It is a wooden cage inside which food is put, so that hens can stretch their necks in to eat but dogs can only look on furiously.) And it was a marvel, considering the size of her feet, how fast she could run.

I was leaving the old house farther and farther behind, while the hills and rivers of my old home were also receding gradually ever farther in the distance. But I felt no regret. I only felt that all round me was an invisible high wall, cutting me off from my fellows, and this depressed me thoroughly. The vision of that small hero with the silver necklet among the watermelons had formerly been as clear as day, but now it suddenly blurred, adding to my depression.

Mother and Hung-erh fell asleep.

I lay down, listening to the water rippling beneath the boat, and knew that I was going my way. I thought: although there is such a barrier between Jun-tu and myself, the children still have much in common, for wasn't Hung-erh thinking of Shui-sheng just now? I hope they will not he like us, that they will not allow a barrier to grow up between them. But again I would not like them, because they want to be akin, all to have a treadmill existence like mine, nor to suffer like Jun-ru until they become stupefied, nor yet, like others, to devote all their energies to dissipation. They should have a new life, a life we have never experienced.

The access of hope made me suddenly afraid. When Jun-tu asked for the incense burner and candlesticks I had laughed up my sleeve at him, to think that he still worshipped idols and could not put them out of his mind. Yet what I now called hope was no more than an idol I had created myself. The only difference was that what he desired was close at hand, while what I desired was less easily realized.

As I dozed, a stretch of jade-green seashore spread itself before my eyes, and above a round golden moon hung in a deep blue sky. I thought: hope cannot be said to exist, nor can it be said not to exist. It is just like roads across the earth. For actually the earth had no roads to begin with, but when many men pass one way, a road is made.

January 1921

The True Story of Ah Q

Chapter 1

INTRODUCTION

*F*or several years now I have been meaning to write the true story of Ah Q. But while wanting to write I was in some trepidation, too, which goes to show that I am not one of those who achieve glory by writing; for an immortal pen has always been required to record the deeds of an immortal man, the man becoming known to posterity through the writing and the writing known to posterity through the man – until finally it is not clear who is making whom known. But in the end, as though possessed by some fiend, I always came back to the idea of writing the story of Ah Q.

And yet no sooner had I taken up my pen than I became conscious of tremendous difficulties in writing this far-from-immortal work. The first was the question of what to call it. Confucius said, "If the name is not correct, the words will not ring true"; and this axiom should be most scrupulously observed. There are many types of biographies: official biographies, autobiographies, unauthorized biographies, legends, supplementary biographies, family histories, sketches . . . but unfortunately none of these suited my purpose. "Official biography?" This account will obviously not be included with those of many eminent people in some authentic history. "Autobiography?" But I am obviously not Ah Q. If I were to call this an "unauthorized biography," then where is his "authenticated biography?" The use of "legend" is impossible, because Ah Q was no legendary figure. "Supplementary biography?" But no president has ever ordered the National Historical Institute to write a "standard life" of Ah Q. It is true that although there are no "lives of gamblers" in authentic English history, the famous author Conan Doyle nevertheless wrote *Rodney Stone;** but while this is permissible for a famous author it is not permissible for such as I. Then there is "family history"; but I do nor know whether I belong to the same family as Ah Q or not, nor have his children or grandchildren ever entrusted me with such a task. If I were to use "sketch," it might be objected that Ah Q has no "complete account." In short, this is really a "life," but since I write in vulgar vein using the language of hucksters and peddlers, I dare not presume to give it so high-sounding a title. So from the stock phrase of the novelists, who are not reckoned among the Three Cults and Nine Schools.† "Enough of this digression, and back to the *true story!*" I will take the last two words as my title; and if this is reminiscent of the *True Story of Calligraphy*‡ of the ancients, it cannot be helped.

The second difficulty confronting me was that a biography of this type should start off something like this: "So-and-so, whose other name was so-and-so, was a native of such-and-such a place"; but I don't really know what Ah Q's surname was. Once, he seemed to be named Chao, but the next day there was some confusion about the matter again. This was after Mr. Chao's son had passed the county examination, and, to the sound of gongs, his success was announced in the village. Ah Q, who had just drunk two bowls of yellow wine, began to prance about declaring that this reflected credit on him too, since he belonged to the same clan as Mr. Chao, and by an exact reckoning was three generations senior to the successful candidate. At the time several bystanders even began to stand slightly in awe of Ah Q. But the next day the

---

* In Chinese this novel was called *Supplementary Biographies of the Gamblers.*

† The Three Cults were Confucianism, Buddhism and Taoism. The Nine Schools included the Confucian, Taoist, Legalist and Moist schools, as well as others. Novelists, who did not belong to any of these, were considered not quite respectable.

‡ A book by Feng Wu of the Ching dynasty (1644-1911).

bailiff summoned him to Mr. Chao's house. When the old gentleman set eyes on him his face turned crimson with fury and he roared:

"Ah Q, you miserable wretch! Did you say I belonged to the same clan as you?"

Ah Q made no reply.

The more he looked at him the angrier Mr. Chao became, and advancing menacingly a few steps he said, "How dare you talk such nonsense! How could I have such a relative as you? Is your surname Chao?"

Ah Q made no reply, and was planning a retreat, when Mr. Chao darted forward and gave him a slap on the face.

"How could *you* be named Chao! — Do you think you are worthy of the name Chao?"

Ah Q made no attempt to defend his right to the name Chao, but rubbing his left cheek went out with the bailiff. Once outside, he had to listen to another torrent of abuse from the bailiff, and thank him to the tune of two hundred cash. All who heard this said Ah Q was a great fool to ask for a beating like that. Even if his surname were Chao — which wasn't likely — he should have known better than to boast like that when there was a Mr. Chao living in the village. After this no further mention was made of Ah Q's ancestry, so that I still don't know what his surname really was.

The third difficulty I encountered in writing this work was that I don't know how Ah Q's personal name should be written either. During his lifetime everybody called him Ah Quei, but after his death not a soul mentioned Ah Quei again; for be was obviously not one of those whose name is "preserved on bamboo tablets and silk."* If there is any question of preserving his name, this essay must be the first attempt at doing so. Hence I am confronted with this difficulty at the outset. I have given the question careful thought: Ah Quei — would that be the "Quei" meaning cassia or the "Quei" meaning nobility? If his other name had been Moon Pavilion, or if he had celebrated his birthday in the month of the Moon Festival, then it would certainly be the "Quei" for cassia.†

---

* A phrase first used in the third century B.C. Bamboo and silk were writing material in ancient China.

† The cassia blooms in the month of the Moon Festival. Also, according

But since he had no other name — or if he had, no one knew it — and since he never sent out invitations on his birthday to secure complimentary verses, it would be arbitrary to write Ah Quei (cassia). Again, if he had had an elder or younger brother called Ah Fu (prosperity), then he would certainly be called Ah Quei (nobility). But he was all on his own: thus there is no justification for writing Ah Quei (nobility). All the other, unusual characters with the sound Quei are even less suitable. I once put this question to Mr. Chao's son, the successful county candidate, but even such a learned man as he was baffled by it. According to him, however, the reason why this name could not be traced was that Chen Tu-hsiu* had brought out the magazine *New Youth*, advocating the use of the Western alphabet, so that the national culture was going to the dogs. As a last resort, I asked someone from my district to go and look up the legal documents recording Ah Q's case, but after eight months he sent me a letter saying that there was no name anything like Ah Quei in those records. Although uncertain whether this was the truth or whether my friend had simply done nothing, after failing to trace the name this way I could think of no other means of finding it. Since I am afraid the new system of phonetics has not yet come into common use, there is nothing for it but to use the Western alphabet, writing the name according to the English spelling as Ah Quei and abbreviating it to Ah Q. This approximates to blindly following the *New Youth* magazine, and I am thoroughly ashamed of myself; but since even such a learned man as Mr. Chao's son could not solve my problem, what else can I do?

My fourth difficulty was with Ah Q's place of origin. If his surname were Chao, then according to the old custom which still prevails of classifying people by their districts, one might look up the commentary in *The Hundred Surnames*† and find "A native of Tienshui in Kansu Province." But

---

to Chinese folklore, it is believed that the shadow on the moon is a cassia tree.

* 1880-1942. A professor of Peking University at this time, he edited the monthly *New Youth*. Later he became a renegade from the Chinese Communist Party.

† An old school primer, in which the surnames were written into verse.

unfortunately this surname is open to question, with the result that Ah Q's place of origin must also remain uncertain. Although he lived for the most part in Weichuang, he often stayed in other places, so that it would be wrong to call him a native of Weichuang. It would, in fact, amount to a distortion of history.

The only thing that consoles me is the fact that the character "Ah" is absolutely correct. This is definitely not the result of false analogy, and is well able to stand the test of scholarly criticism. As for the other problems, it is not for such unlearned people as myself to solve them, and I can only hope that disciples of Dr. Hu Shih, who has such "a passion for history and antiquities,"* may be able in future to throw new light on them. I am afraid, however, that by that time my *True Story of Ah Q* will have long since passed into oblivion.

The foregoing may be considered as an introduction.

Chapter 2

A BRIEF ACCOUNT OF AH Q'S VICTORIES

*I*n addition to the uncertainty regarding Ah Q's surname, personal name, and place of origin, there is even some uncertainty regarding his "background." This is because the people of Weichuang only made use of his services or treated him as a laughingstock, without ever paying the slightest attention to his "background." Ah Q himself remained silent on this subject, except that when quarreling with someone he might glance at him and say, "We used to be much better off than you! Who do you think you are anyway?"

Ah Q had no family but lived in the Tutelary God's Temple at Weichuang. He had no regular work either, simply doing odd jobs for others: were there wheat to be cut he would cut

---

* This phrase was often used in self-praise by Hu Shih, the well-known reactionary politician and writer.

it, were there rice to be ground he would grind it, were there a boat to be punted he would punt it. If the work lasted for a considerable period he might stay in the house of his temporary employer, but as soon as it was finished he would leave. Thus whenever people had work to be done they would remember Ah Q, but what they remembered was his service and not his "background"; and by the time the job was done even Ah Q himself was forgotten, to say nothing of his "background." Once indeed an old man remarked, "What a good worker Ah Q is!" At that time Ah Q, stripped to the waist, listless and lean, was standing before him, and other people did not know whether the remark was meant seriously or derisively, but Ah Q was overjoyed.

Ah Q, again, had a very high opinion of himself. He looked down on all the inhabitants of Weichuang, thinking even the two young "scholars" not worth a smile, though most young scholars were likely to pass the official examinations. Mr. Chao and Mr. Chien were held in great respect by the villagers, for in addition to being rich they were both the fathers of young scholars. Ah Q alone showed them no exceptional deference, thinking to himself, "My sons may be much greater!"

Moreover, after Ah Q had been to town several times, he naturally became even more conceited, although at the same time he had the greatest contempt for townspeople. For instance, a bench made of a wooden plank three feet by three inches the Weichuang villagers called a "long bench." Ah Q called it a "long bench" too; but the townspeople called it a "straight bench," and he thought, "This is wrong. How ridiculous!" Again, when they fried large-headed fish in oil the Weichuang villagers all added shallot leaves sliced half an inch long, whereas the townspeople added finely shredded shallots, and he thought, "This is wrong too. How ridiculous!" But the Weichuang villagers were really ignorant rustics who had never seen fish fried in town!

Ah Q who "used to be much better off," who was a man of the world and "a good worker," would have been almost the perfect man had it nor been for a few unfortunate physical blemishes. The most annoying were some places on his scalp where in the past, at some uncertain dare, shiny ringworm scars had appeared. Although these were on his own head, apparently Ah Q did not consider them as altogether honorable, for he refrained from using the word "ringworm" or any words that sounded anything like it. Later he improved on this, making "bright" and "light" forbidden words, while later still even "lamp" and "candle" were taboo. Whenever this taboo was disregarded, whether intentionally or not, Ah Q would fly into a rage, his ringworm scars turning scarlet. He would look over the offender, and if it were someone weak in repartee he would curse him, while if it were a poor fighter he would hit him. Yet, curiously enough, it was usually Ah Q who was worsted in these encounters, until finally he adopted new tactics, contenting himself in general with a furious glare.

It so happened, however, that after Ah Q had taken to using this furious glare, the idlers in Weichuang grew even more fond of making jokes at his expense. As soon as they saw him they would pretend to give a start, and say:

"Look! It's lighting up."

Ah Q would rise to the bait as usual, and glare furiously.

"So there is a paraffin lamp here," they would continue, not in the least intimidated.

Ah Q could do nothing but rack his brains for some retort: "You don't even deserve. . . ." At this juncture it seemed as if the scars on his scalp were noble and honorable, not just ordinary ringworm scars. However, as we said above, Ah Q was a man of the world: he knew at once that he had neatly broken the "taboo" and refrained from saying anymore.

If the idlers were still not satisfied, but continued to bait him, they would in the end come to blows. Then only after Ah Q had, to all appearances, been defeated, had his brownish pigtail pulled and his head bumped against the wall four or five times, would the idlers walk away, satisfied at having won. Ah Q would stand there for a second, thinking to himself, "It is as if I were beaten by my son. What is the world coming to nowadays. . . ." Thereupon he too would walk away, satisfied at having won.

Whatever Ah Q thought he was sure to tell people later; thus almost all who made fun of Ah Q knew that he had this means of winning a psychological victory. So after this anyone who pulled or twisted his brown pigtail would forestall him by saying: "Ah Q, this is not a son beating his father, it is a man beating a beast. Let's hear you say it: A man bearing a beast!"

Then Ah Q, clutching at the root of his pigtail, his head on one side, would say: "Beating an insect — how about that? I am an insect — now will you let me go?"

But although he was an insect the idlers would not let him go until they had knocked his head five or six times against something nearby, according to their custom, after which they would walk away satisfied that they had won, confident that this time Ah Q was done for. In less than ten seconds, however, Ah Q would walk away also satisfied that he had won, thinking that he was the "foremost self-belittler," and that after subtracting "self-belittler" what remained was "foremost." Was not the highest successful candidate in the official examination also the "foremost?" "And who do you think you are anyway?"

After employing such cunning devices to get even with his enemies, Ah Q would make his way cheerfully to the wine shop to drink a few bowls of wine, joke with the others again, quarrel with them again, come off victorious again, and return cheerfully to the Tutelary God's Temple, there to fall asleep as soon as his head touched the pillow. If he had money he would gamble. A group of men would squat on the ground, Ah Q sandwiched in their midst, his face streaming with perspiration; and his voice would shout the loudest: "Four hundred on the Green Dragon!"

"Hey — open there!" the stakeholder, his face streaming with perspiration too, would open the box and chant: "Heavenly Gate. . . ! Nothing for the Corner. . . ! No stakes on the Popularity Passage! Pass over Ah Q's coppers!"

"The Passage — one hundred — one hundred and fifty."

To the tune of this chanting, Ah Q's money would gradually vanish into the pockets of other perspiring people. Finally he would be forced to squeeze his way out of the crowd and watch from the back, taking a vicarious interest in the game until it broke up, when he would return reluctantly to the Tutelary God's Temple. The next day he would go to work with swollen eyes.

However, the truth of the proverb "misfortune may be a blessing in disguise" was shown when Ah Q was unfortunate enough to win and almost suffered defeat in the end.

This was the evening of the Festival of the Gods in Weichuang. According to custom there was a play; and close to the stage, also according to custom, were numerous gambling tables. The drums and gongs of the play sounded about three miles away to Ah Q who had ears only for the stakeholder's chant. He staked successfully again and again, his coppers turning into silver coins, his silver coins into dollars, and his dollars mounting up. In his excitement he cried our, "Two dollars on Heavenly Gate!"

He never knew who started the fight, nor for what reason. Curses, blows and footsteps formed a confused medley of sound in his head, and by the time he clambered to his feet the gambling tables had vanished and so had the gamblers. Several parts of his body seemed to be aching as if he had been kicked and knocked about, while a number of people were looking at him in astonishment. Feeling as if there were something amiss, he walked back to the Tutelary God's Temple, and by the time he regained his composure he realized that his pile of dollars had disappeared. Since most of the people who ran gambling tables at the Festival were not natives of Weichuang, where could he look for the culprits?

So white and glittering a pile of silver! It had all been his . . . but now it had disappeared. Even to consider it tantamount to being robbed by his son did not comfort him. To consider himself as an insect did not comfort him either. This time he really tasted something of the bitterness of defeat.

But presently he changed defeat into victory. Raising his right hand he slapped his own face hard twice, so that it tingled with pain. After this slapping his heart felt lighter, for it seemed as if the one who had given the slap was himself, the one slapped some other self, and soon it was just as if he had beaten someone else — in spite of the fact that his face was still tingling. He lay down satisfied that he had gained the victory.

Soon he was asleep.

Chapter 3

A FURTHER ACCOUNT OF AH Q'S VICTORIES

*A*lthough Ah Q was always gaining victories, it was only after he was favored with a slap on the face by Mr. Chao that he became famous.

After paying the bailiff two hundred cash he lay down angrily. Later he said to himself, "What is the world coming to nowadays, with sons beating their parents. . . ." Then the thought of the prestige of Mr. Chao, who was now his son, gradually raised his spirits, and he got up and went to the wine shop singing *The Young Widow at Her Husband's Grave.* At that time he did feel that Mr. Chao was a cut above most people.

After this incident, strange to relate, it was true that every-body seemed to pay him unusual respect. He probably attrib-uted this to the fact that he was Mr. Chao's father, but actually such was not the case. In Weichuang, as a rule, if the seventh child hit the eighth child or Li So-and-so hit Chang So-and-so, it was not taken seriously. A heating had to be connected with some important personage like Mr. Chao before the villagers thought it worth talking about. But once they thought it worth talking about, since the beater was famous, the one beaten enjoyed some of his reflected fame. As for the fault being Ah Q's, that was naturally taken for granted, the reason being that Mr. Chao could not possibly be wrong. But if Ah Q were wrong, why did everybody seem to treat him with unusual respect? This is difficult to explain. We may put forward the hypothesis that it was because Ah Q had said he belonged to the same family as Mr. Chao; thus, although he had been beaten, people were still afraid there might be some truth in what he said and therefore thought it safer to treat him more respectfully. Or, alternatively, it may have been like the case of the sacrificial beef in the Confucian temple:

although the beef was in the same category as the sacrificial pork and mutton, being of animal origin just as they were, later Confucians did not dare touch it since the sage had enjoyed it.

After this Ah Q prospered for several years.

One spring, when he was walking along in a state of happy intoxication, he saw Whiskers Wang sitting stripped to the waist in the sunlight at the foot of a wall, catching lice; and at this sight his own body began to itch. Since Whiskers Wang was scabby and bewhiskered, everybody called him "Ring-worm Whiskers Wang." Although Ah Q omitted the word "Ringworm," he had the greatest contempt for the man. Ah Q felt that while scabs were nothing to take exception to, such hairy cheeks were really too outlandish, and could excite nothing but scorn. So Ah Q sat down by his side. If it had been any other idler, Ah Q would never have dared sit down so casually; but what had he to fear by the side of Whiskers Wang? To tell the truth, the fact that he was willing to sit down was an honor for Wang.

Ah Q took off his tattered lined jacket, and turned it inside out; but either because he had washed it recently or because he was too clumsy, a long search yielded only three or four lice. He saw that Whiskers Wang, on the other hand, was catching first one and then another in swift succession, cracking them in his teeth with a popping sound.

Ah Q felt first disappointed, then resentful: the despicable Whiskers Wang could catch so many while he himself had caught so few — what a great loss of face! He longed to catch one or two big ones, but there were none, and it was only with considerable difficulty that he managed to catch a mid-dle-sized one, which he thrust fiercely into his mouth and bit savagely; but it only gave a small sputtering sound, again inferior to the noise Whiskers Wang was making.

All Ah Q's scars turned scarlet. Flinging his jacket on the ground, he spat and said, "Hairy worm!"

"Mangy dog, who are you calling names?" Whiskers Wang looked up contemptuously.

Although the relative respect accorded him in recent years had increased Ah Q's pride, when confronted by loafers who were accustomed to fighting he remained rather timid. On this occasion, however, he was feeling exceptionally pugnacious. How dare a hairy-cheeked creature like this insult him?

"Anyone who the name fits," said Ah Q standing up, his hands on his hips.

"Are your bones itching?" demanded Whiskers Wang, standing up too and putting on his coat.

Thinking that Wang meant to run away, Ah Q stepped forward raising his fist to punch him. But before his fist came down, Whiskers Wang had already seized him and given him a tug which sent him staggering. Then Whiskers Wang seized Ah Q's pigtail and started dragging him towards the wall to knock his head in the time-honored manner.

"'A gentleman uses his tongue but not his hands!'" protested Ah Q, his head on one side.

Apparently Whiskers Wang was no gentleman, for without paying the slightest attention to what Ah Q said he knocked his head against the wall five times in succession, and gave him a great shove which sent him staggering two yards away. Only then did Whiskers Wang walk away satisfied.

As far as Ah Q could remember, this was the first humiliation of his life, because he had always scoffed at Whiskers Wang on account of his ugly bewhiskered cheeks, but had never been scoffed at, much less beaten by him. And now, contrary to all expectations, Whiskers Wang had beaten him. Perhaps what they said in the marketplace was really true: "The Emperor has abolished the official examinations, so that scholars who have passed them are no longer in demand." As a result of this the Chao family must have lost prestige. Was it a result of this, too, that people were treating him contemptuously?

Ah Q stood there irresolutely.

From the distance approached another of Ah Q's enemies. This was Mr. Chien's eldest son whom Ah Q also despised. After studying in a foreign school in the city, it seemed he had gone to Japan. When he came home half a year later his legs were straight and his pigtail had disappeared. His mother cried bitterly a dozen times, and his wife tried three times to jump into the well. Later his mother told everyone, "His pigtail was cut off by some scoundrel when he was drunk. He would have been able to be an official, but now he will have to wait until it has grown again before he thinks of that." Ah Q did not, however, believe this, and insisted on calling him "Imitation Foreign Devil" and "Traitor in Foreign Pay." As soon as Ah Q saw him he would start cursing under his breath.

*W*hat Ah Q despised and detested most in him was his false pigtail. When it came to having a false pigtail, a man could scarcely be considered human; and the fact that his wife had not attempted to jump into the well a fourth time showed that she was not a good woman either.

Now this "Imitation Foreign Devil" was approaching.

"Baldhead — Ass —" In the past Ah Q had cursed under his breath only, inaudibly; but today, because he was in a bad temper and wanted to work off his feelings, the words slipped out involuntarily.

Unfortunately this "baldhead" was carrying a shiny, brown stick which Ah Q called a "staff carried by the mourner." With great strides he bore down on Ah Q who, guessing at once that a beating was impending, hastily braced himself to wait with a stiffened back. Sure enough, there was a resounding thwack which seemed to have alighted on his head.

"I meant him!" explained Ah Q, pointing to a nearby child.

Thwack! Thwack! Thwack!

As far as Ah Q could remember, this was the second humiliation of his life. Fortunately after the thwacking stopped it seemed to him that the matter was closed, and he even felt somewhat relieved. Moreover, the precious "ability to forget" handed down by his ancestors stood him in good stead. He walked slowly away and by the time he approached the wine shop door he felt quite happy again.

Just then, however, a small nun from the Convent of Quiet Self-improvement came walking towards him. The sight of a nun always made Ah Q swear; how much more so, then, after these humiliations? When he recalled what had happened, all his anger revived.

"So all my bad luck today was because I had to see you!" he thought to himself.

He went up to her and spat noisily. "Ugh. . . ! Pah!"

The small nun paid not the least attention, but walked on with lowered head. Ah Q went up to her and shot out a hand to rub her newly shaved scalp, then laughing stupidly said, "Baldhead! Go back quickly, your monk is waiting for you. . . ."

"Who are you pawing. . . ?" demanded the nun, blushing crimson as she began to hurry away.

The men in the wine shop roared with laughter. Seeing that his feat was admired, Ah Q began to feel elated.

"If the monk paws you, why can't I?" said he, pinching her cheek.

Again the men in the wine shop roared with laughter. Ah Q felt even more pleased, and in order to satisfy those who were expressing approval, he pinched her hard again before letting her go.

During this encounter he had already forgotten Whiskers Wang and the Imitation Foreign Devil, as if all the day's bad luck had been avenged. And, strange to relate, even more relaxed than after the beating, he felt light and buoyant as if ready to float into the air.

"Ah Q, may you die sonless!" sounded the little nun's voice tearfully in the distance.

Ah Q roared with delighted laughter.

The men in the wine shop roared too, with only slightly less satisfaction.

Chapter 4

THE TRAGEDY OF LOVE

*T*here are said to be some victors who take no pleasure in a victory unless their opponents are as fierce as tigers or eagles: if their adversaries are as timid as sheep or chickens they find their triumph empty. There are other victors who, having carried all before them, with the enemy slain or surrendered, cowering in utter subjection, realize that now no foe, rival, or friend is left — they have only themselves, supreme, solitary, desolate, and forlorn. Then they find their triumph a tragedy. But our hero was not so spineless. He was always exultant. This may be a proof of the moral supremacy of China over the rest of the world.

Look at Ah Q, light and elated, as if about to fly!

This victory was not without strange consequences, though. For quite a time he seemed to be flying, and he flew into the Tutelary God's Temple, where he would normally have snored as soon as he lay down. This evening, however, he found it very difficult to close his eyes, for he felt as if there were something the matter with his thumb and first finger, which seemed to be smoother than usual. It is impossible to say whether something soft and smooth on the little nun's face had stuck to his fingers, or whether his fingers had been rubbed smooth against her cheek.

"Ah Q, may you die sonless!"

These words sounded again in Ah Q's ears, and he thought, "Quite right, I should take a wife; for if a man dies sonless he has no one to sacrifice a bowl of rice to his spirit . . . I ought to have a wife." As the saying goes, "There are three forms of unfilial conduct, of which the worst is to have no descendants,"* and it is one of the tragedies of life that "spirits without descendants go hungry."† Thus his view was absolutely in accordance with the teachings of the saints and sages, and it is indeed a pity that later he should have run amok.

"Woman, woman!" he thought.

". . . The monk paws. . . . Woman, woman. . . ! Woman!" he thought again.

We shall never know when Ah Q finally fell asleep that evening. After this, however, he probably always found his fingers rather soft and smooth, and always remained a little lightheaded. "Woman. . . ." he kept thinking.

From this we can see that woman is a menace to mankind.

---

* A quotation from Mencius (372-289 B.C.).
† A quotation from the old classic *Zuo Zhuan*.

The majority of Chinese men could become saints and sages, were it not for the unfortunate fact that they are ruined by women. The Shang dynasty was destroyed by Ta Chi, the Chou dynasty was undermined by Pao Szu; as for the Chin dynasty, although there is no historical evidence to that effect, if we assume that it fell on account of some woman we shall probably not be far wrong. And it is a fact that Tung Cho's death was caused by Tiao Chan.*

Ah Q, too, was a man of strict morals to begin with. Although we do not know whether he was guided by some good teacher, he had always shown himself most scrupulous in observing "strict segregation of the sexes," and was righteous enough to denounce such heretics as the little nun and the Imitation Foreign Devil. His view was, "All nuns must carry on in secret with monks. If a woman walks alone on the street, she must want to seduce bad men. When a man and a woman talk together, it must be to arrange to meet." In order to correct such people, he would glare furiously, pass loud, cutting remarks, or, if the place were deserted, throw a small stone from behind.

Who could tell that close on thirty, when a man should "stand firm,"† he would lose his head like this over a little nun? Such lightheadedness, according to the classical canons, is most reprehensible; thus women certainly are hateful creatures. For if the little nun's face had not been soft and smooth, Ah Q would not have been bewitched by her; nor would this have happened if the little nun's face had been covered by a cloth. Five or six years before, when watching an open-air opera, he had pinched the leg of a woman in the audience; but because it was separated from him by the cloth of her trousers he had not had this lightheaded feeling afterwards. The little nun had not covered her face, however, and this is another proof of the odiousness of the heretic.

"Woman . . ." thought Ah Q.

---

* Ta Chi, of the twelfth century B.C., was the concubine of the last king of the Shang dynasty. Pao Szu, of the eighth century B.C., was the concubine of the last king of the Western Chou dynasty. Tiao Chan was the concubine of Tung Cho, a powerful minister of the third century A.D.

† Confucius said that at thirty he "stood firm." The phrase was later used to indicate that a man was thirty years old.

He kept a close watch on those women who he believed must "want to seduce bad men," but they did not smile at him. He listened very carefully to those women who talked to him, but not one of them mentioned anything relevant to a secret rendezvous. Ah! This was simply another example of the odiousness of women: they all assumed a false modesty.

One day when Ah Q was grinding rice in Mr. Chao's house, he sat down in the kitchen after supper to smoke a pipe. If it had been anyone else's house, he could have gone home after supper, but they dined early in the Chao family. Although it was the rule that you must not light a lamp, but go to bed after eating, there were occasional exceptions to the rule. Before Mr. Chao's son passed the county examination he was allowed to light a lamp to study the examination essays, and when Ah Q went to do odd jobs he was allowed to light a lamp to grind rice. Because of this latter exception to the rule, Ah Q still sat in the kitchen smoking before going on with his work.

When Amah Wu, the only maidservant in the Chao household, had finished washing the dishes, she sat down on the long bench too and started chatting to Ah Q:

"Our mistress hasn't eaten anything for two days, because the master wants to get a concubine. . . ."

"Woman . . . Amah Wu . . . this little widow," thought Ah Q.

"Our young mistress is going to have a baby in the eighth moon . ."

"Woman . . ." thought Ah Q.

He put down his pipe and stood up.

"Our young mistress —" Amah Wu chattered on.

"Sleep with me!" Ah Q suddenly rushed forward and threw himself at her feet.

There was a moment of absolute silence.

"Aiya!" Dumbfounded for an instant, Amah Wu suddenly began to tremble, then rushed out shrieking and could soon be heard sobbing.

Ah Q kneeling opposite the wall was dumbfounded too. He grasped the empty bench with both hands and stood up slowly, dimly aware that something was wrong. In fact, by this time he was in rather a nervous state himself. In a flurry, he stuck his pipe into his belt and decided to go back to the rice. But — bang! — a heavy blow landed on his head, and he spun round to see the successful county candidate standing before him brandishing a big bamboo pole.

"How dare you . . . you. . . . ."

The big bamboo pole came down across Ah Q's shoulders. When he put up both hands to protect his head, the blow landed on his knuckles, causing him considerable pain. As he escaped through the kitchen door it seemed as if his back also received a blow.

"Turtle's egg!" shouted the successful candidate, cursing him in mandarin from behind.

Ah Q fled to the hulling-floor where he stood alone, still feeling a pain in his knuckles and still remembering that "turtle's egg" because it was an expression never used by the Weichuang villagers, but only by the rich who had seen something of official life. This made him more frightened, and left an exceptionally deep impression on his mind. By now, however, all thought of "Woman . . ." had flown. After this cursing and beating it seemed as if something were done with, and quite lightheartedly he began to grind rice again. After grinding for some time he felt hot, and stopped to take off his shirt.

While he was taking off his shirt he heard an uproar outside, and since Ah Q always liked to join in any excitement that was going, he went Out in search of the sound. He traced it gradually right into Mr. Chao's inner courtyard. Although it was dusk he could see many people there: all the Chao family including the mistress who had not eaten for two days. In addition, their neighbor Mrs. Tsou was there, as well as their relatives Chao Pai-yen and Chao Szu-chen.

The young mistress was leading Amah Wu out of the servants' quarters, saying as she did so:

"Come outside . . . don't stay brooding in your own room."

"Everybody knows you are a good woman," put in Mrs. Tsou from the side. "You mustn't think of committing suicide."

Amah Wu merely wailed, muttering something inaudible.

"This is interesting," thought Ah Q. "What mischief can this little widow be up to?" Wanting to find out, he was approaching Chao Szu-chen when suddenly he caught sight of Mr. Chao's eldest son rushing towards him with, what was worse, the big bamboo pole in his hand. The sight of this big bamboo pole reminded him that he had been beaten by it, and be realized that apparently he was connected in some way with this scene of excitement. He turned and ran, hoping to escape to the hulling-floor, not foreseeing that the bamboo pole would cut off his retreat; thereupon he turned and ran in the other direction, leaving without further ado by the back door. In a short time he was back in the Tutelary God's Temple.

After Ah Q had sat down for a time, his skin began to form goose pimples and he felt cold, because although it was spring the nights were still quite frosty and nor suited to bare backs. He remembered that he had left his shirt in the Chaos' house, but he was afraid if he went to fetch it he might get another taste of the successful candidate's bamboo pole.

Then the bailiff came in.

"Curse you, Ah Q!" said the bailiff. "So you can't even keep your hands off the Chao family servants, you rebel! You've made me lose my sleep, curse you. . . !"

Under this torrent of abuse Ah Q naturally had nothing to say. Finally, since it was night-time, Ah Q had to pay double and give the bailiff four hundred cash. Because he happened to have no ready money by him, he gave his felt hat as security, and agreed to the following five terms:

1.The next morning Ah Q must take a pair of red candles, weighing one pound, and a bundle of incense sticks to the Chao family to atone for his misdeeds.

2.Ah Q must pay for the Taoist priests whom the Chao family had called to exorcize evil spirits.

3.Ah Q must never again set foot in the Chao household.

4.If anything unfortunate should happen to Amah Wu, Ah Q must be held responsible.

5.Ah Q must not go back for his wages or shirt.

Ah Q naturally agreed to everything, but unfortunately he had no ready money. Luckily it was already spring, so it was possible to do without his padded quilt which he pawned for two thousand cash to comply with the terms stipulated. After kowtowing with bare back he still had a few cash left, but instead of using these to redeem his felt hat from the bailiff, he spent them all on drink.

Actually, the Chao family burned neither the incense nor the candles, because these could be used when the mistress worshipped Buddha and were put aside for that purpose. Most of the ragged shirt was made into diapers for the baby which was born to the young mistress in the eighth moon, while the tattered remainder was used by Amah Wu to make shoe soles.

Chapter 5

THE PROBLEM OF LIVELIHOOD

*A*fter Ah Q had kowtowed and complied with the Chao family's terms, he went back as usual to the Tutelary God's Temple. The sun had gone down, and he began to feel that something was wrong. Careful thought led him to the conclusion that this was probably because his back was bare. Remembering that he still had a ragged lined jacket, he put it on and lay down, and when he opened his eyes again the sun was already shining on the top of the west wall. He sat up, saying, "Curse it. . . ."

After getting up he loafed about the streets as usual, until he began to feel that something else was wrong, though this was not to be compared to the physical discomfort of a bare back. Apparently, from that day onwards all the women in Weichuang became shy of Ah Q: whenever they saw him coming they took refuge indoors. In fact, even Mrs. Tsou who was nearly fifty years old retreated in confusion with the rest, calling her eleven-year-old daughter to go inside. This struck Ah Q as very strange. "The bitches!" he thought. "They have suddenly become as coy as young ladies. . . ."

A good many days later, however, he felt even more strongly that something was wrong. First, the wine shop refused him credit; secondly, the old man in charge of the Tutelary God's Temple made some uncalled-for remarks, as if he wanted Ah Q to leave; and thirdly, for many days — how many exactly he could not remember — not a soul had come to hire him. To be refused credit in the wine shop he could put up with; if the old man kept urging him to leave, Ah Q could just ignore his complaints; but when no one came to hire him he had to go hungry; and this was really a "cursed" state to be in.

When Ah Q could stand it no longer he went to his regular employers' houses to find out what was the matter — it was only Mr. Chao's threshold that he was not allowed to cross. But he met with a very strange reception. The one to appear was always a man, who looked thoroughly annoyed and waved Ah Q away as if he were a beggar, saying:

"There is nothing, nothing at all! Go away!"

Ah Q found it more and more extraordinary. "These people always needed help in the past," he thought. "They can't suddenly have nothing to be done. This looks fishy." After making careful enquiries he found out that when they had any odd jobs they all called in Young D. Now this Young D was a lean and weakly pauper, even lower in Ah Q's eyes than Whiskers Wang. Who could have thought that this low fellow would steal his living from him? So this time Ah Q's indignation was greater than usual, and going on his way, fuming, he suddenly raised his arm and sang: *"I'll thrash you with a steel mace*. . . ."*

A few days later he did indeed meet Young D in front of Mr. Chien's house. "When two foes meet, their eyes flash fire." As Ah Q went up to him, Young D stood still.

"Stupid ass!" hissed Ah Q, glaring furiously and foaming at the mouth.

"I'm an insect — will that do?" asked Young D.

Such modesty only made Ah Q angrier than ever, but since he had no steel mace in his hand all he could do was to rush

---

* A line from *The Battle of Dragon and Tiger*, an opera popular in Shaohsing. It told how Chao Kuang-yin, the first emperor of the Sung dynasty, fought with another general.

forward with outstretched hand to seize Young D's pigtail. Young D, while protecting his pigtail with one hand, tried to seize Ah Q's with the other, whereupon Ah Q also used one free hand to protect his own pigtail. In the past Ah Q had never considered Young D worth taking seriously, but since he had recently suffered from hunger himself he was now as thin and weak as his opponent, so that they presented a spectacle of evenly matched antagonists. Four hands clutched at two heads, both men bending at the waist, cast a blue, rainbow-shaped shadow on the Chien family's white wall for over half an hour.

"All right! All right!" exclaimed some of the onlookers, probably trying to make peace.

"Good, good!" exclaimed others, but whether to make peace, applaud the fighters or incite them on to further efforts, is not certain.

The two combatants turned deaf ears to them all, however. If Ah Q advanced three paces, Young D would recoil three paces, and so they would stand. If Young D advanced three paces, Ah Q would recoil three paces, and so they would stand again. After about half an hour — Weichuang had few striking clocks, so it is difficult to tell the time; it may have been twenty minutes — when steam was rising from their heads and sweat pouring down their cheeks, Ah Q let fall his hands, and in the same second Young D's hands fell too. They straightened up simultaneously and stepped back simultaneously, pushing their way out through the crowd.

"You'll be hearing from me again, curse you. . . !" said Ah Q over his shoulder.

"Curse you! You'll be hearing from me again . . ." echoed Young D, also over his shoulder.

This epic struggle had apparently ended neither in victory nor defeat, and it is not known whether the spectators were satisfied or not, for none of them expressed any opinion. But still not a soul came to hire Ah Q.

One warm day, when a balmy breeze seemed to give some foretaste of summer, Ah Q actually felt cold; but he could put up with this — his greatest worry was an empty stomach. His cotton quilt, felt bar and shirt had long since disappeared, and after that he had sold his padded jacket. Now nothing was left but his trousers, and these of course he could not take off. He had a ragged lined jacket, it is true; but this was certainly worthless, unless he gave it away to be made into shoe soles. He had long hoped to pick up a sum of money on the road, but hitherto he had not been successful; he had also hoped he might suddenly discover a sum of money in his tumbledown room, and had looked wildly all through it, but the room was quite, quite empty. Thereupon he made up his mind to go out in search of food.

As he walked along the road "in search of food" he saw the familiar wine shop and the familiar steamed bread, but he passed them by without pausing for a second, without even hankering after them. It was not these he was looking for, although what exactly he was looking for he did nor know himself.

Since Weichuang was not a big place, he soon left it behind. Most of the country outside the village consisted of paddy fields, green as far as the eye could see with the tender shoots of young rice, dotted here and there with round, black, moving objects, which were peasants cultivating the fields. But blind to the delights of country life, Ah Q simply went on his way, for he knew instinctively that this was far removed from his "search for food." Finally, however, he came to the walls of the Convent of Quiet Self-improvement.

The convent too was surrounded by paddy fields, its white walls standing out sharply in the fresh green, and inside the low earthen wall at the back was a vegetable garden. Ah Q hesitated for a time, looking around him. Since there was no one in sight he scrambled on to the low wall, holding on to some milkwort. The mud wall started crumbling, and Ah Q shook with fear; however, by clutching at the branch of a mulberry tree he managed to jump over it. Within was a wild profusion of vegetation, but no sign of yellow wine, steamed bread, or anything edible. A clump of bamboos, with many young shoots, grew by the west wall but unfortunately these shoots were not cooked. There was also rape which had long since gone to seed; the mustard was already about to flower, and the small cabbages looked very tough.

Ah Q felt as resentful as a scholar who has failed in the examinations. As he walked slowly towards the gate of the garden he gave a start of joy, for there before him what did he see but a patch of turnips! He knelt down and began pulling, when suddenly a round head appeared from behind the gate, only to be withdrawn again at once. This was no other than the little nun. Now though Ah Q had always had the greatest contempt for such people as little nuns, there are times when "Discretion is the better part of valor." He hastily pulled up four turnips, tore off the leaves and folded them in his jacket. By this time an old nun had already come out.

"May Buddha preserve us, Ah Q! What made you climb into our garden to steal turnips. . . ! Oh dear, what a wicked thing to do! Oh dear, Buddha preserve us. . . !"

"When did I ever climb into your garden and steal turnips?" retorted Ah Q, as he started off, still looking at her.

"Now — aren't you?" said the old nun, pointing at the folds of his jacket.

"Are these yours? Can you make them answer you? You. . . ."

Leaving his sentence unfinished, Ah Q took to his heels as fast as he could, followed by an enormously fat, black dog. Originally this dog had been at the front gate, and how it reached the back garden was a mystery. With a snarl the black dog gave chase and was just about to bite Ah Q's leg when most opportunely a turnip fell from his jacket, and the dog, taken by surprise, stopped for a second. During this time Ah Q scrambled up the mulberry tree, scaled the mud wall and fell, turnips and all, outside the convent. He left the black dog still barking by the mulberry tree, and the old nun saying her prayers.

Fearing that the nun would let the black dog our again, Ah Q gathered together his turnips and ran, picking up a few small stones as he went. But the black dog did not reappear. Ah Q threw away the stones and walked on, eating as he went, thinking to himself: "There is nothing to be had here; I had better go to town. . . ."

By the time he had finished the third turnip, he had made up his mind to go to town.

Chapter 6

FROM RESTORATION TO
DECLINE

*W*eichuang did not see Ah Q again till just after the Moon Festival that year. Everybody was surprised to hear of his return, and this made them think back and wonder where he had been all that time. The few previous occasions on which Ah Q had been to town, he had usually informed people in advance with great gusto; but since he had not done so this time, no one had noticed his going. He might have told the old man in charge of the Tutelary God's Temple, but according to the custom of Weichuang it was only when Mr. Chao, Mr. Chien, or the successful county candidate went to town that it was considered important. Even the Imitation Foreign Devil's going was not talked about, much less Ah Q's. This would explain why the old man had not spread the news for him, with the result that the villagers had had no means of knowing.

Ah Q's return this time was very different from before, and in fact quite enough to occasion astonishment. The day was growing dark when he appeared blinking sleepily before the door of the wine shop, walked up to the counter, pulled a handful of silver and coppers from his belt and tossed them on the counter. "Cash!" he said. "Bring the wine!" He was wearing a new, lined jacket, and at his waist evidently hung a large purse, the great weight of which caused his belt to sag in a sharp curve. It was the custom in Weichuang that when there seemed to be something unusual about anyone, he should be treated with respect rather than insolence, and now, although they knew quite well that this was Ah Q, still he was very different from the Ah Q of the ragged coat. The ancients say, "A scholar who has been away three days must be looked at with new eyes." So the waiter, innkeeper, customers and passers-by, all quite naturally expressed a kind of suspicion mingled with respect. The innkeeper started by nodding, then said:

"Hullo, Ah Q, so you're back!"

"Yes, I'm back."

"You've made money . . . er . . . where. . . .?"

"I went to town."

By the next day this piece of news had spread through Weichuang. And since everybody wanted to hear the success story of this Ah Q of the ready money and the new lined jacket, in the wine shop, tea-house, and under the temple eaves, the villagers gradually ferreted out the news. The result was that they began to treat Ah Q with a new deference.

According to Ah Q, he had been a servant in the house of a successful provincial candidate. This part of the story filled all who heard it with awe. This successful provincial candidate was named Pai, but because he was the only successful provincial candidate in the whole town there was no need to use his surname: whenever anyone spoke of the successful provincial candidate, it meant him. And this was so not only in Weichuang but everywhere within a radius of thirty miles, as if everybody imagined his name to be Mr. Successful Provincial Candidate. To have worked in the household of such a man naturally called for respect; but according to Ah Q's further statements, he was unwilling to go on working there because this successful candidate was really too much of a "turtle's egg." This part of the story made all who heard it sigh, but with a sense of pleasure, because it showed that Ah Q was actually not fit to work in such a man's household, yet not to work was a pity.

According to Ah Q, his return was also due to the fact that he was not satisfied with the townspeople because they called a long bench a straight bench, used shredded shallots to fry fish, and — a defect he had recently discovered — the women did not sway in a very satisfactory manner as they walked. However, the town had its good points too; for instance, in Weichuang everyone played with thirty-two bamboo counters, and only the Imitation Foreign Devil could play mah-jong, but in town even the street urchins excelled at mah-jong. You had only to place the Imitation Foreign Devil in the

hands of these young rascals in their teens, for him straightway to become like "a small devil before the King of Hell."
This part of the story made all who heard it blush.

"Have you seen an execution?" asked Ah Q. "Ah, that's a
fine sight. . . . When they execute the revolutionaries. . . . Ah,
that's a fine sight, a fine sight. . . ." " As he shook his head,
his spittle flew on to the face of Chao Szu-chen who stood
directly opposite. This part of the story made all who heard
it tremble. Then with a glance around, he suddenly raised his
right hand and dropped it on the neck of Whiskers Wang,
who, his head thrust forward, was listening with rapt attention.

"Kill!" shouted Ah Q.

Whiskers Wang gave a start, and drew in his head as fast
as lightning or a spark struck from a flint, while the bystanders shivered with pleasurable apprehension. After this, Whiskers Wang went about in a daze for many days, and dared not
go near Ah Q, nor did the others.

Although we cannot say that in the eyes of the inhabitants
of Weichuang Ah Q's status at this time was superior to that
of Mr. Chao, we can at least affirm without any danger of
inaccuracy that it was about the same.

Not long after, Ah Q's fame suddenly spread into the
women's apartments of Weichuang too. Although the only
two families of any pretensions in Weichuang were those of
Chien and Chao, and nine-tenths of the rest were poor, still
women's apartments are women's apartments, and the way
Ah Q's fame spread into them was something of a miracle.
When the womenfolk met they would say to each other, "Mrs.
Tsou bought a blue silk skirt from Ah Q. Although it was
old, it only cost ninety cents. And Chao Pai-yen's mother
(this has yet to be verified, because some say it was Chao
Szu-chen's mother) bought a child's costume of crimson
foreign calico, which was nearly new, for only three hundred
cash, less eight per cent discount."

Then those who had no silk skirt or needed foreign calico
were most anxious to see Ah Q in order to buy from him.
Far from avoiding him now, they sometimes followed him
when he passed, calling to him to stop.

"Ah Q, have you anymore silk skirts?" they would ask. "No? We want foreign calico too. Do you have any?"

This news later spread from the poor households to the rich ones, because Mrs. Tsou was so pleased with her silk skirt that she took it to Mrs. Chao for her approval, and Mrs. Chao told Mr. Chao, speaking very highly of it.

Mr. Chao discussed the matter that evening at dinner with his son, the successful county candidate, suggesting that there must be something queer about Ah Q, and that they should be more careful about their doors and windows. They did not know, though, whether Ah Q had any things left or not, and thought he might still have something good. Since Mrs. Chao happened to want a good, cheap, fur jacket, after a family council it was decided to ask Mrs. Tsou to find Ah Q for them at once. For this a third exception was made to the rule, special permission being given that evening for a lamp to be lit.

A considerable amount of oil had been burned, but still there was no sign of Ah Q. The whole Chao household was yawning with impatience, some of them resented Ah Q's undisciplined ways, others angrily blamed Mrs. Tsou for not trying harder to get him there. Mrs. Chao was afraid that Ah Q dared not come because of the terms agreed upon that spring, but Mr. Chao did nor think this anything to worry about, because, as he said, "This time I sent for him." Sure enough, Mr. Chao proved himself a man of insight, for Ah Q finally arrived with Mrs. Tsou.

"He keeps saying he has nothing left," panted Mrs. Tsou as she came in. "When I told him to come and tell you so himself he went on talking. I told him. . . ."

"Sir!" said Ah Q with an attempt at a smile, coming to a halt under the eaves.

"I hear you got rich out there, Ah Q," said Mr. Chao, going up to him and looking him over carefully. "Very good. Now . . . they say you have some old things. . . . Bring them all here for us to look at. . . . This is simply because I happen to want. . . ."

"I told Mrs. Tsou — there is nothing left."

"Nothing left?" Mr. Chao could not help sounding disappointed. "How could they go so quickly?"

"They belonged to a friend, and there was not much to begin with. People bought some. . . . ."

"There must be something left."

"There is only a door curtain left."

"Then bring the door curtain for us to see," said Mrs. Chao hurriedly.

"Well, it will be all right if you bring it tomorrow," said Mr. Chao without much enthusiasm. "When you have anything in future, Ah Q, you must bring it to us first. . . . ."

"We certainly will not pay less than other people!" said the successful county candidate. His wife shot a hasty glance at Ah Q to see his reaction.

"I need a fur jacket," said Mrs. Chao.

Although Ah Q agreed, he slouched out so carelessly that they did not know whether he had taken their instructions to heart or not. This made Mr. Chao so disappointed, annoyed and worried that he even stopped yawning. The successful candidate was also far from satisfied with Ah Q's attitude, and said, "People should be on their guard against such a turtle's egg. It might be best to order the bailiff to forbid him to live in Weichuang."

Mr. Chao did not agree, saying that he might bear a grudge, and that in a business like this it was probably a case of "the eagle does not prey on its own nest": his own village need not worry, and they need only be a little more watchful at night. The successful candidate, much impressed by this parental instruction, immediately withdrew his proposal for driving Ah Q away, but cautioned Mrs. Tsou on no account to repeat what he had said.

The next day, however, when Mrs. Tsou took her blue skirt to be dyed black she repeated these insinuations about Ah Q, although not actually mentioning what the successful candidate had said about driving him away. Even so, it was most damaging to Ah Q. In the first place, the bailiff appeared at his door and took away the door curtain. Although Ah Q protested that Mrs. Chao wanted to see it, the bailiff would not give it back, and even demanded a monthly payment of hush-money. In the second place, the villagers' respect for him suddenly changed. Although they still dared not take liberties, they avoided him as much as possible. While this differed from their previous fear of his "Kill!," it closely resembled the attitude of the ancients to spirits: they kept a respectful distance.

Some idlers who wanted to get to the bottom of the business went to question Ah Q carefully. And with no attempt at concealment, Ah Q told them proudly of his experiences. They learned that he had merely been a petty thief, not only unable to climb walls, but even unable to go through openings: he simply stood outside an opening to receive the stolen goods.

One night he had just received a package and his chief had gone in again, when he heard a great uproar inside, and took to his heels as fast as he could. He fled from the town that same night, back to Weichuang; and after this he dared not return to such a business. This story, however, was even more damaging to Ah Q, since the villagers had been keeping a respectful distance because they did not want to incur his enmity; for who could have guessed that he was only a thief who dared not steal again? Now they knew he was really too low to inspire fear.

Chapter 7

THE REVOLUTION

On the fourteenth day* of the ninth moon of the third year in the reign of Emperor Hsuan Tung — the day on which Ah Q sold his purse to Chao Pai-yen — at midnight, after the fourth stroke of the third watch, a large boat with a big black awning came to the Chao family's landing place. This boat floated up in the darkness while the villagers were sound asleep, so that they knew nothing about it; but it left again about dawn, when quite a number of people saw it. Investi-

---

* The day on which Shaohsing was freed in the 1911 Revolution.

gation revealed that this boat actually belonged to the successful provincial candidate!

This incident caused great uneasiness in Weichuang, and before midday the hearts of all the villagers were beating faster. The Chao family kept very quiet about the errand of the boat, but according to the gossip in the tea-house and wine shop, the revolutionaries were going to enter the town and the successful provincial candidate had come to the country to take refuge. Mrs. Tsou alone thought otherwise, maintaining that the successful provincial candidate merely wanted to deposit a few battered cases in Weichuang, but that Mr. Chao had sent them back. Actually the successful provincial candidate and the successful county candidate in the Chao family were not on good terms, so that it was scarcely logical to expect them to prove friends in adversity; moreover, since Mrs. Tsou was a neighbor of the Chao family and had a better idea of what was going on, she ought to have known.

Then a rumor spread to the effect that although the scholar had not arrived himself, he had sent a long letter tracing some distant relationship with the Chao family; and since Mr. Chao after thinking it over had decided it could, after all, do him no harm to keep the cases, they were now stowed under his wife's bed. As for the revolutionaries, some people said they had entered the town that night in white helmets and white armor — in mourning for Emperor Chung Chen.*

Ah Q had long since known of revolutionaries, and this year with his own eyes had seen revolutionaries being decapitated. But since it had occurred to him that the revolutionaries were rebels and that a rebellion would make things difficult for him, he had always detested and kept away from them. Who could have guessed they could so frighten a successful provincial candidate renowned for thirty miles around? In consequence, Ah Q could not help feeling rather "entranced," the terror of all the villagers only adding to his delight.

---

* Chung Chen, the last emperor of the Ming dynasty, reigned from 1628 to 1644. He hanged himself before the insurgent peasants army under Li Tzu-cheng entered Peking.

"Revolution is not a bad thing," thought Ah Q. "Finish off the whole lot of them . . . curse them. . . ! I would like to go over to the revolutionaries myself."

Ah Q had been hard up recently, and was probably rather dissatisfied; added to this, he had drunk two bowls of wine at noon on an empty stomach. Consequently, he became drunk very quickly; and as he walked along thinking to himself, he felt again as if he were treading on air. Suddenly, in some curious way, he felt as if the revolutionaries were himself, and all the people in Weichuang were his captives. Unable to contain himself for joy, he could not help shouting loudly:

"Rebellion! Rebellion!"

All the villagers looked at him in consternation. Ah Q had never seen such pitiful looks before, and found them as refreshing as a drink of iced water in midsummer. So he walked on even more happily, shouting:

"All right . . . I shall take what I want! I shall like whom I please!

"Tra la, tra la!

"I regret to have killed by mistake my sworn brother Cheng, in my cups.

"I regret to have killed . . . yah, yah, yah!

"Tra la, tra la, tum ti tum tum!

"I'll thrash you with a steel mace."

Mr. Chao and his son were standing at their gate with two relatives discussing the revolution. Ah Q did not see them as he passed with his head thrown back, singing, *"Tra la la, tum ti tum!"*

"Q, old chap!" called Mr. Chao timidly in a low voice.

"Tra la!" sang Ah Q, unable to imagine that his name could be linked with those words "old chap." Sure that he had heard wrongly and was in no way concerned, he simply went on singing, *"Tra la la, tum ti tum!"*

"Q, old chap!"

"I regret to have killed. . . ."

"Ah Q!" The successful candidate had to call his name.

Only then did Ah Q come to a stop. "Well?" he asked with his head on one side.

"Q, old chap . . . now. . . ." But Mr. Chao was at a loss for words again. "Are you getting rich now?"

"Getting rich? Of course. I take what I like. . . ."

"Ah — Q, old man, poor friends of yours like us can't possibly matter . . ." said Chao Pai-yen apprehensively, as if sounding out the revolutionaries' attitude.

"Poor friends? Surely you are richer than I am," replied Ah Q, and walked away.

They stood there despondent and speechless; then Mr. Chao and his son went back to the house, and that evening discussed the question until it was time to light the lamps. When Chao Pai-yen went home he took the purse from his waist and gave it to his wife to hide for him at the bottom of a chest.

For some time Ah Q seemed to be walking on air, but by the time he reached the Tutelary God's Temple he was sober again. That evening the old man in charge of the temple was also unexpectedly friendly and offered him tea. Then Ah Q asked him for two flat cakes, and after eating these demanded a four-ounce candle that had been used, and a candlestick. He lit the candle and lay down alone in his little room. He felt inexpressibly refreshed and happy, while the candlelight leaped and flickered as on the Lantern Festival and his imagination soared with it.

"Revolt? It would be fun. . . . A group of revolutionaries would come, all wearing white helmets and white armor, carrying swords, steel maces, bombs, foreign guns, double-edged knives with sharp points and spears with hooks. They would come to the Tutelary God's Temple and call out, 'Ah Q! Come with us, come with us!' And then I would go with them. . . .

"Then all those villagers would be in a laughable plight, kneeling down and pleading, 'Ah Q, spare our lives.' But who would listen to them! The first to die would be Young D and Mr. Chao, then the successful county candidate and the Imitation Foreign Devil . . . but perhaps I would spare a few. I would once have spared Whiskers Wang, but now I don't even want him. . . .

"Things . . . I would go straight in and open the cases: silver ingots, foreign coins, foreign calico jackets. . . . First I would move the Ningpo bed of the successful county candidate's wife to the temple, and also move in the Chien family tables and chairs — or else just use the Chao family's. I would not lift a finger myself, but order Young D to move the things for me, and to look smart about it, unless he wanted a slap in the face. . . .

"Chao Szu-chen's younger sister is very ugly. In a few years Mrs. Tsou's daughter might be worth considering. The Imitation Foreign Devil's wife is willing to sleep with a man without a pigtail, hah! She can't be a good woman! The successful county candidate's wife has scars on her eyelids. . . . I have not seen Amah Wu for a long time, and don't know where she is — what a pity her feet are so big."

Before Ah Q had reached a satisfactory conclusion, there was a sound of snoring. The four-ounce candle had burned down only half an inch, and its flickering red light lit up his open mouth.

"Ho, ho!" shouted Ah Q suddenly, raising his head and looking wildly around. But when he saw the four-ounce candle, he lay back and went to sleep again.

The next morning he got up very late, and when he went out in to the street everything was the same as usual. He was still hungry, but though he racked his brains he did not seem able to think of anything. Suddenly an idea came to him, and he walked slowly off, until either by design or accident he reached the Convent of Quiet Self-improvement.

The convent was as peaceful as it had been that spring, with its white wall and shining black gate. After a moment's reflection, he knocked at the gate, whereupon a dog started barking within. He hastily picked up several pieces of broken brick, then went up again to knock more heavily, knocking until a number of small dents appeared on the black gate. At last he heard someone coming to open the door.

Holding his broken bricks, Ah Q hastily stood with his legs wide apart, prepared to do battle with the black dog. The convent door opened a crack, and no black dog rushed out. When he looked in all he could see was the old nun.

"What are you here for again?" she asked, giving a start.

"There is a revolution . . . don't you know?" said Ah Q vaguely.

"Revolution, revolution . . . there has already been one," said the old nun, her eyes red from crying. "What do you think will become of us with all your revolutions?"

"What?" asked Ah Q in astonishment.

"Didn't you know? The revolutionaries have already been here!"

"Who?" asked Ah Q in even greater astonishment.

"The successful county candidate and the Imitation Foreign Devil."

This came as a complete surprise to Ah Q, who could not help being taken aback. When the old nun saw that he had lost his aggressiveness, she quickly shut the gate, so that when Ah Q pushed it again he could not budge it, and when he knocked again there was no answer.

It had happened that morning. The successful county candidate in the Chao family learned the news quickly, and as soon as he heard that the revolutionaries had entered the town that night, he immediately wound his pigtail up on his head and went out first thing to call on the Imitation Foreign Devil in the Chien family, with whom he had never been on good terms before. Because this was a time for all to work for reforms, they had a very pleasant talk and on the spot became comrades who saw eye to eye and pledged themselves to become revolutionaries.

After racking their brains for some time, they remembered that in the Convent of Quiet Self-improvement there was an imperial tablet inscribed "Long Live the Emperor" which ought to be done away with at once. Thereupon they lost no time in going to the convent to carry out their revolutionary activities. Because the old nun tried to stop them, and put in a few words, they considered her as the Ching government and knocked her on the head many times with a stick and with their knuckles. The nun, pulling herself together after they had gone, made an inspection. Naturally the imperial tablet had been smashed into fragments on the ground, and the valuable Hsuan Te censer* before the shrine of Kuanyin, the goddess of mercy, had also disappeared.

---

* Highly decorative bronze censers were made during the Hsuan Te period (1426–1435) of the Ming dynasty.

Ah Q only learned this later. He deeply regretted having been asleep at the time, and resented the fact that they had not come to call him. Then he said to himself, "Maybe they still don't know I have joined the revolutionaries."

Chapter 8

BARRED FROM THE REVOLUTION

*T*he people of Weichuang became more reassured every day. From the news that was brought they knew that, although the revolutionaries had entered the town, their coming had not made a great deal of difference. The magistrate was still the highest official, it was only his title that had changed; and the successful provincial candidate also had some post — the Weichuang villagers could not remember these names clearly — some kind of official post; while the head of the military was still the same old captain. The only cause for alarm was that, the day after their arrival, some bad revolutionaries made trouble by cutting off people's pigtails. It was said that the boatman "Seven Pounder" from the next village had fallen into their clutches, and that he no longer looked presentable. Still, the danger of this was not great, because the Weichuang villagers seldom went to town to begin with, and those who had been considering a trip to town at once changed their minds in order to avoid this risk. Ah Q had been thinking of going to town to look up his old friends, but as soon as he heard the news he became resigned and gave up the idea.

It would be wrong, however, to say that there were no reforms in Weichuang. During the next few days the number of people who coiled their pigtails on their heads gradually increased, and, as has already been said, the first to do so was naturally the successful county candidate; the next were Chao Szu-chen and Chao Pai-yen, and after them Ah Q. If it had been summer it would not have been considered strange if everybody had coiled their pigtails on their heads or tied them in knots; but this was late autumn, so that this autumn observance of a summer practice on the part of those who coiled their pigtails could be considered nothing short of a heroic decision, and as far as Weichuang was concerned it could not be said to have had no connection with the reforms.

When Chao Szu-chen approached with the nape of his neck bare, people who saw him remarked, "Ah! Here comes a revolutionary!"

When Ah Q heard this he was greatly impressed. Although he had long since heard how the successful county candidate had coiled his pigtail on his head, it had never occurred to him to do the same. Only now when he saw that Chao Szuchen had followed suit was he struck with the idea of doing the same himself. He made up his mind to copy them. He used a bamboo chopstick to twist his pigtail up on his head, and after some hesitation eventually summoned up the courage to go out.

As he walked along the street people looked at him, but nobody said anything. Ah Q was very displeased at first, then he became very resentful. Recently he had been losing his temper very easily. As a matter of fact his life was no harder than before the revolution, people treated him politely, and the shops no longer demanded payment in cash, yet Ah Q still felt dissatisfied. He thought since a revolution had taken place, it should involve more than this. When he saw Young D, his anger boiled over.

Young D had also coiled his pigtail up on his head and, what was more, he had actually used a bamboo chopstick to do so too. Ah Q had never imagined that Young D would also have the courage to do this; he certainly could not tolerate such a thing! Who was Young D anyway? He was greatly tempted to seize him then and there, break his bamboo chopstick, let down his pigtail and slap his face several times into the bargain to punish him for forgetting his place and for his presumption in becoming a revolutionary. But in the end he let him off, simply fixing him with a furious glare, spitting, and exclaiming, "Pah!"

These last few days the only one to go to town was the Imitation Foreign Devil. The successful county candidate in the Chao family had thought of using the deposited cases as a pretext to call on the successful provincial candidate, but the danger that he might have his pigtail cut off had made him defer his visit. He had written an extremely formal letter, and asked the Imitation Foreign Devil to take it to town; he had also asked the latter to introduce him to the Liberty Party. When the Imitation Foreign Devil came back he asked the successful county candidate for four dollars, after which the successful county candidate wore a silver peach on his chest. All the Weichuang villagers were overawed, and said that this was the badge of the Persimmon Oil Party,* equivalent to the rank of a Han Lin.† As a result, Mr. Chao's prestige suddenly increased, far more so in fact than when his son first passed the official examination; consequently he started looking down on everyone else, and, when he saw Ah Q, tended to ignore him a little.

Ah Q was thoroughly discontented at finding himself continually ignored, but as soon as he heard of this silver peach he realized at once why he was left out in the cold. Simply to say that you had gone over was not enough to make anyone a revolutionary; nor was it enough merely to wind your pigtail up on your head; the most important thing was to get into touch with the revolutionary party. In all his life he had known only two revolutionaries, one of whom had already lost his head in town, leaving only the Imitation Foreign Devil. Unless he went at once to talk things over with the Imitation Foreign Devil, no way would be left open to him.

The front gate of the Chien house happened to be open, and Ah Q crept timidly in. Once inside he gave a start, for there he saw the Imitation Foreign Devil standing in the middle of the courtyard dressed entirely in black, no doubt

---

* The Liberty Party was called *Zi You Dang*. The villagers, not understanding the word Liberty, turned *Zi You* into *Shi You*, which means persimmon oil.

† The highest literary degree in the Ching dynasty (1644-1911).

in foreign dress, and also wearing a silver peach. In his hand he held the stick with which Ah Q was already acquainted to his cost, and the foot or so of hair which he had grown again fell over his shoulders, hanging disheveled like Saint Liu's.* Standing erect before him were Chao Pai-yen and three others, all of them listening with the utmost deference to what the Imitation Foreign Devil was saying.

Ah Q tiptoed inside and stood behind Chao Pai-yen, wanting to utter a greeting, but not knowing what to say. Obviously he could not call the man "Imitation Foreign Devil," and neither "Foreigner" nor "Revolutionary" seemed suitable. Perhaps the best form of address would be "Mr. Foreigner."

But Mr. Foreigner had not seen him, because with eyes raised he was saying with great animation:

"I am so impulsive that when we met I kept saying, 'Old Hung, we should get on with it!' But he always answered 'Nein!' — that's a foreign word which you wouldn't understand. Otherwise we should have succeeded long ago. This is an instance of how cautious he is. He asked me again and again to go to Hupeh, but I wouldn't agree. Who wants to work in a small district town. . . ?"

"Er — er —" Ah Q waited for him to pause, and then screwed up his courage to speak. But for some reason or other he still did not call him Mr. Foreigner.

The four men who had been listening gave a start and turned to stare at Ah Q. Mr. Foreigner too caught sight of him for the first time.

"What?"

"I. . . ."

"Clear out!"

"I want to join. . . ."

"Get out!" said Mr. Foreigner, lifting the "mourner's stick."

Then Chao Pai-yen and the others shouted, "Mr. Chien tells you to get out, don't you hear!"

Ah Q put up his hands to protect his head, and without knowing what he was doing fled through the gate; but this time Mr. Foreigner did not give chase. After running more

---

* An immortal in Chinese folk legend, always portrayed with flowing hair.

than sixty steps Ah Q slowed down, and began to feel most upset, because if Mr. Foreigner would not allow him to be a revolutionary, there was no other way open to him. In future he could never hope to have men in white helmets and white armor come to call him. All his ambition, aims, hope and future had been blasted at one stroke. The fact that people might spread the news and make him a laughingstock for the likes of Young D and Whiskers Wang was only a secondary consideration.

Never before had he felt so flat. Even coiling his pigtail on his head now struck him as pointless and ridiculous. As a form of revenge he was very tempted to let his pigtail down at once, but he did not do so. He wandered about till evening, when after drinking two bowls of wine on credit he began to feel in better spirits, and in his mind's eye saw fragmentary visions of white helmets and white armor once more.

One day he loafed about until late at night. Only when the wine shop was about to close did he start to stroll back to the Tutelary God's Temple.

"Bang — bump!"

He suddenly heard an unusual sound, which could not have been firecrackers. Ah Q, who always liked excitement and enjoyed poking his nose into other people's business, went looking for the noise in the darkness. He thought he heard footsteps ahead, and was listening carefully when a man suddenly rushed out in front of him. As soon as Ah Q saw him, he turned and followed as fast as he could. When that man turned, Ah Q turned too, and when after turning a corner that man stopped, Ah Q stopped too. He saw there was no one behind, and that the man was Young D.

"What is the matter?" asked Ah Q resentfully.

"Chao . . . the Chao family has been robbed," panted Young D.

Ah Q's heart went pit-a-pat. After telling him this, Young D left. Ah Q ran on, then stopped two or three times. However, since he had once been in the business himself, he felt exceptionally courageous. Emerging from the street corner, he listened carefully and thought he heard shouting; he also looked carefully and thought he could see a lot of men in white helmets and white armor, carrying off cases, carrying

off furniture, even carrying off the Ningpo bed of the successful county candidate's wife; he could not, however, see
them very clearly. He wanted to go nearer, but his feet were
rooted to the ground.

There was no moon that night, and Weichuang was very
still in the pitch darkness, as quiet as in the peaceful days of
the ancient Emperor Fu Hsi.* Ah Q stood there until he lost
interest, yet everything still seemed the same as before; in the
distance people moved to and fro, carrying things, carrying
off cases, carrying off furniture, carrying off the Ningpo bed
of the successful county candidate's wife . . . carrying until
he could hardly believe his own eyes. But he decided not to
go nearer, and went back to the temple.

It was even darker in the Tutelary God's Temple. When he
had closed the big gate he groped his way into his room, and
only after he had been lying down for some time did he feel
calm enough to begin thinking how this affected him. The
men in white helmets and white armor had evidently arrived,
but they had not come to call him; they had taken away many
things, but there was no share for him — this was all the fault
of the Imitation Foreign Devil, who had barred him from the
rebellion. Otherwise how could he have failed to have a share
this time?

The more Ah Q thought of it the angrier he grew, until he
was in a towering rage. "So no rebellion for me, only for you,
eh?" he exclaimed, nodding maliciously. "Curse you, you
Imitation Foreign Devil — all right, be a rebel! A rebel is
punished by having his head chopped off. I'll turn informer,
and see you carried into town to have your head cut off —
you and all your family. . . . Kill, kill!"

---

* One of the earliest legendary monarchs in China.

Chapter 9

THE GRAND FINALE

*A*fter the Chao family was robbed most of the people in Weichuang felt pleased yet fearful, and Ah Q was no exception. But four days later Ah Q was suddenly dragged into town in the middle of the night. It happened to be a dark night. A squad of soldiers, a squad of militia, a squad of police and five secret servicemen made their way quietly to Weichuang, and, after posting a machine-gun opposite the entrance, under cover of darkness they surrounded the Tutelary God's Temple. Ah Q did not rush out. For a long time nothing stirred in the temple. The captain grew impatient and offered a reward of twenty thousand cash. Only then did two militiamen summon up courage to jump over the wall and enter. With their co-operation from within, the others rushed in and dragged Ah Q out. But not until he had been carried out of the temple to somewhere near the machine-gun did he begin to sober up.

It was already midday by the time they reached town, and Ah Q found himself carried to a dilapidated yamen where, after taking five or six turnings, he was pushed into a small room. No sooner had he stumbled inside than the door, made of wooden bars to form a grating, closed upon his heels. The rest of the room consisted of three blank walls, and when he looked round carefully he saw two other men in a corner of the room.

Although Ah Q was feeling rather uneasy, he was by no means too depressed, because the room where he slept in the Tutelary God's Temple was in no way superior to this. The two other men also seemed to be villagers. They gradually fell into conversation with him, and one of them told him that the successful provincial candidate wanted to dun him for the rent owed by his grandfather; the other did not know why he was there. When they questioned Ah Q, he answered quite frankly, "Because I wanted to revolt."

That afternoon he was dragged out through the barred door and taken to a big hall, at the far end of which sat an old man with a cleanly shaven head. Ah Q took him for a monk at first, but when he saw soldiers standing guard and a dozen men in long coats on both sides, some with their heads clean-shaven like this old man and some with a foot or so of hair hanging over their shoulders like the Imitation Foreign Devil, all glaring furiously at him with grim faces, he knew this man must be someone important. At once the joints of his knees relaxed of their own accord, and he sank down.

"Stand up to speak! Don't kneel!" shouted all the men in the long coats.

Although Ah Q understood, he felt incapable of standing up: his body had involuntarily dropped to a squatting position, and improving on it he finally knelt down.

"Slave!" exclaimed the long-coated men contemptuously. They did not insist on his getting up, however.

"Tell the truth and you will receive a lighter sentence," said the old man with the shaven head, in a low but clear voice, fixing his eyes on Ah Q. "I know everything already. When you have confessed, I will let you go."

"Confess!" repeated the long-coated men loudly.

"The fact is I wanted . . . to come . . ." muttered Ah Q disjointedly, after a moment's confused thinking.

"In that case, why didn't you come?" asked the old man gently.

"The Imitation Foreign Devil wouldn't let me!"

"Nonsense! It is too late to talk now. Where are your accomplices?"

"What. . . ?"

"The people who robbed the Chao family that night."

"They didn't come to call me. They moved the things away themselves." Mention of this made Ah Q indignant.

"Where did they go? When you have told me I will let you go," repeated the old man even more gently.

"I don't know . . . they didn't come to call me. . . ."

Then, at a sign from the old man, Ah Q was dragged back through the barred door. The following morning he was dragged out once more.

Everything was unchanged in the big hall. The old man with the clean-shaven head was still sitting there, and Ah Q knelt down again as before.

"Have you anything else to say?" asked the old man gently.

Ah Q thought, and decided there was nothing to say, so he answered, "Nothing."

Then a man in a long coat brought a sheet of paper and held a brush in front of Ah Q, which he wanted to thrust into his hand. Ah Q was now nearly frightened out of his wits, because this was the first time in his life that his hand had ever come into contact with a writing brush. He was just wondering how to hold it when the man pointed out a place on the paper, and told him to sign his name.

"I – I – can't write," said Ah Q, shamefaced, nervously holding the brush.

"In that case, to make it easy for you, draw a circle!"

Ah Q tried to draw a circle, but the hand with which he grasped the brush trembled, so the man spread the paper on the ground for him. Ah Q bent down and, as painstakingly as if his life depended on it, drew a circle. Afraid people would laugh at him, he determined to make the circle round; however, not only was that wretched brush very heavy, but it would not do his bidding. Instead it wobbled from side to side; and just as the line was about to close it swerved out again, making a shape like a melon seed.

While Ah Q was ashamed because he had nor been able to draw a round circle, the man had already taken back the paper and brush without any comment. A number of people then dragged him back for the third time through the barred door.

This time he did not feel particularly irritated. He supposed that in this world it was the fate of everybody at some time to be dragged in and out of prison, and to have to draw circles on paper; it was only because his circle had not been round that he felt there was a stain on his reputation. Presently, however, he regained composure by thinking, "Only idiots can make perfect circles." And with this thought he fell asleep.

That night, however, the successful provincial candidate was unable to go to sleep, because he had quarreled with the captain. The successful provincial candidate had insisted that the most important thing was to recover the stolen goods, while the captain said the most important thing was to make a public example. Recently the captain had come to treat the successful provincial candidate quite disdainfully. So, banging his fist on the table, he said, "Punish one to awe one hundred! See now, I have been a member of the revolutionary party for less than twenty days, but there have been a dozen cases of robbery, none of them solved yet; and think how badly that reflects on me. Now this one has been solved, you come and argue like a pedant. It won't do! This is my affair."

The successful provincial candidate was very upset, but he still persisted, saying that if the stolen goods were nor recovered, he would resign immediately from his post as assistant civil administrator. "As you please!" said the captain.

In consequence the successful provincial candidate did not sleep that night, but happily he did not hand in his resignation the next day after all.

The third time that Ah Q was dragged out of the barred door, was the morning following the night on which the successful provincial candidate had been unable to sleep. When he reached the big ball, the old man with the clean-shaven head was still sitting there as usual, and Ah Q also knelt down as usual.

Very gently the old man questioned him: "Have you anything more to say?"

Ah Q thought, and decided there was nothing to say, so he answered, "Nothing."

A number of men in long coats and short jackets put a white vest of foreign cloth on him. It had some black characters on it. Ah Q felt considerably disconcerted, because this was very like mourning dress, and to wear mourning was unlucky. At the same time his hands were bound behind his back, and he was dragged out of the yamen.

Ah Q was lifted on to an uncovered cart, and several men in short jackets sat down with him. The cart started off at once. In front were a number of soldiers and militiamen shouldering foreign rifles, and on both sides were crowds of gaping spectators, while what was behind Ah Q could not see. Suddenly it occurred to him — "Can I be going to have my head cut off?" Panic seized him and everything turned dark before his eyes, while there was a humming in his ears as if he had fainted. But he did not really faint. Although he felt frightened some of the time, the rest of the time he was quite calm. It seemed to him that in this world probably it was the fate of everybody at some time to have his head cur off.

He still recognized the road and felt rather surprised: why were they not going to the execution ground? He did not know that he was being paraded round the streets as a public example. But if he had known, it would have been the same; he would only have thought that in this world probably it was the fate of everybody at some time to be made a public example of.

Then he realized that they were making a detour to the execution ground, so, after all, he must be going to have his head cut off. He looked round him regretfully at the people swarming after him like ants, and unexpectedly in the crowd of people by the road he caught sight of Amah Wu. So that was why he had not seen her for so long: she was working in town.

Ah Q suddenly became ashamed of his lack of spirit, because he had not sung any lines from an opera. His thoughts revolved like a whirlwind: *The Young Widow at Her Husband's Grave* was not heroic enough. The words of "I regret to have killed" in *The Battle of Dragon and Tiger* were too poor. *I'll thrash you with a steel mace* was still the best. But when he wanted to raise his hands, he remembered that they were bound together; so he did not sing *I'll thrash you* either.

"In twenty years I shall be another. . . ."* In his agitation Ah Q uttered half a saying which he had picked up himself but never used before. The crowd's roar "Good!!!" sounded like the growl of a wolf.

The cart moved steadily forward. During the shouting Ah Q's eyes turned in search of Amah Wu, but she did not seem

---

* "In twenty years I shall be another stout young fellow" was a phrase often used by criminals before execution, to show their scorn of death.

to have seen him for she was looking intently at the foreign rifles carried by the soldiers.

So Ah Q took another look at the shouting crowd.

At that instant his thoughts revolved again like a whirlwind. Four years before, at the foot of the mountain, he had met a hungry wolf which had followed him at a set distance, wanting to eat him. He had nearly died of fright, but luckily he happened to have an axe in his hand, which gave him the courage to get back to Weichuang. He had never forgotten that wolf's eyes, fierce yet cowardly, gleaming like two will-o'-the-wisps, as if boring into him from a distance. Now he saw eyes more terrible even than the wolf's: dull yet penetrating eyes that, having devoured his words, still seemed eager to devour something beyond his flesh and blood. And these eyes kept following him at a set distance.

These eyes seemed to have merged into one, biting into his soul.

"Help, help!"

But Ah Q never uttered these words. All had turned black before his eyes, there was a buzzing in his ears, and he felt as if his whole body were being scattered like so much light dust.

As for the after-effects of the robbery, the most affected was the successful provincial candidate, because the stolen goods were never recovered. All his family lamented bitterly. Next came the Chao household; for when the successful county candidate went into town to report the robbery, nor only did he have his pigtail cut off by bad revolutionaries, but he had to pay a reward of twenty thousand cash into the bargain; so all the Chao family lamented bitterly too. From that day forward they gradually assumed the air of the survivors of a fallen dynasty.

*A*s for any discussion of the event, no question was raised in Weichuang. Naturally all agreed that Ah Q had been a bad man, the proof being that he had been shot; for if he had not been bad, how could he have been shot? But the consensus of opinion in town was unfavorable. Most people were dissatisfied, because a shooting was nor such a fine spectacle as a decapitation; and what a ridiculous culprit he had been too, to pass through so many streets without singing a single line from an opera They had followed him for nothing.

December 1921

Village Opera

*D*uring the past twenty years I have been to the Chinese opera only twice. During the first ten years I never went, having neither the desire nor the Opportunity. The two occasions on which I went were in the past ten years, but each time I left without seeing anything in it.

The first time was in 1912 when I was new to Peking. A friend told me Peking had the best opera and that seeing it was an experience I shouldn't miss. I thought it might be interesting to see an opera, especially in Peking, and hurried in high spirits to some theater, the name of which I have forgotten. The performance had already started. Even outside I could hear the beat of the drums. As we squeezed in, bright colors flashed in view, and I saw many heads in the auditorium; as I scanned the theater I saw a few seats in the middle still empty. But when 1 squeezed in to sit down, someone spoke up. There was such a throbbing in my ears I had to listen attentively to catch what he was saying — "Sorry, these seats are taken!"

We went to the back, but then a man with a glossy queue led us to a side aisle, and indicated an unoccupied place. This was a bench only three-quarters the width of my thighs, but with legs nearly twice as long as mine. To begin with I hadn't the courage to get up there, and then it reminded me of some instrument of torture, and with an involuntary shudder I fled.

I had gone some distance, when I heard my friend's voice, asking: "Well, what's the matter?" Looking over my shoulder I saw he had followed me out. He seemed very surprised. "Why do you march along without a word?" he demanded.

"I'm sorry," I told him. "There's such a pounding in my ears, I couldn't hear you."

Whenever I thought back on the incident, it struck me as very strange, and I supposed that the opera had been a very poor one — or else a theater was no place for me.

I forget in what year I made the second venture, but funds were being raised for flood victims in Hupeh, and Tan Hsin-pei* was still alive. By paying two dollars for a ticket, you contributed money and could go to the Number One Theater to see an opera with a cast made up for the most part of famous actors, one being Tan Hsin-pei himself. I bought a ticket primarily to satisfy the collector, but then some busybody seized the opportunity to tell me why Tan Hsin-pei simply had to be seen. At that, I forgot the disastrous din and crash of a few years before, and went to the theater — probably half because I had paid so much for that precious ticket that I wouldn't feel comfortable if I didn't use it. I learned that Tan Hsin-pei made his appearance late in the evening, and Number One Theater was a modern one where you didn't have to fight for your seat. That reassured me, and I waited till nine o'clock before setting out. To my surprise, just as before, it was full. There was hardly any standing room and I had to squeeze into the crowd at the rear to watch an actor singing an old woman's part. He had a paper spill burning at each corner of his mouth and there was a devil-soldier beside him. I racked my brains and guessed that this might be Maudgalyayana's† mother, because the next to come on was a monk. Not recognizing the actor, I asked a fat gentleman who was squeezed in on my left. "Kung Yun-fu!"‡ he said, throwing me a withering look from the corner of his eye. My face burned with shame for my ignorant blunder, and I mentally resolved that at all costs I would ask no more questions. Then I watched a heroine and her maid sing, next an old man and some other characters I couldn't identify. After that, I watched a whole group fight a free-for-all, and after that, two or three people fighting together — from after

---

* A famous actor in Peking opera.

† Maudgalyayana was a disciple of Buddha. Legend has it that his mother went to hell for her sins, and he rescued her.

‡ Another famous actor in Peking opera, who played old women's roles.

nine till ten, from ten till eleven, from eleven till eleven thirty, from eleven thirty till twelve: but there was no sign of Tan Hsin-pei.

Never in my life have I waited for anything so patiently. But the wheezes of the fat gentleman next to me, the clanging, tinkling, drumming and gonging on the stage, the whirl of bright colors and the lateness of the hour suddenly made me realize that this was no place for me. Mechanically I turned round, and tried with might and main to shove my way out. I felt the place behind me fill up at once — no doubt the elastic fat gentleman had expanded his right side into my empty place. With my retreat cut off, naturally there was nothing to do but push and push till at last I was out of the door. Apart from the rickshaws waiting for the playgoers, there was practically no one walking outside, but there were still a dozen people by the gate looking up at the program, and another group not looking at anything, who must, I thought, be waiting to watch the women come out after the show was over. There was no sign of Tan Hsin-pei. . . .

But the night air was so brisk, it went right through me. This seemed to be the first time I had known such good air in Peking.

I said goodbye to Chinese opera that night. I never thought about it again, and, if by any chance I passed a theater, it meant nothing to me for in spirit we were poles apart.

A few days ago, however, I happened to read a Japanese book — unfortunately I have forgotten the title and author, but it was about the Chinese opera. One chapter made the point that Chinese opera is so full of gongs and cymbals, shouting and jumping, that it makes the onlookers' heads swim. It is quite unsuited for presentation in a theater but, if performed in the open air and watched from a distance, it has its charm. I felt this put into words what had remained unformulated in my mind, because as a matter of fact I clearly remembered seeing a really good opera in the country, and it was under its influence, perhaps, that after coming to Peking, I went twice to the theater. It's a pity that, somehow or other, I've forgotten the name of that book.

As to when I saw that good opera, it was really "long, long ago," and I could not have been much more than eleven or twelve. It was the custom in Luchen where we lived for married women who were not yet in charge of the household to go back to their parents' home for the summer. Although my father's mother was then still quite strong, my mother had quite a few household duties. She could not spend many days at her own home during the summer. She could take a few days only after visiting the ancestral graves. At such times I always went with her to stay in her parents' house. It was in a place called Pingchao Village, not far from the sea, a very out-of-the-way little village on a river, with less than thirty households, peasants and fishermen, and just one tiny grocery. In my eyes, however, it was heaven, for not only was I treated as a guest of honor, but I could skip reading the *Book of Songs.**

There were many children for me to play with. For with the arrival of a visitor from such a distance they got permission from their parents to do less work in order to play with me. In a small village the guest of one family is virtually the guest of the whole community. We were all about the same age, but when it came to determining seniority, many were at least my uncles or grand-uncles, since everybody in the village had the same family name and belonged to one clan. But we were all good friends, and if by some chance we fell out and I hit one of my grand-uncles, it never occurred to any child or grown-up in the village to call it "disrespect to elders." Ninety-nine out of a hundred of them could neither read nor write.

We spent most of our days digging up worms, putting them on little hooks made of copper wire, and lying on the riverbank to catch shrimps. Shrimps are the silliest water creatures: they willingly use their own pincers to push the point of the hook into their mouths; so in a few hours we could catch a big bowlful. It became the custom to give these shrimps to me. Another thing we did was to take the buffaloes out together, but, maybe because they are animals of a higher species, oxen and buffaloes are hostile to strangers, and they treated me with contempt so that I never dared get too close to them. I could only follow at a distance and stand there. At

---

* The earliest anthology of poetry in China.

such times my small friends were no longer impressed by the fact that I could recite classical poetry, but would hoot with laughter.

What I looked forward to most was going to Chaochuang to see the opera. Chaochuang was a slightly larger village about two miles away. Since Pingchiao was too small to afford to put on operas, every year it contributed some money for a performance at Chaochuang. At the time, I wasn't curious why they should have operas every year. Thinking about it now, I dare say it may have been for the late spring festival or for the village sacrifice.

That year when I was eleven or twelve, the long-awaited day arrived. But as ill luck would have it, there was no boat for hire that morning. Pingchiao Village had only one sailing boat, which left in the morning and came back in the evening. This was a large boat which it was out of the question to hire; and all the other boats were unsuitable because they were too small. Someone was sent round to the neighboring villages to ask if they had boats, but no — they had all been hired already. My grandmother was very upset, blamed my cousins for not hiring one earlier, and began to complain. Mother tried to comfort her by saying the operas at Luchen were much better than in these little villages, and there were several every year, so there was no need to go today. But I was nearly in tears from disappointment, and mother did her best to impress on me that no matter what, I must not make a scene, because it would upset my grandmother; and I mustn't go with other people either, for then grandmother would be worried.

In a word, it had fallen through. After lunch, when all my friends had left and the opera had started, I imagined I could hear the sound of gongs and drums, and saw them, with my mind's eye, in front of the stage buying soya-bean milk.

I didn't catch shrimps that day, and didn't eat much either. Mother was very upset, but there was nothing she could do. By supper time grandmother realized how I felt, and said I was quite right to be angry, they had been too negligent, and never before had guests been treated so badly. After the meal, youngsters who had come back from the opera gathered round and gaily described it all for us. I was the only one

silent; they all sighed and said how sorry they were for me.
Suddenly one of the brightest, called Shuang-hsi, had an
inspiration, and said: "A big boat — hasn't Eighth Grand-uncle's boat come back?" A dozen other boys picked up the idea
in a flash, and at once started agitating to take the boat and
go with me. I cheered up. But grandmother was nervous,
thinking we were all children and undependable. And mother
said that since the grown-ups all had to work the next day, it
wouldn't be fair to ask them to go with us and stay up all
night. While our fate hung in the balance, Shuang-hsi went
to the root of the question and declared loudly: "I give my
word it'll be all right! It's a big boat, Brother Hsun never
jumps around, and we can all swim!"

It was true. There wasn't one boy in the dozen who wasn't
a fish in water, and two or three of them were first-rate
swimmers.

Grandmother and mother were convinced and did not
raise anymore objections. They both smiled, and we immediately rushed out.

My heavy heart suddenly became light, and I felt as though
I were floating on air. When we got outside, I saw in the
moonlight a boat with a white awning moored at the bridge.
We jumped aboard, Shuang-hsi seized the front pole and
Ah-fa the back one; the younger boys sat down with me in
the middle of the boat, while the older ones went to the stern.
By the time mother followed us out to say "Be careful!" we
had already cast off. We pushed off from the bridge, floated
back a few feet, then moved forward under the bridge. Two
oars were set up, each manned by two boys who changed shifts
every third of a mile. Chatter, laughter and shouts mingled
with the lapping of the water against the bow of our boat; to
our right and left, as we flew forward towards Chaochuang,
were emerald green fields of beans and wheat.

The mist hung over the water, the scent of beans, wheat
and river weeds wafted towards us, and the moonlight shone
faintly through the mist. In the distance, grey hills, undulat-
ing like the backs of some leaping iron beasts, seemed to be
racing past the stern of our boat; but still I felt our progress
was slow. When the oarsmen had changed shifts four times,
it was just possible to see the faint outline of Chauchuang,

and catch the sound of singing. There were several lights too, which we guessed must be on the stage, unless they were fishermen's lights.

The music we heard was probably flutes. Eddying round and round and up and down, it soothed me and set me dreaming at the same time, till I felt as though I were about to drift far away with it through the night air heavy with the scent of beans and wheat and river weeds.

As we approached the lights, we found they were fishermen's lights after all, and I realized I hadn't been looking at Chaochuang at all. Directly ahead of us was a pine wood where I had played the year before, and seen the broken stone horse that had fallen on its side, and a stone sheep couched in the grass. When we passed the wood, the boat rounded a bend into a cove, and Chaochuang was really before us.

Our eyes were drawn to the stage standing in a plot of empty ground by the river outside the village, hazy in the distant moonlight, barely distinguishable from its surroundings. It seemed that the fairyland I had seen in pictures had come alive here. The boat was moving faster now, and presently we could make out figures on the stage and a blaze of bright colors, and the river close to the stage was black with the boat awnings of people who had come to watch the play.

"There's no room near the stage, let's watch from a distance," suggested Ah-fa,

The boat had slowed down now, and soon we arrived. True enough, it was impossible to get close to the stage. We had to make our boat fast even further from the stage than the shrine opposite it. We did not regret it, though, for we did not want our boat with its white awning to mix with those common black boats; and there was no room for us anyway. . . .

While we hastily moored, there appeared on the stage a man with a long black beard who had four pennons fixed to his back. With a spear he fought a whole group of bare-armed men. Shuang-hsi told us this was a famous acrobat who could turn eighty-four somersaults, one after the other. He had counted for himself earlier in the day.

We all crowded to the bow to watch the fighting, but the acrobat didn't turn any somersaults. Some of the bare-armed men turned head over heels a few times, then trooped off.

Then a girl came out, and sang in a long drawn-out voice. "There aren't many people in the evening," said Shuang-hsi, "and the acrobat's taking it easy. Nobody wants to show his skill without an audience." That was common sense, because by then there really weren't many people left to watch. The country folk had work the next day, and couldn't stay up all night, so they had all gone to bed. Just a score or so of idlers from Chaochuang and the villages around remained sprinkled about. The families of the local rich were still there in the boats with black awnings, but they weren't really interested in the opera. Most of them had gone to the foot of the stage to eat cakes, fruit or melon seeds. So it didn't really amount to an audience.

As a matter of fact, I wasn't keen on the somersaults. What I wanted to see most was a snake spirit swathed in white, its two hands clasping on its head a wandlike snake's head. My second choice was a leaping tiger dressed in yellow. But though I waited a long time, they didn't appear. The girl was followed at once by a very old man acting the part of a young man. I was rather tired and asked Kuei-sheng to buy me some soya-bean milk. He came back in a little while to say: "There isn't any. The deaf man who sells it has gone. There was some in the daytime, I drank two bowls then. I'll get you a dipperful of water to drink."

I didn't drink the water, but stuck it out as best I could. I can't say what I saw, but it seemed that the faces of the players gradually became very strange, the features blurred as though they had melted into one flat surface. Most of the younger boys yawned, while the older ones chatted among themselves. It was only when a clown in a red shirt was fastened to a pillar on the stage, and a greybeard started horsewhipping him that we all roused ourselves to watch again and laughed. I really think that was the best scene of the evening.

But then the old woman came out. This was the character I most dreaded, especially when she sat down to sing. Now I saw by everybody's disappointment that they felt as I did. In the beginning, the old woman just walked to and fro singing, then she sat on a chair in the middle of the stage. I was really distressed, and Shuang-hsi and the others started swearing. I waited patiently until, after a long time, the old woman raised her hand, and I thought she was going to stand up. But despite my hopes she lowered her hand slowly to its original position, and went on singing just as before. Some of the boys in the boat couldn't help groaning, and the rest began to yawn again. Finally Shuang-hsi couldn't stand it any longer. He said he was afraid the old woman would go on singing till dawn, and we had better leave. We all promptly agreed, and became as eager as when we had set out. Three or four boys ran to the stern, seized the poles to punt back several yards, and headed the boat around. Cursing the old singer, they set up the oars, and started back for the pine wood.

Judging from the position of the moon, we had not been watching very long, and once we left Chaochuang the moonlight seemed unusually bright. When we turned back to see the lantern-lit stage, it looked just as it had when we came, hazy as a fairy pavilion, covered in a rosy mist. Once again the flutes piped melodiously in our ears. I thought the old woman must have finished, but couldn't very well suggest going back again to see.

Soon the pine wood was behind us. Our boat was moving rather fast, but there was such thick darkness all around you could tell it was very late. As they discussed the players, laughing and swearing, the towers pulled faster on the oars. Now the plash of water against our bow was even more distinct. The boat seemed like a great white fish carrying a freight of children on its back through the foam. Some old fishermen who fished all night stopped their punts to cheer at the sight.

We were still about a third of a mile from Pingchiao when our boat slowed down, and the oarsmen said they were tired after rowing so hard. We'd had nothing to eat for hours. It was Kuei-sheng who had a brilliant idea this time. He said the *lohan* beans were ripe, and we had fuel on the boat — we could use a little to cook the beans. Everybody agreed, and we immediately headed towards the bank. The pitch-black fields were filled with succulent beans.

"Hey! Ah-fa! It's your family's over here, and Old Liu Yi's over there. Which shall we take?" Shuang-hsi had been the first to leap ashore, and was calling from the bank.

As we all jumped ashore too, Ah-fa said: "Wait a minute and I'll take a look." He walked up and down feeling the beans, then straightened up to say: "Take ours, they're much bigger." With a shout we scattered through the bean field of Ah-fa's family, each picking a big handful of beans and throwing them into the boat. Shuang-hsi thought that if we took anymore and Ah-fa's mother found out, there would be trouble, so we all went to Old Liu Yi's field to pick another handful each.

Then a few of the older boys started rowing slowly again, while others lit a fire in the stern, and the younger boys and I shelled the beans. Soon they were cooked, and we let the boat drift while we gathered round and ate them with our fingers. When we had finished eating we went on again, washing the pot and throwing the pods into the river, to destroy all traces. Shuang-hsi was uneasy because we had used the salt and firewood on Eighth Grand-uncle's boat, and the old man was so sharp he would be sure to find out and scold us. But after some discussion we decided there was nothing to fear. If he did scold us we would ask him to return the pine branch he had taken the previous year from the riverbank, and call him "Old Scabby" to his face.

"We're all back! How could anything have happened? Didn't I guarantee it would be all right!" Shuang-hsi's voice suddenly rang out from the bow.

Looking past him, I saw we were already at Pingchiao, and someone was standing at the foot of the bridge — it was mother. It was to her that Shuang-hsi had called. As I walked up to the bow the boat passed under the bridge, then stopped, and we all went ashore. Mother was rather annoyed, and asked why we had come back so late — it was after midnight. But she was soon in a good humor again, and smiled as she invited everybody to come back and have some puffed rice.

They told her we had all eaten something, and were sleepy, so they had better get to bed at once, and off we all went to our own homes.

I didn't get up till noon the next day, and there was no word of any trouble with Eighth Grand-uncle over the salt or firewood. In the afternoon we went to catch shrimps as usual.

"Shuang-hsi, you young rascals stole my beans yesterday! And you didn't pick them properly, you trampled down quite a few." I looked up and saw Old Liu Yi on a punt, coming back from selling beans. There was still a heap of left-over beans at the bottom of the punt.

"Yes. We were treating a visitor. We didn't mean to take yours to begin with," said Shuang-hsi. "Look! You've frightened away my shrimp!"

When the old man saw me, he stopped punting, and chuckled. "Treating a visitor? So you should." Then he asked me: "Was yesterday's opera good?"

"Yes." I nodded.

"Did you enjoy the beans?"

"Very much." I nodded again.

To my surprise, the old man was greatly pleased. He stuck up a thumb, and declared with satisfaction: "People from big towns who have studied really know what's good. I select my bean seeds one by one. Country folk can't tell good from bad, and say my beans aren't as good as other people's. I'll give some to your mother today for her to try. . . . ." Then he punted off.

When mother called me home for supper, there was a large bowl of boiled beans on the table, which Old Liu Yi had brought for her and me to eat. I heard he had praised me highly to mother, saying, "He's so young, yet he knows what's what. He's sure to pass all the official examinations in future. Your fortune's as good as made." But when I ate the beans, they didn't taste as good as the ones we'd eaten the night before.

It's a fact, right up till now, I've really never eaten such good beans, or seen such a good opera, as I did that night.

October 1922

The New Year's Sacrifice

New Year's Eve of the old calendar* seems after all more like the real New Year's Eve; for, to say nothing of the villages and towns, even in the air there is a feeling that New Year is coming. From the pale, lowering evening clouds issue frequent flashes of lightning, followed by a rumbling sound of firecrackers celebrating the departure of the Hearth God; while, nearer by, the firecrackers explode even more violently, and before the deafening report dies away the air is filled with a faint smell of powder. It was on such a night that I returned to Luchen, my native place. Although I call it my native place, I had had no home there for some time, so I had to put up temporarily with a certain Mr. Lu, the fourth son of his family. He is a member of our clan, and belongs to the generation before mine, so I ought to call him "Fourth Uncle." An old student of the imperial college† who went in for Neo-Confucianism, I found him very little changed in any way, simply slightly older, but without any moustache as yet. When we met, after exchanging a few polite remarks he said I was fatter, and after saying that immediately started a violent attack on the revolutionaries. I knew this was not meant personally, because the object of the attack was still Kang Yu-wei.‡ Nevertheless, conversation proved difficult, so that in a short time I found myself alone in the study.

---

* The Chinese lunar calendar.
† The highest institute of learning in the Ching dynasty.
‡ A famous reformist who lived from 1858 to 1927 and advocated constitutional monarchy.

The next day I got up very late, and after lunch went out to see some relatives and friends. The day after I did the same. None of them was greatly changed, simply slightly older; but every family was busy preparing for "the sacrifice." This is the great end-of-year ceremony in Luchen, when people reverently welcome the God of Fortune and solicit good fortune for the coming year. They kill chickens and geese and buy pork, scouring and scrubbing until all the women's arms turn red in the water. Some of them still wear twisted silver bracelets. After the meat is cooked some chopsticks are thrust into it at random, and this is called the "offering." It is set out at dawn when incense and candles are lit, and they reverently invite the God of Fortune to come and partake of the offering. Only men can be worshippers, and after the sacrifice they naturally continue to let off firecrackers as before. This happens every year, in every family, provided they can afford to buy the offering and firecrackers; and this year they naturally followed the old custom.

The day grew overcast. In the afternoon it actually started to snow, the biggest snow-flakes as large as plum blossom petals fluttered about the sky; and this, combined with the smoke and air of activity, made Luchen appear in a ferment. When I returned to my uncle's study the roof of the house was already white with snow. The room also appeared brighter, the great red rubbing hanging on the wall showing up very clearly the character for Longevity written by the Taoist saint Chen Tuan.* One of a pair of scrolls had fallen down and was lying loosely rolled up on the long table, but the other was still hanging there, bearing the words: "By understanding reason we achieve tranquility of mind." Idly, I went to turn over the books on the table beneath the window, but all I could find was a pile of what looked like an incomplete set of *Kang Hsi's Dictionary,*† a volume of Chiang Yung's *Notes to Chu Hsi's Philosophical Writings* and a volume of *Commentaries on the Four Books.*‡ At all events, I made up my mind to leave the next day.

---

* A hermit at the beginning of the tenth century.
† A Chinese dictionary compiled under the auspices of Emperor Kang Hsi who reigned from 1662 to 1722.
‡ Confucian classics.

Besides, the very thought of my meeting with Hsiang Lin's Wife the day before made me uncomfortable. It happened in the afternoon. I had been visiting a friend in the eastern part of the town. As I came out I met her by the river, and seeing the way she fastened her eyes on me I knew very well she meant to speak to me. Of all the people I had seen this time at Luchen none had changed as much as she: her hair, which had been streaked with white five years before, was now completely white, quite unlike someone in her forties. Her face was fearfully thin and dark in its sallowness, and had moreover lost its former expression of sadness, looking as if carved out of wood. Only an occasional flicker of her eyes showed she was still a living creature. In one hand she carried a wicker basket, in which was a broken bowl, empty; in the other she held a bamboo pole longer than herself, split at the bottom: it was clear she had become a beggar.

I stood still, waiting for her to come and ask for money.

"You have come back?" she asked me first.

"Yes."

"That is very good. You are a scholar, and have traveled too and seen a lot. I just want to ask you something." Her lusterless eyes suddenly gleamed.

I never guessed she would talk to me like this. I stood there taken by surprise.

"It is this." She drew two paces nearer, and whispered very confidentially: "After a person dies, does he turn into a ghost or not?"

As she fixed her eyes on me I was seized with foreboding. A shiver ran down my spine and I felt more nervous than during an unexpected examination at school, when unfortunately the teacher stands by one's side. Personally, I had never given the least thought to the question of the existence of spirits. In this emergency how should I answer her? Hesitating for a moment, I reflected: "It is the tradition here to believe in spirits, yet she seems to be skeptical — perhaps it would be better to say she hopes: hopes that there is immortality and yet hopes that there is not. Why increase the sufferings of the wretched? To give her something to look forward to, it would be better to say there is."

"There may be, I think," I told her hesitantly.

"Then, there must also be a Hell?"

"What, Hell?" Greatly startled, I could only try to evade the question. "Hell? According to reason there should be one too — but not necessarily. Who cares about it anyway. . . ?"

"Then will all the people of one family who have died see each other again?"

"Well, as to whether they will see each other again or not. . . ." I realized now that I was a complete fool; for all my hesitation and reflection I had been unable to answer her three questions. Immediately I lost confidence and wanted to say the exact opposite of what I had previously said. "In this case . . . as a matter of fact, I am not sure. . . . Actually, regarding the question of ghosts, I am not sure either."

In order to avoid further importunate questions, I walked off, and beat a hasty retreat to my uncle's house, feeling exceedingly uncomfortable. I thought to myself: "I am afraid my answer will prove dangerous to her. Probably it is just that when other people are celebrating she feels lonely by herself, but could there be another reason? Could she have had some premonition? If there is another reason, and as a result something happens, then, through my answer, I shall be held responsible to a certain extent." Finally, however, I ended by laughing at myself, thinking that such a chance meeting could have no great significance, and yet I was taking it so to heart; no wonder certain educationalists called me a neurotic. Moreover I had distinctly said, "I am not sure," contradicting my previous answer; so that even if anything did happen, it would have nothing at all to do with me.

"I am not sure" is a most useful phrase.

Inexperienced and rash young men often take it upon themselves to solve people's problems for them or choose doctors for them, and if by any chance things turn out badly, they are probably held to blame; but by simply concluding with this phrase "I am not sure," one can free oneself of all responsibility. At this time I felt even more strongly the necessity for such a phrase, since even in speaking with a beggar woman there was no dispensing with it.

However, I continued to feel uncomfortable, and even after a night's rest my mind kept running on this, as if I had a premonition of some untoward development. In that oppressive snowy weather, in the gloomy study, this discomfort increased. It would be better to leave: I should go back to town the next day. The boiled shark's fins in the Fu Hsing Restaurant used to cost a dollar for a large portion, and I wondered if this cheap and delicious dish had increased in price or not. Although the friends who had accompanied me in the old days had scattered, even if I was alone the shark's fins still had to be tasted. At all events, I made up my mind to leave the next day.

After experiencing many times that things which I hoped would not happen and felt should not happen invariably did happen, I was desperately afraid this would prove another such case. And, indeed, strange things did begin to happen. Towards evening I heard talking — it sounded like a discussion — in the inner room; but soon the conversation ended, and all I heard was my uncle saying loudly as he walked out: "Not earlier nor later, but just at this time — sure sign of a bad character!"

At first I felt astonished, then very uncomfortable, thinking these words must refer to me. I looked outside the door, but no one was there. I contained myself with difficulty till their servant came in before dinner to brew a pot of tea, when at last I had a chance to make some enquiries.

"With whom was Mr. Lu angry just now?" I asked.

"Why, still with Hsiang Lin's Wife," he replied briefly.

"Hsiang Lin's Wife? How was that?" I asked again.

"She's dead."

"Dead?" My heart suddenly missed a beat. I started, and probably changed color too. But since he did not raise his head, he was probably quite unaware of how I felt. Then I controlled myself, and asked:

"When did she die?"

"When? Last night, or else today, I'm not sure."

"How did she die?"

"How did she die? Why, of poverty of course." He answered placidly and, still without having raised his head to look at me, went out.

However, my agitation was only short-lived, for now that something I had felt imminent had already taken place, I no longer had to take refuge in my "I'm not sure," or the servant's expression "dying of poverty" for comfort. My heart already felt lighter. Only from time to time something still seemed to weigh on it. Dinner was served, and my uncle solemnly accompanied me. I wanted to ask about Hsiang Lin's Wife, but knew that although he had read, "Ghosts and spirits are properties of Nature,"* he had retained many superstitions, and on the eve of this sacrifice it was out of the question to mention anything like death or illness. In case of necessity one could use veiled allusions, but unfortunately I did not know how to, so although questions kept rising to the tip of my tongue, I had to bite them back. From his solemn expression I suddenly suspected that he looked on me as choosing not earlier nor later but just this time to come and trouble him, and that I was also a bad character; therefore to set his mind at rest I told him at once that I intended to leave Luchen the next day and go back to the city. He did not press me greatly to stay. So we quietly finished the meal.

In winter the days are short and, now that it was snowing, darkness already enveloped the whole town. Everybody was busy beneath the lamplight, but outside the windows it was very quiet. Snow-flakes fell on the thickly piled snow, as if they were whispering, making me feel even more lonely. I sat by myself under the yellow gleam of the vegetable oil lamp and thought, "This poor woman, abandoned by people in the dust as a tiresome and worn-out toy, once left her own imprint in the dust, and those who enjoy life must have wondered at her for wishing to prolong her existence; but now at least she has been swept clear by eternity. Whether spirits exist or not I do not know; but in the present world when a meaningless existence ends, so that someone whom others are tired of seeing is no longer seen, it is just as well, both for the individual concerned and for others." I listened quietly to see if I could hear the snow falling outside the window, still pursuing this train of thought, until gradually I felt less ill at ease.

---

* A Confucian saying.

Fragments of her life, seen or heard before, now combined to form one whole.

She did not belong to Luchen. One year at the beginning of winter, when my uncle's family wanted to change their maidservant, Old Mrs. Wei brought her in and introduced her. Her hair was tied with white bands, she wore a black skirt, blue jacket and pale green bodice, and was about twenty-six, with a pale skin but rosy cheeks. Old Mrs. Wei called her Hsiang Lin's Wife, and said that she was a neighbor of her mother's family, and because her husband was dead she wanted to go out to work. My uncle knitted his brows and my aunt immediately understood that he disapproved of her because she was a widow. She looked very suitable, though, with big strong feet and hands, and a meek expression; and she had said nothing but showed every sign of being tractable and hard-working. So my aunt paid no attention to my uncle's frown, but kept her. During the period of probation she worked from morning till night, as if she found resting dull, and she was so strong that she could do a man's work; accordingly on the third day it was settled, and each month she was to be paid five hundred cash.

Everybody called her Hsiang Lin's Wife. They did not ask her her own name; but since she was introduced by someone from Wei Village who said she was a neighbor, presumably her name was also Wei. She was not very talkative, only answering when other people spoke to her, and her answers were brief. It was not until a dozen days or so had passed that they learned little by little that she still had a severe mother-in-law at home and a younger brother-in-law more than ten years old, who could cut wood. Her husband, who had been a woodcutter too, had died in the spring. He had been ten years younger than she.* This little was all that people learned from her.

The days passed quickly. She worked as hard as ever; she would eat anything, and did not spare herself. Everybody agreed that the Lu family had found a very good maidservant, who really got through more work than a hard-working man.

---

* In old China it used to be common in country districts for young women to be married to boys of ten or eleven. The bride's labor could then he exploited by her husband's family.

At the end of the year she swept, mopped, killed chickens and geese and sat up to boil the sacrificial meat, single-handed, so the family did not have to hire extra help. Nevertheless she, on her side, was satisfied; gradually the trace of a smile appeared at the corner of her mouth. She became plumper and her skin whiter.

New Year was scarcely over when she came back from washing rice by the river looking pale, and said that in the distance she had just seen a man wandering on the opposite bank who looked very like her husband's cousin, and probably he had come to look for her. My aunt, much alarmed, made detailed enquiries, but failed to get any further information. As soon as my uncle learned of it he frowned and said, "This is bad. She must have run away from her husband's family."

Before long this inference that she had run away was confirmed.

About a fortnight later, just as everybody was beginning to forget what had happened, Old Mrs. Wei suddenly called, bringing with her a woman in her thirties who, she said, was the maidservant's mother-in-law. Although the woman looked like a villager, she behaved with great self-possession and had a ready tongue in her head. After the usual polite remarks she apologized for coming to take her daughter-in-law home, saying there was a great deal to be done at the beginning of spring, and since there were only old people and children at home they were short-handed.

"Since it is her mother-in-law who wants her to go back, what is there to be said?" was my uncle's comment.

Thereupon her wages were reckoned up. They amounted to one thousand seven hundred and fifty cash, all of which she had left with her mistress without using a single coin. My aunt gave the entire amount to her mother-in-law. The latter also took her clothes, thanked Mr. and Mrs. Lu and went out. By this time it was already noon.

"Oh, the rice! Didn't Hsiang Lin's Wife go to wash the rice?" my aunt exclaimed some time later. Probably she was rather hungry, so that she remembered lunch.

Thereupon everybody set about looking for the rice basket. My aunt went first to the kitchen, then to the hall, then to the bedroom; but not a trace of it was to be seen anywhere. My uncle went outside, but could not find it either; only when he went right down to the riverside did he see it, set down fair and square on the bank, with a bundle of vegetables beside it.

Some people there told him that a boat with a white awning had moored there in the morning, but since the awning covered the boat completely they did not know who was inside, and before this incident no one had paid any attention to it. But when Hsiang Lin's Wife came to wash rice, two men looking like country people jumped off the boat just as she was kneeling down and seizing hold of her carried her on board. After several shouts and cries, Hsiang Lin's Wife became silent: they had probably stopped her mouth. Then two women walked up, one of them a stranger and the other Old Mrs. Wei. When the people who told this story tried to peep into the boat they could not see very clearly, but Hsiang Lin's Wife seemed to be lying bound on the floor of the boat.

"Disgraceful! Still . . ." said my uncle.

That day my aunt cooked the midday meal herself, and my cousin Ah Niu lit the fire.

After lunch Old Mrs. Wei came again.

"Disgraceful!" said my uncle.

"What is the meaning of this? How dare you come here again!" My aunt, who was washing dishes, started scolding as soon as she saw her. "You recommended her yourself, and then plotted to have her carried off, causing all this stir. What will people think? Are you trying to make a laughingstock of our family?"

"Aiya, I was really taken in! Now I have come specially to clear up this business. When she asked me to find her work, how was I to know that she had left home without her mother-in-law's consent? I am very sorry, Mr. Lu, Mrs. Lu. Because I am so old and foolish and careless, I have offended my patrons. However, it is lucky for me that your family is always so generous and kind, and unwilling to be hard on your inferiors. This time I promise to find you someone good to make up for my mistake."

"Still . . ." said my uncle.

Thereupon the business of Hsiang Lin's Wife was concluded, and before long it was also forgotten.

O nly my aunt, because the maidservants taken on afterwards were all lazy or fond of stealing food, or else both lazy and fond of stealing food, with not a good one in the lot, still often spoke of Hsiang Lin's Wife. On such occasions she would always say to herself, "I wonder what has become of her now?" meaning that she would like to have her back. But by the following New Year she too gave up hope.

The New Year's holiday was nearly over when Old Mrs. Wei, already half tipsy, came to pay her respects, and said it was because she had been back to Wei Village to visit her mother's family and stayed a few days that she had come late. During the course of conversation they naturally came to speak of Hsiang Lin's Wife.

"She?" said Mrs. Wei cheerfully. "She is in luck now. When her mother-in-law dragged her home, she had already promised her to the sixth son of the Ho family in Ho Village. Not long after she reached home they put her in the bridal chair and sent her off."

"Aiya! What a mother-in-law!" exclaimed my aunt in amazement.

"Ah, madam, you really talk like a great lady! We country folk, poor women, think nothing of that. She still had a younger brother-in-law who had to be married. And if they hadn't found her a husband, where would they have found the money for his wedding? But her mother-in-law is a clever and capable woman, who knows how to drive a good bargain, so she married her off into the mountains. If she had married her to someone in the same village, she wouldn't have got so much money; but since very few women are willing to marry someone living deep in the mountains, she got eighty thousand cash. Now the second son is married, the presents only cost her fifty thousand, and after paying the wedding expenses she still has over ten thousand left. Just think, doesn't this show she knows how to drive a good bargain. . . ?"

"But was Hsiang Lin's Wife willing?"

"It wasn't a question of being willing or not. Of course anyone would have protested. They just tied her up with a rope, stuffed her into the bridal chair, carried her to the man's house, put on the bridal headdress, performed the ceremony in the hall and locked them in their room; and that was that. But Hsiang Lin's Wife is quite a character. I heard she really put up a great struggle, and everybody said she was different from other people because she had worked in a scholar's family. We go-betweens, madam, see a great deal. When widows remarry, some cry and shout, some threaten to commit suicide, some when they have been carried to the man's house won't go through the ceremony, and some even smash the wedding candlesticks. But Hsiang Lin's Wife was different from the rest. They said she shouted and cursed all the way, so that by the time they had carried her to Ho Village she was completely hoarse. When they dragged her out of the chair, although the two chairbearers and her young brother-in-law used all their strength, they couldn't force her to go through the ceremony. The moment they were careless enough to loosen their grip — gracious Buddha! — she threw herself against a corner of the table and knocked a big hole in her head. The blood poured out; and although they used two handfuls of incense ashes and bandaged her with two pieces of red cloth, they still couldn't stop the bleeding. Finally it took all of them together to get her shut up with her husband in the bridal chamber, where she went on cursing. Oh, it was really dreadful!" She shook her head, cast down her eyes and said no more.

"And after that what happened?" asked my aunt.

"They said the next day she still didn't get up," said Old Mrs. Wei, raising her eyes.

"And after?"

"After? She got up. At the end of the year she had a baby, a boy, who was two this New Year.* These few days when I was at home some people went to Ho Village, and when they came back they said they had seen her and her son, and that both mother and baby are fat. There is no mother-in-law over

---

* It was the custom in China to reckon a child as one year old at birth, and to add another year to his age as New Year.

her, the man is a strong fellow who can earn a living, and the house is their own. Well, well, she is really in luck."

After this even my aunt gave up talking of Hsiang Lin's Wife.

*B*ut one autumn, two New Years after they heard how lucky Hsiang Lin's Wife had been, she actually reappeared on the threshold of my uncle's house. On the table she placed a round bulb-shaped basket, and under the eaves a small roll of bedding. Her hair was still wrapped in white bands, and she wore a black skirt, blue jacket and pale green bodice. But her skin was sallow and her cheeks had lost their color; she kept her eyes downcast, and her eyes, with their tear-stained rims, were no longer bright. Just as before, it was Old Mrs. Wei, looking very benevolent, who brought her in, and who explained at length to my aunt:

"It was really a bolt from the blue. Her husband was so strong, nobody could have guessed that a young fellow like that would die of typhoid fever. First he seemed better, but then he ate a bowl of cold rice and the sickness came back. Luckily she had the boy, and she can work, whether it is chopping wood, picking tea leaves or raising silkworms; so at first she was able to carry on. Then who could believe that the child, too, would be carried off by a wolf? Although it was nearly the end of spring, still wolves came to the village — how could anyone have guessed that? Now she is all on her own. Her brother-in-law came to take the house, and turned her out; so she has really no way open to her but to come and ask help from her former mistress. Luckily this time there is nobody to stop her, and you happen to be wanting a new servant, so I have brought her here. I think someone who is used to your ways is much better than a new hand. . . ."

"I was really stupid, really . . ." Hsiang Lin's Wife raised her listless eyes to say. "I only knew that when it snows the wild beasts in the glen have nothing to eat and may come to the villages; I didn't know that in spring they came too. I got up at dawn and opened the door, filled a small basket with beans and called our Ah Mao to go and sit on the threshold and shell the beans. He was very obedient and always did as I told him: he went out. Then I chopped wood at the back of the house and washed the rice, and when the rice was in the pan and I wanted to boil the beans I called Ah Mao, but there was no answer; and when I went our to look, all I could see was beans scattered on the ground, but no Ah Mao. He never went to other families to play; and in fact at each place where I went to ask, there was no sign of him. I became desperate, and begged people to go to look for him. Only in the afternoon, after looking everywhere else, did they go to look in the glen and see one of his little shoes caught on a bramble. 'That's bad,' they said, 'he must have met a wolf.' And sure enough when they went further in there he was, lying in the wolf's lair, with all his entrails eaten away, his hand still tightly clutching that little basket. . . ." At this point she started crying, and was unable to complete the sentence.

My aunt had been undecided at first, but by the end of this story the rims of her eyes were rather red. After thinking for a moment she told her to take the round basket and bedding into the servants' quarters. Old Mrs. Wei heaved a long sigh as if relieved of a great burden. Hsiang Lin's Wife looked a little more at ease than when she first came and, without having to be told the way, quietly took away her bedding. From this time on she worked again as a maidservant in Luchen.

Everybody still called her Hsiang Lin's Wife.

However, she had changed a great deal. She had not been there more than three days before her master and mistress realized that she was not as quick as before. Since her memory was much worse, and her impassive face never showed the least trace of a smile, my aunt already expressed herself very far from satisfied. When the woman first arrived, although my uncle frowned as before, because they invariably had such difficulty in finding servants he did not object very strongly, only secretly warned my aunt that while such people may seem very pitiful they exert a bad moral influence. Thus although it would be all right for her to do ordinary work she must not join in the preparations for sacrifice; they would have to prepare all the dishes themselves, for otherwise they would be unclean and the ancestors would not accept them.

The most important event in my uncle's household was the ancestral sacrifice, and formerly this had been the busiest time for Hsiang Lin's Wife; but now she had very little to do. When the table was placed in the center of the hall and the curtain fastened, she still remembered how to set out the wine cups and chopsticks in the old way.

"Hsiang Lin's Wife, put those down!" said my aunt hastily.

She sheepishly withdrew her hand and went to get the candlesticks.

"Hsiang Lin's Wife, put those down!" cried my aunt hastily again. "I'll fetch them."

After walking round several times without finding anything to do, Hsiang Lin's Wife could only go hesitantly away. All she did that day was to sit by the stove and feed the fire.

The people in the town still called her Hsiang Lin's Wife, but in a different tone from before; and although they talked to her still, their manner was colder. She did not mind this in the least, only, looking straight in front of her, she would tell everybody her story, which night or day was never out of her mind.

"I was really stupid, really," she would say. "I only knew that when it snows the wild beasts in the glen have nothing to eat and may come to the villages; I didn't know that in spring they came too. I got up at dawn and opened the door, filled a small basket with beans and called our Ah Mao to go and sit on the threshold and shell them. He was very obedient and always did as I told him: he went out. Then I chopped wood at the back of the house and washed the rice, and when the rice was in the pan and I wanted to boil the beans I called Ah Mao, but there was no answer; and when I went out to look, all I could see was beans scattered on the ground, but no Ah Mao. He never went to other families to play; and in fact at each place where I went to ask, there was no sign of him. I became desperate, and begged people to go to look for him. Only in the afternoon, after looking everywhere else, did they go to look in the glen and see one of his little shoes caught on a bramble. 'That's bad,' they said, 'he must have met a wolf.' And sure enough when they went further in there he was, lying in the wolf's lair, with all his entrails eaten away, his hand still tightly clutching that small basket. . . ." At this point she would start crying and her voice would trail away.

This story was rather effective, and when men heard it they often stopped smiling and walked away disconcerted, while the women not only seemed to forgive her but their faces immediately lost their contemptuous look and they added their tears to hers. There were some old women who had not heard her speaking in the street, who went specially to look for her, to hear her sad tale. When her voice trailed away and she started to cry, they joined in, shedding the tears which had gathered in their eyes. Then they sighed, and went away satisfied, exchanging comments.

She asked nothing better than to tell her sad story over and over again, often gathering three or four hearers. But before long everybody knew it by heart, until even in the eyes of the most kindly, Buddha fearing old ladies not a trace of tears could be seen. In the end, almost everyone in the town could recite her tale, and it bored and exasperated them to hear it.

"I was really stupid, really . . ." she would begin.

"Yes, you only knew that in snowy weather the wild beasts in the mountains had nothing to eat and might come down to the villages." Promptly cutting short her recital, they walked away.

She would stand there open-mouthed, looking at them with a dazed expression, and then go away too, as if she also felt disconcerted. But she still brooded over it, hoping from other topics such as small baskets, beans and other people's children, to lead up to the story of her Ah Mao. If she saw a child of two or three, she would say, "Oh dear, if my Ah Mao were still alive, he would be just as big. . . ."

Children seeing the look in her eyes would take fright and, clutching the hems of their mothers' clothes, try to tug them away. Thereupon she would be left by herself again, and finally walk away disconcerted. Later everybody knew what she was like, and it only needed a child present for them to ask her with an artificial smile, "Hsiang Lin's Wife, if your Ah Mao were alive, wouldn't he be just as big as that?"

She probably did not realize that her story, after having been turned over and tasted by people for so many days, had long since become stale, only exciting disgust and contempt; but from the way people smiled she seemed to know that they were cold and sarcastic, and that there was no need for her to say anymore. She would simply look at them, not answering a word.

In Luchen people celebrate New Year in a big way: preparations start from the twentieth day of the twelfth month onwards. That year my uncle's household found it necessary to hire a temporary manservant, but since there was still a great deal to do they also called in another maidservant, Liu Ma, to help. Chickens and geese had to be killed; but Liu Ma was a devout woman who abstained from meat, did not kill living things, and would only wash the sacrificial dishes. Hsiang Lin's Wife had nothing to do but feed the fire. She sat there, resting, watching Liu Ma as she washed the sacrificial dishes. A light snow began to fall.

"Dear me, I was really stupid," began Hsiang Lin's Wife, as if to herself, looking at the sky and sighing.

"Hsiang Lin's Wife, there you go again," said Liu Ma, looking at her impatiently. "I ask you: that wound on your forehead, wasn't it then you got it?"

"Uh, huh," she answered vaguely.

"Let me ask you: what made you willing after all?"

"Me?"

"Yes. What I think is, you must have been willing; otherwise. . . ."

"Oh dear, you don't know how strong he was."

"I don't believe it. I don't believe he was so strong that you really couldn't keep him off. You must have been willing, only you put the blame on his being so strong."

"Oh dear, you . . . you try for yourself and see." She smiled.

Liu Ma's lined face broke into a smile too, making it wrinkled like a walnut; her small beady eyes swept Hsiang Lin's Wife's forehead and fastened on her eyes. As if rather embarrassed, Hsiang Lin's Wife immediately stopped smiling, averted her eyes and looked at the snow-flakes.

"Hsiang Lin's Wife, that was really a bad bargain," continued Liu Ma mysteriously. "If you had held out longer or knocked yourself to death, it would have been better. As it is, after living with your second husband for less than two years, you are guilty of a great crime. Just think: when you go down to the lower world in future, these two men's ghosts will fight over you. To which will you go? The King of Hell will have no choice but to cut you in two and divide you between them. I think, really. . . . ."

Then terror showed in her face. This was something she had never heard in the mountains.

"I think you had better take precautions beforehand. Go to the Tutelary God's Temple and buy a threshold to be your substitute, so that thousands of people can walk over it and trample on it, in order to atone for your sins in this life and avoid torment after death."

At the time Hsiang Lin's Wife said nothing, but she must have taken this to heart, for the next morning when she got up there were dark circles beneath her eyes. After breakfast she went to the Tutelary God's Temple at the west end of the village, and asked to buy a threshold. The temple priests would not agree at first, and only when she shed tears did they give a grudging consent. The price was twelve thousand cash.

She had long since given up talking to people, because Ah Mao's story was received with such contempt; but news of her conversation with Liu Ma that day spread, and many people took a fresh interest in her and came again to tease her into talking. As for the subject, that had naturally changed to deal with the wound on her forehead.

"Hsiang Lin's Wife, I ask you: what made you willing after all that time?" one would cry.

"Oh, what a pity, to have had this knock for nothing," another looking at her scar would agree.

Probably she knew from their smiles and tone of voice that they were making fun of her, for she always looked steadily at them without saying a word, and finally did not even turn her head. All day long she kept her lips tightly closed, bearing. on her head the scar which everyone considered a mark of shame, silently shopping, sweeping the floor, washing vegetables, preparing rice. Only after nearly a year did she take from my aunt her wages which had accumulated. She changed them for twelve silver dollars, and asking for leave went to the west end of the town. In less time than it takes for a meal she was back again, looking much comforted, and with an unaccustomed light in her eyes. She told my aunt happily that she had bought a threshold in the Tutelary God's Temple.

When the time came for the ancestral sacrifice at the winter equinox, she worked harder than ever, and seeing my aunt take out the sacrificial utensils and with Ah Niu carry the table into the middle of the hall, she went confidently to fetch the wine cups and chopsticks.

"Put those down, Hsiang Lin's Wife!" my aunt called out hastily.

She withdrew her hand as if scorched, her face turned ashen-grey, and instead of fetching the candlesticks she just stood there dazed. Only when my uncle came to burn incense and told her to go, did she walk away. This time the change in her was very great, for the next day not only were her eyes sunken, but even her spirit seemed broken. Moreover she became very timid, not only afraid of the dark and shadows, but also of the sight of anyone. Even her own master or mistress made her look as frightened as a little mouse that has come out of its hole in the daytime. For the rest, she would sit stupidly, like a wooden statue. In less than half a year her hair began to turn grey, and her memory became much worse, reaching a point when she was constantly forgetting to go and prepare the rice.

"What has come over Hsiang Lin's Wife? It would really have been better not to have kept her that time." My aunt would sometimes speak like this in front of her, as if to warn her.

However, she remained this way, so that it was impossible to see any hope of her improving. They finally decided to get rid of her and tell her to go back to Old Mrs. Wei. While I was at Luchen they were still only talking of this; but judging by what happened later, it is evident that this was what they must have done. Whether after leaving my uncle's household she became a beggar, or whether she went first to Old Mrs. Wei's house and later became a beggar, I do not know.

I was woken up by firecrackers exploding noisily close at hand, saw the glow of the yellow oil lamp as large as a bean, and heard the splutter of fireworks as my uncle's household celebrated the sacrifice. I knew that it was nearly dawn. I felt bewildered, hearing as in a dream the confused continuous sound of distant crackers which seemed to form one dense cloud of noise in the sky, joining the whirling snow-flakes to envelop the whole town. Wrapped in this medley of sound, relaxed and at ease, the doubt which had preyed on me from dawn to early night was swept clean away by the atmosphere of celebration, and I felt only that the saints of heaven and earth had accepted the sacrifice and incense and were all reeling with intoxication in the sky, preparing to give the people of Luchen boundless good fortune.

February 7, 1924

In the Wine Shop

*D*uring my travels from the North to the Southeast I made a detour to my home, then to S———. This town is only about ten miles from my native place, and by small boat can be reached in less than half a day. I had taught in a school here for a year. In the depth of winter, after snow, the landscape was bleak. Indolence and nostalgia combined finally made me put up for a short time in the Lo Szu Inn, one which had not been there before. The town was small. I looked for several old colleagues I thought I might find, but not one was there: they had long since gone their different ways. When I passed the gate of the school, I found that too had changed its name and appearance, which made me feel quite a stranger. In less than two hours my enthusiasm had waned, and I rather reproached myself for coming.

The inn in which I stayed let rooms but did not supply meals; rice and dishes could be ordered from outside, but they were quite unpalatable, tasting like mud. Outside the window was only a stained and spotted wall, covered with withered moss. Above was the slatey sky, dead white without any coloring; moreover a light flurry of snow had begun to fall. I had had a poor lunch to begin with, and had nothing to do to while away the time, so quite naturally I thought of a small wine shop I had known very well in the old days, called "One Barrel House," which, I reckoned, could not be far from the hotel. I immediately locked the door of my room and set out for this tavern. Actually, all I wanted was to escape the boredom of my stay. I did not really want to drink. "One Barrel House" was still there, its narrow, moldering front and dilapidated signboard unchanged. But from the landlord down to the waiter there was not a single person I knew – in "One Barrel House" too I had become a complete stranger. Still I walked up the familiar flight of stairs in the corner of the room to the little upper storey. Up here were the same five small wooden tables, unchanged. Only the back window, which had originally had a wooden lattice, had been fitted with panes of glass.

"A catty of yellow wine. Dishes? Ten slices of fried bean curd, with plenty of pepper sauce!"

As I gave the order to the waiter who had come up with me, I walked to the back and sat down at the table by the window. This upstairs room was absolutely empty, which enabled me to take possession of the best seat from which I could look out on to the deserted courtyard beneath. The courtyard probably did not belong to the wine shop. I had looked out at it many times before in the past, sometimes in snowy weather too. Now, to eyes accustomed to the North, the sight was sufficiently striking: several old plum trees, rivals of the snow, were actually in full blossom as if entirely oblivious of winter; while beside the crumbling pavilion there was still a camellia with a dozen crimson blossoms standing out against its thick, dark green foliage, blazing in the snow as bright as fire, indignant and arrogant, as if despising the wanderer's wanderlust. I suddenly remembered the moistness of the heaped snow here, clinging, glistening and shining, quite unlike the dry northern snow which, when a high wind blows, will fly up and fill the sky like mist. . . .

"Your wine, sir," said the waiter carelessly, and put down the cup, chopsticks, wine pot and dish. The wine had come. I turned to the table, set everything straight and filled my cup. I felt that the North was certainly not my home, yet when I came South I could only count as a stranger. The dry snow up there, which flew like powder, and the soft snow here, which clung lingeringly, seemed equally alien to me. In a slightly melancholy mood, I took a leisurely sip of wine. The wine was quite pure, and the fried bean curd was excellently cooked. The only pity was that the pepper sauce was too thin, but then the people of S—— had never understood pungent flavors .

Probably because it was only afternoon, the place had none of the atmosphere of a tavern. I had already drunk three cups, but apart from myself there were still only four bare wooden tables in the place. Looking at the deserted courtyard I began to feel lonely, yet I did not want any other customers to come up. I could not help being irritated by the sound of footsteps on the stairs, and was relieved to find it was only the waiter. And so I drank another two cups of wine.

"This time it must be a customer," I thought, for the footsteps sounded much slower than those of the waiter. When I judged that he must be at the top of the stairs, I raised my head rather apprehensively to look at this unwelcome company. I gave a start and stood up. I never guessed that here of all places I should unexpectedly meet a friend — if such he would still let me call him. The newcomer was an old classmate who had been my colleague when I was a teacher, and although he had changed a great deal I knew him as soon as I saw him. Only he had become much slower in his movements, very unlike the nimble and active Lu Wei-fu of the old days.

"Ah, Wei-fu, is it you? I never expected to meet you here."

"Oh, it's you? Neither did I ever. . . ."

I urged him to join me, but only after some hesitation did he seem willing to sit down. At first I thought this very strange, and felt rather hurt and displeased. When I looked closely at him he had still the same disorderly hair and beard and pale oblong face, but he was thinner and weaker. He looked very quiet, or perhaps dispirited, and his eyes beneath their thick black brows had lost their alertness; but when he looked slowly around in the direction of the deserted courtyard, from his eyes suddenly flashed one of those piercing looks which I had seen so often at school.

"Well," I said cheerfully but somewhat awkwardly, "we have not seen each other now for about ten years. I heard long ago that you were at Tsinan, but I was so wretchedly lazy I never wrote. . . ."

"I was just the same. I have been at Taiyuan for more than two years now, with my mother. When I came back to fetch her I learned that you had already left, left for good and all."

"What are you doing in Taiyuan?" I asked.

"Teaching in the family of a fellow-provincial."

"And before that?"

"Before that?" He took a cigarette from his pocket, lit it and put it in his mouth, then, watching the smoke as he puffed, said reflectively, "Simply futile work, equivalent to doing nothing at all."

He also asked what had happened to me since we separated. I gave him a rough idea, at the same time calling the waiter to bring a cup and chopsticks, so that he could share my wine while we had another two catties heated. We also ordered dishes. In the past we had never stood on ceremony, but now we began to be so formal that neither would choose a dish, and finally we fixed on four suggested by the waiter: peas spiced with aniseed, cold meat, fried bean curd, and salted fish.

"As soon as I came back I knew I was a fool." Holding his cigarette in one hand and the wine cup in the other, he spoke with a bitter smile. "When I was young, I saw the way bees or flies stopped in one place. If they were frightened they would fly off, but after flying in a small circle they would come back again to stop in the same place; and I thought this really very foolish, as well as pathetic. But I didn't think that I would fly back myself, after only flying in a small circle. And I didn't think you would come back either. Couldn't you have flown a little further?"

"That's difficult to say. Probably I too have simply flown in a small circle." I also spoke with a rather bitter smile. "But why did you fly back?"

"For something quite futile." In one gulp he emptied his cup, then took several pulls at his cigarette, and opened his eyes a little wider. "Futile — but you may as well hear about it."

*T*he waiter brought up the freshly heated wine and dishes, and set them on the table. The smoke and the fragrance of fried bean curd seemed to make the upstairs room more cheerful, while outside the snow fell still more thickly.

"Perhaps you knew," he went on, "that I had a little brother who died when he was three, and was buried here in the country. I can't even remember clearly what he looked like, but I have heard my mother say he was a very lovable child, and very fond of me. Even now it brings tears to her eyes to speak of him. This spring an elder cousin wrote to tell us that the ground beside his grave was gradually being swamped, and he was afraid before long it would slip into the river: we should go at once and do something about it. As soon as my mother knew this, she became very upset, and couldn't sleep for several nights — she can read letters by herself, you know. But what could I do? I had no money, no time: there was nothing that could be done.

"Only now, taking advantage of my New Year's holiday, I have been able to come South to move his grave." He drained another cup of wine, looked out of the window and exclaimed: "Could you find anything like this up North? Flowers in thick snow, and beneath the snow unfrozen ground. So the day before yesterday I bought a small coffin, because I reckoned that the one under the ground must have rotted long ago — I took cotton and bedding, hired four workmen, and went into the country to move his grave. At the time I suddenly felt very happy, eager to dig up the grave, eager to see the body of the little brother who had been so fond of me: this was a new sensation for me. When we reached the grave, sure enough, the river water was encroaching on it and was already less than two feet away. The poor grave had not had any earth added to it for two years, and had sunk in. I stood in the snow, firmly pointed it out to the workmen, and said: 'Dig it up!'

"I really am a commonplace fellow. I felt that my voice at this juncture was rather unnatural, and that this order was the greatest I had given in all my life. But the workmen didn't find it at all strange, and simply set to work to dig. When they reached the enclosure I had a look, and indeed the wood of the coffin had rotted almost completely away, leaving only a heap of splinters and small fragments of wood. My heart beat faster and I set these aside myself very carefully, wanting to see my little brother. However, I was taken by surprise. Bedding, clothes, skeleton, all had gone! I thought: 'These have all rotted away, but I always heard that the most difficult substance to rot is hair; perhaps there is still some hair.' So I bent down and looked carefully in the mud where the pillow should have been, but there was none. Not a trace remained." I suddenly noticed that the rims of his eyes had become rather red, but realized at once that this was the effect of the wine. He had scarcely touched the dishes, but had been drinking incessantly, so that he had already drunk more than a catty, and his looks and gestures had all become more vigorous, so that he gradually resembled the Lu Wei-fu I had known. I called the waiter to heat two more measures of wine, then turned back and, taking my wine cup, face to face with him, listened in silence to what he had to tell.

"Actually it need not really have been moved again; I had only to level the ground, sell the coffin, and that would have been the end of it. Although there would have been something rather singular in my going to sell the coffin, still, if the price were low enough the shop from which I bought it would have taken it, and at least I could have saved a little money for wine. But I didn't do so. I still spread out the bedding, wrapped up in cotton some of the clay where his body had been, covered it up, put it in the new coffin, moved it to the grave where my father was buried, and buried it beside him. Because I used bricks for an enclosure of the coffin I was busy again most of yesterday, supervising the work. In this way I can count the affair ended, at least enough to deceive my mother and set her mind at rest. Well, well, you look at me like that! Do you blame me for being so changed? Yes, I still remember the time when we went together to the Tutelary God's Temple to pull off the images' beards, how all day long we used to discuss methods of revolutionizing China until we even came to blows. But now I am like this, willing to let things slide and to compromise. Sometimes I think: 'If my old friends were to see me now, probably they would no longer acknowledge me as a friend.' But this is what I am like now."

He took out another cigarette, put it in his mouth and lit it.

"Judging by your expression, you still seem to have hope for me. Naturally I am much more obtuse than before, but

there are still some things I realize. This makes me grateful
to you, at the same time rather uneasy. I am afraid I am only
letting down the old friends who even now still have some
hope for me. . . ." He stopped and puffed several times at his
cigarette before going on slowly: "Only today, just before
coming to this 'One Barrel House,' I did something futile,
and yet it was something I was glad to do. My former
neighbor on the east side was called Chang Fu. He was a
boatman and had a daughter called Ah Shun. When you came
to my house in those days you might have seen her, but you
certainly wouldn't have paid any attention to her, because
she was so small then. Nor did she grow up to be pretty,
having just an ordinary thin oval face and pale skin. Only
her eyes were unusually large, with very long lashes, and the
whites were as clear as a cloudless night sky — I mean the
cloudless sky of the North when there is no wind; here it is
not so clear. She was very capable. She lost her mother when
she was in her teens, and it was her job to look after a small
brother and sister; also she had to wait on her father, and all
this she did very competently. She was economical too, so
that the family gradually grew better off. There was scarcely
a neighbor who did not praise her, and even Chang Fu often
expressed his appreciation. When I left on my journey this
time, my mother remembered her — old people's memories
are so long. She recalled that in the past Ah Shun once saw
someone wearing artificial red flowers in her hair, and wanted
a spray for herself. When she couldn't get one she cried nearly
all night, so that she was beaten by her father, and her eyes
remained red and swollen for two or three days. These red
flowers came from another province, and couldn't be bought
even in S———, so how could she ever hope to have any?
Since I was coming South this time, my mother told me to
buy two sprays to give her.

"Far from feeling vexed at this commission, I was actually
delighted. I was really glad to do something for Ah Shun. The
year before last, I came back to fetch my mother, and one day
when Chang Fu was at home I happened to start chatting
with him. He wanted to invite me to take a bowl of gruel
made of buckwheat flour, telling me that they added white
sugar to it. You see, a boatman who could keep white sugar

in his house was obviously not poor, and must eat very well.
I let myself be persuaded and accepted, but begged that they
would only give me a small bowl. He quite understood, and
said to Ah Shun: 'These scholars have no appetite. You can
use a small bowl, but add more sugar!' However when she
had prepared the concoction and brought it in, I gave a start,
for it was a large bowl, as much as I would eat in a whole day.
Compared with Chang Fu's bowl, it is true, it did appear
small. In all my life I had never eaten this buckwheat gruel,
and now that I tasted it, it was really unpalatable, though
extremely sweet. I carelessly swallowed a few mouthfuls, and
had decided not to eat anymore when I happened to catch a
glimpse of Ah Shun standing far off in one corner of the
room. Then I hadn't the heart to put down my chopsticks. I
saw in her face both hope and fear — fear, no doubt, that she
had prepared it badly, and hope that we would find it to our
liking. I knew that if I left most of mine she would feel very
disappointed and apologetic. So I screwed up my courage,
opened my mouth wide and shoveled it down, eating almost
as fast as Chang Fu. It was then that I learned the agony of
forcing oneself to eat; I remember when I was a child and had
to finish a bowl of brown sugar mixed with medicine for
worms I experienced the same difficulty. I felt no resentment,
though, because her half suppressed smile of satisfaction,
when she came to take away our empty bowls, repaid me
amply for all my discomfort. That night, although indiges-
tion kept me from sleeping well and I had a series of night-
mares, I still wished her a lifetime of happiness, and hoped
the world would change for the better for her sake. Such
thoughts were only the traces of my dreams in the old days.
The next instant I laughed at myself, and promptly forgot
them.

"I did not know before that she had been beaten on account
of a spray of artificial flowers, but when my mother spoke of
it I remembered the buckwheat gruel incident, and became
unaccountably diligent. First I made a search in Taiyuan, but
none of the shops had them. It was only when I went to
Tsinan. . . ."

There was a rustle outside the window, as a pile of snow
slipped down from the camellia which it had bent beneath

its weight; then the branches of the tree straightened themselves, showing even more clearly their dark thick foliage and blood-red flowers. The color of the sky became more slatey. Small sparrows chirped, probably because evening was near, and since the ground was covered with snow they could find nothing to eat and would go early to their nests to sleep.

"It was only when I went to Tsinan," he looked out of the window for a moment, turned back and drained a cup of wine, took several puffs at his cigarette, and went on, "only then did I buy the artificial flowers. I didn't know whether those she had been beaten for were this kind or not; but at least these were also made of velvet. I didn't know either whether she liked a deep or a light color, so I bought one spray of red, one spray of pink, and brought them both here.

"Just this afternoon, as soon as I had finished lunch, I went to see Chang Fu, having specially stayed an extra day for this. His house was there all right, only looking rather gloomy; or perhaps that was simply my imagination. His son and second daughter — Ah Chao — were standing at the gate. Both of them had grown. Ah Chao was quite different from her sister, and looked very plain; but when she saw me come up to their house, she quickly ran inside. When I asked the little boy, I found that Chang Fu was not at home. 'And your elder sister?' At once he stared at me wide-eyed, and asked me what I wanted her for; moreover he seemed very fierce, as if he wanted to attack me. Hesitantly I walked away. Nowadays I just let things slide. . . .

"You have no idea how much more afraid I am of calling on people than I used to be. Because I know very well how unwelcome I am, I have even come to dislike myself and, knowing this, why should I inflict myself on others? But this time I felt my errand had to be carried out, so after some reflection I went back to the firewood shop almost opposite their house. The shopkeeper's mother, Old Mrs. Fa, was there at least, and still recognized me. She actually asked me into the shop to sit down. After an exchange of polite remarks I told her why I had come back to S—— and was looking for Chang Fu. I was taken aback when she heaved a sigh and said:

"What a pity Ah Shun had not the good luck to wear these flowers you have brought.'

"Then she told me the whole story, saying, 'It was probably last spring that Ah Shun began to look pale and thin. Later she would often start crying suddenly, and if you asked her why, she wouldn't say. Sometimes she even cried all night, until Chang Fu lost his temper and scolded her, saying she had waited too long to marry and had gone mad. When autumn came, first she had a slight cold and then she took to her bed, and after that she never got up again. Only a few days before she died, she told Chang Fu that she had long ago become like her mother, often spitting blood and per-spiring at night. She had hidden it, afraid that he would worry about her. One evening her uncle Chang Keng came to demand money — he was always doing that — and when she would not give him any he smiled coldly and said, "Don't be so proud; your man is not even up to me!" That upset her, but she was too shy to ask, and could only cry. As soon as Chang Fu knew this, he told her what a decent fellow her future husband was; but it was too late. Besides, she didn't believe him. "It's a good thing I'm already like this," she said. "Now nothing matters anymore."'

"The old woman also said, 'If her man was really not as good as Chang Keng, that would be truly frightful! He would not be up to a chicken thief, and what sort of fellow would that be! But when he came to the funeral I saw him with my own eyes: his clothes were clean and he was very presentable. He said with tears in his eyes that he had worked hard all those years on the boat to save up money to marry, but now the girl was dead. Obviously he must really have been a good man, and everything Chang Keng said was false. It was only a pity Ah Shun believed such a rascally liar, and died for nothing. But we can't blame anyone else: this was Ah Shun's fate.'

"Since that was the case, my business was finished too. But what about the two sprays of artificial flowers I had brought with me? Well, I asked her to give them to Ah Chao. This Ah Chao no sooner saw me than she fled as if I were a wolf or some monster; I really didn't want to give them to her. However, I did give them to her, and I have only to tell my mother that Ah Shun was delighted with them, and that will be that. Who cares about such futile affairs anyway? One only wants to muddle through them somehow. When I have muddled through New Year I shall go back to teaching the Confucian classics as before."

"Are you teaching that?" I asked in astonishment.

"Of course. Did you think I was teaching English? First I had two pupils, one studying the *Book of Songs*, the other *Mencius*. Recently I have got another, a girl, who is studying the *Canon for Girls*.* I don't even teach mathematics; not that I wouldn't teach it, but they don't want it taught."

"I could really never have guessed that you would be teaching such books."

"Their father wants them to study these. I'm an outsider, so it's all the same to me. Who cares about such futile affairs anyway? There's no need to take them seriously."

His whole face was scarlet as if he were quite drunk, but the gleam in his eyes had died down. I gave a slight sigh, and for a time found nothing to say. There was a clatter on the stairs as several customers came up. The first was short, with a round bloated face; the second was tall with a conspicuous, red nose. Behind them were others, and as they walked up the small upper floor shook. I turned to Lu Wei-fu, who was trying to catch my eyes; then I called the waiter to bring the bill.

"Is your salary enough to live on?" I asked as I prepared to leave.

"I have twenty dollars a month, not quite enough to manage on."

"Then what do you mean to do in future?"

"In future? I don't know. Just think: Has any single thing turned out as we hoped of all we planned in the past? I'm not sure of anything now, not even of what I will do tomorrow, nor even of the next minute. . . ."

The waiter brought up the bill and gave it to me. Wei-fu did not behave so formally as before, just glanced at me, then went on smoking and allowed me to pay.

We went out of the wine shop together. His hotel lay in the opposite direction to mine, so we said goodbye at the door. As I walked alone towards my hotel, the cold wind and

---

* A book giving the feudal standard of behavior for girls, and the virtues they should cultivate.

snow beat against my face, but I felt refreshed. I saw that the sky was already dark, woven together with houses and streets into the white, shifting web of thick snow.

February 16, 1924

A Happy Family

After the style of Hsu Chin-wen's "An Ideal Companion."

"... One writes simply as one feels: such a work is like sunlight, radiating from a source of infinite brightness, not like a spark from a flint struck on iron or stone. This alone is true art. And such a writer alone is a true artist. . . . But I . . . what do I rank as?"

Having thought so far he suddenly jumped out of bed. It occurred to him that he must make some money by writing to support his family, and he had already decided to send his manuscripts to the *Happy Monthly* publishers, because the remuneration appeared to be comparatively generous. But in that case the choice of subjects would be limited, otherwise the work would probably not be accepted. All right let it be limited. What were the chief problems occupying the minds of the younger generation. . . ? Undoubtedly there must be not a few, perhaps a great many, concerning love, marriage, the family. . . . Yes, there were certainly many people perplexed by such questions, even now discussing them. In that case, write about the family! But how to write. . . ? Otherwise it would probably not be accepted. Why predict anything unlucky? Still. . . .

Jumping out of bed, in four or five steps he reached the desk, sat down, took out a piece of paper with green lines, and promptly yet with resignation wrote the title: A Happy Family.

His pen immediately came to a standstill. He raised his head, fixed his two eyes on the ceiling, and tried to decide on an environment for this Happy Family.

"Peking?" he thought. "That won't do; it's too dead, even the atmosphere is dead. Even if a high wall were built round this family, still the air could scarcely be kept separate. No, that would never do! Kiangsu and Chekiang may start fighting any day, and Fukien is even more out of the question. Szechuan? Kwangtung? They are in the midst of fighting.* What about Shantung or Honan. . . ? No, one of them might be kidnapped, and if that happened the happy family would become an unhappy one. The rents in the foreign concessions in Shanghai and Tientsin are too high. . . . Somewhere abroad? Ridiculous. I don't know what Yunnan and Kweichow are like, but communications are too poor. . . ."

He racked his brains but, unable to think of a good place, decided tentatively to fix on A———. Then, however, he thought: "Nowadays many people object to the use of the Western alphabet to represent the names of people and places, saying it lessens the readers' interest. Probably, to be on the safe side, I had better not use it in my story this time. In that case what would be a good place? There is fighting in Hunan too; the rents in Dairen have gone up again. In Chahar, Kirin and Heilungkiang I have heard there are brigands, so they won't do either. . . !"

Again he racked his brains to think of a good place, but in vain; so finally he made up his mind tentatively to fix A——— as the name of the place where his Happy Family should be.

"After all this Happy Family will have to be at A———. There can't be any question about that. The family naturally consists of a husband and wife — the master and mistress — who married for love. Their marriage contract contains over forty terms going into great detail, so that they have extraordinary equality and absolute freedom. Moreover they have both had a higher education and belong to the cultured élite . . . . Japanese-returned students are no longer the fashion, so let them be Western-returned students. The master of the

---

* During this period there was civil war between warlords in many parts of China.

house always wears a foreign suit, his collar is always snowy white. His wife's hair is always curled up like a sparrow's nest in front, her pearly white teeth are always peeping out, but she wears Chinese dress. . . ."

"That won't do, that won't do! Twenty-five catties!"

Hearing a man's voice outside the window he involuntarily turned his head to look. The sun shone through the curtains hanging by the window, dazzling his eyes, while he heard a sound like small bundles of wood being thrown down. "It doesn't matter," he thought, turning back again. "'Twenty-five catties' of what. . . ? They are the cultured élite, devoted to the arts. But because they have both grown up in happy surroundings, they don't like Russian novels. Most Russian novels describe the lower classes, so they are really quite out of keeping with such a family. 'Twenty-five catties'? Never mind. In that case, what books do they read. . . ? Byron's poetry? Keats? That won't do, neither of them are safe. . . . Ah, I have it: they both like reading *An Ideal Husband.* Although I haven't read the book myself, even university professors praise it so highly that I am sure this couple must enjoy it too. You read it, I read it — they each have a copy, two copies altogether in the family. . . ."

Becoming aware of a hollow feeling in his stomach, he put down the pen and rested his head on his hands, like a globe supported by two axles.

". . . The two of them are just having lunch," he thought. "The table is spread with a snowy white table cloth, and the cook brings in the dishes — Chinese food. 'Twenty-five catties.' Of what? Never mind. Why should it be Chinese food? Westerners say Chinese cooking is the most progressive, the best to eat, the most hygienic; so they eat Chinese food. The first dish is brought in, but what is this first dish. . . ?"

"Firewood. . . ."

He turned his head with a start, to see the mistress of his own family standing on his left, her two gloomy eyes fastened on his face.

"What?" He spoke rather indignantly, feeling that her coming disturbed his work.

"*T*he firewood is all used up, so today I have bought some more. Last time it was still two hundred and forty cash for ten catties, but today he wants two hundred and sixty. Suppose I give him two hundred and fifty?"

"All right, two hundred and fifty, let it be."

"He has weighed it very unfairly. He insists that there are twenty-four and a half catties, but suppose I count it as twenty-three and a half?"

"All right. Count it as twenty-three and a half catties."

"Then, five fives are twenty-five, three fives are fifteen. . . . ."

"Oh, five fives are twenty-five, three fives are fifteen. . . ." He could get no further either, but after stopping for a moment suddenly took up his pen and started working out a sum on the lined paper on which he had written "A Happy Family." After working at it for some time he raised his head to say:

"Five hundred and eighty cash."

"In that case I haven't enough here; I am still eighty or ninety short. . . . ."

He pulled open the drawer of the desk, took out all the money in it — somewhere between twenty and thirty coppers — and put it in her outstretched hand. Then he watched her go out, and finally turned back to the desk. His head seemed to be bursting as if filled to the brim with sharp faggots. Five fives are twenty-five — scattered Arabic numerals were still imprinted on his brain. He gave a long sigh and breathed out again deeply, as if by this means he might expel the firewood, the "five fives are twenty-five," and the Arabic numerals which had stuck in his head. Sure enough after breathing out his heart seemed much lighter, whereupon he started thinking vaguely again:

"What dish? It doesn't matter, so long as it is something out of the way. Fried pork or prawns' roe and sea-slugs are really too common. I must have them eating 'Dragon and Tiger.' But what is that exactly? Some people say it's made of snakes and cats, and is an upper-class Cantonese dish, only eaten at big feasts. I've seen the name on the menu in a

Kiangsu restaurant; still, Kiangsu people aren't supposed to eat snakes or cats, so it must be made, as someone else said, of frogs and eels. Now what part of the country shall this couple he from? Never mind. After all, people from any part of the country can eat a dish of snake and car (or frog and eel), without injuring their Happy Family. At any rate, this first dish is to be 'Dragon and Tiger'; there can be no question about that.

"Now that this bowl of 'Dragon and Tiger' is placed in the middle of the table, they take up their chopsticks simultaneously, point to the dish, smile sweetly at each other and say, in a foreign tongue:

"*Chérie, s'il vous plait!*'

"*Voulez-vous commencer, chéri!*'

"*Mais non, après vous!*'

"Then they lift their chopsticks simultaneously, and simultaneously take a morsel of snake — no, no, snake's flesh really sounds too peculiar; it would be better after all to say a morsel of eel. It is settled then that 'Dragon and Tiger' is made of frogs and eels. They pick out two morsels of eel simultaneously, exactly the same size. Five fives are twenty-five, three fives. . . . Never mind. And simultaneously put them in their mouths. . . . Against his will he wanted to turn round, because he was conscious of a good deal of excitement behind him, and considerable coming and going. Nevertheless he persevered, and pursued his train of thought distractedly:

"This seems rather sentimental; no family would behave like this. Whatever makes me so woolly-minded? I'm afraid this good subject will never be written up. . . . Or perhaps there is no need for them to be returned students; people who have received higher education in China would do just as well. They are both university graduates, the cultured élite, the élite . . . . The man is a writer; the woman is also a writer, or else a lover of literature. Or else the woman is a poetess; the man is a lover of poetry, a respecter of womanhood. Or else. . ."

Finally he could contain himself no longer, and turned round.

Beside the bookcase behind him appeared a mound of cabbages, three at the bottom, two above, and one at the top, confronting him like a large letter A.

"Oh!" He started and gave a sigh, feeling his cheeks burn, while prickles ran up and down his spine. "Ah!" He took a very deep breath to get rid of the prickly feeling in his spine, then went on thinking: "The house of the Happy Family must have plenty of rooms. There is a store-room where things like cabbages are put. The master's study is apart, its walls lined with bookshelves; there are naturally no cabbages there. The shelves are filled with Chinese books and foreign books, including of course *An Ideal Husband* — two copies *altogether.* There is a separate bedroom, a brass bedstead, or something simpler like one of the elmwood beds made by the convicts of Number One Prison would do equally well. It is very clean beneath the bed. . . ." He glanced beneath his own bed. The firewood had all been used up, and there was only a piece of straw rope left, still coiled there like a dead snake.

"Twenty-three and a half catties. . . ." He felt that the firewood was just about to pour in a never-ending stream under his bed. His head ached again. He got up and went quickly to the door to close it. But he had scarcely put his hand on the door when he felt that this was overhasty and let it go instead, dropping the door curtain that was thick with dust. At the same time he thought: "This method avoids the severity of shutting oneself in, as well as the discomfort of keeping the door open; it is quite in keeping with the *Doctrine of the Mean.*"*

". . . So the master's study door is always closed." He walked back, sat down and thought, "Anyone with business must first knock at the door, and have his permission to come in; that is really the only thing to be done. Now suppose the master is sitting in his study and the mistress comes to discuss literature, she knocks too. . . . Of this at least one can be assured — she will nor bring in any cabbages.

"*Entrez, chérie, s'il vous plait.*'

"But what happens when the master has no time to discuss literature? Hearing her stand outside tapping gently on the

---

* A Confucian classic, advocating the principle of moderation in all things.

door, does he ignore her? That probably wouldn't do. Maybe it is all described in *An Ideal Husband* — that must really be an excellent novel. If I get paid for this article I must buy a copy to read!"

Slap!

His back stiffened, because he knew from experience that this slapping sound was made by his wife's hand striking their three-year-old daughter's head.

"In a Happy Family . . ." he thought, his back still rigid, hearing the child sob, "children are born late, yes, born late. Or perhaps it would be better to have none at all, just two people without any ties. . . . Or it might be better to stay in a hotel and let them look after everything, a single man without. . . ." Hearing the sobs increase in volume, he stood up and brushed past the curtain, thinking, "Karl Marx wrote his *Das Kapital* while his children were crying around him. He must really have been a great man. . . ." He walked out, opened the outer door, and was assailed by a strong smell of paraffin. The child was lying to the right of the door, face downwards. As soon as she saw him she started crying aloud.

"There, there, all right! Don't cry, don't cry! There's a good girl." He bent down to pick her up. Having done so he turned round to see his wife standing furiously to the left of the door, also with a rigid back, her hands on her hips as if she were preparing to start physical exercises.

"Even you have to come and bully me! You can't help, you only make trouble — even the paraffin lamp had to turn over. What shall we light this evening. . . ?"

"There, there, all right! Don't cry, don't cry!" Ignoring his wife's trembling voice, he carried the child into the house, and stroked her head. "There's a good girl," he repeated. Then he put her down, pulled out a chair and sat down. Setting her between his knees, he raised his hand. "Don't cry, there's a good girl," he said. "Daddy will do 'Pussy Washing' for you. At the same time he craned his neck, licked his palms from a distance twice, then with them traced circles towards his face.

"Aha! Pussy!" She started laughing.

"That's right, that's right. Pussy." He traced several more circles, and then stopped, seeing her smiling at him with tears still in her eyes. It struck him suddenly that her sweet, innocent face was just like her mother's had been five years ago, especially her bright red lips, although the general outline was smaller. That had been another bright winter's day when she heard his decision to overcome all obstacles and sacrifice everything for her; when she too looked at him in the same way, smiling, with tears in her eyes. He sat down disconsolately, as if a little drunk.

"Ah, sweet lips," he thought.

The door curtain was suddenly fastened back and the firewood brought in.

Suddenly coming to himself again, he saw that the child, still with tears in her eyes, was looking at him with her bright red lips parted. "Lips. . . ." He glanced sidewards to where the firewood was being brought in. ". . . Probably it will be nothing but five fives are twenty-five, nine nines are eighty-one, all over again. . . ! And two gloomy eyes. . . ." So thinking he snatched up the green-lined paper with the heading and the figures written on it, crumpled it up and then unfolded it again to wipe the child's eyes and nose. "Good girl, run along and play by yourself." He pushed her away as he spoke, at the same time throwing the ball of paper into the waste-paper basket.

But at once he felt rather sorry for the child, and, turning his head, followed her with his eyes as she walked forlornly away, while his ears were filled with the sound of firewood. Determined to concentrate, he turned back again and closed his eyes to put a stop to all distracting thoughts, sitting there quietly and peacefully.

He saw passing before him a flat, round, black-freckled flower with an orange center, which floated from the left of his left eye right over to the opposite side where it disappeared; then a bright green flower, with a dark green center; and finally a pile of six cabbages which formed themselves before him into an enormous letter A.

March 18, 1924

Soap

*W*ith her back to the north window in the slanting sunlight, Ssu-min's wife with her eight-year-old daughter, Hsiu-erh, was pasting paper money for the dead when she heard the slow, heavy footsteps of someone in cloth shoes and knew her husband was back. Paying no attention, she simply went on pasting coins. But the tread of cloth shoes drew nearer and nearer, till it finally stopped beside her. Then she could not help looking up to see Ssu-min before her, bunching his shoulders and stooping forward to fumble desperately under his cloth jacket in the inner pocket of his long gown.

By dint of twisting and turning at last he extracted his hand with a small oblong package in it, which he handed to his wife. As she took it, she smelt an indefinable fragrance rather reminiscent of olive. On the green paper wrapper was a bright golden seal with a network of tiny designs. Hsiu-erh bounded forward to seize this and look at it, but her mother promptly pushed her aside.

"Been shopping. . . ?" she asked as she looked at it.

"Er — yes." He stared at the package in her hand.

The green paper wrapper was opened. Inside was a layer of very thin paper, also sunflower-green, and nor till this was unwrapped was the object itself exposed — glossy and hard, besides being sunflower-green, with another network of fine designs on it. The thin paper was a cream color, it appeared. The indefinable fragrance rather reminiscent of olive was stronger now.

"My, this is really good soap!"

She held the soap to her nose as gingerly as if it were a child, and sniffed at it as she spoke.

"Er — yes. Just use this in future. . . ."

As he spoke, she noticed him eyeing her neck, and felt herself flushing up to her cheekbones. Sometimes when she rubbed her neck, especially behind the ears, her fingers detected a roughness; and though she knew this was the accumulated dirt of many years, she had never given it much thought. Now, under his scrutiny, she could not help blushing as she looked at this green, foreign soap with the curious scent, and this blush spread right to the tips of her ears. She mentally resolved to have a thorough wash with this soap after supper.

"There are places you can't wash clean just with honey locust pods,"* she muttered to herself.

"Ma, can I have this?" As Hsiu-erh reached out for the sunflower-green paper, Chao-erh, the younger daughter who had been playing outside, came running in too. Mrs. Ssu-min promptly pushed them both aside, folded the thin paper in place, wrapped the green paper round it as before, then leaned over to put it on the highest shelf of the wash-stand. After one final glance, she turned back to her paper coins.

"Hsueh-cheng!" Ssu-min seemed to have remembered something. He gave a long-drawn-out shout, sitting down on a high-backed chair opposite his wife.

"Hsueh-cheng!" she helped him call.

She stopped pasting coins to listen, but not a sound could she hear. When she saw him with upturned head waiting so impatiently, she felt quite apologetic.

"Hsueh-cheng!" she called shrilly at the top of her voice.

This call proved effective, for they heard the tramp of leather shoes draw near, and Hsueh-cheng stood before her. He was in shirt sleeves, his plump round face shiny with perspiration.

"What were you doing?" she asked disapprovingly. "Why didn't you hear your father call?"

---

* In many parts of China, honey locust pods were used for washing. They were cheaper than soap, but not so effective.

"I was practicing Hexagram Boxing. . . ." He turned at once to his father and straightened up, looking at him as if to ask what he wanted.

"Hsueh-cheng, I want to ask you the meaning of o-du-fu."*

"O-du-fu. . . ? Isn't it a very fierce woman?"

"What nonsense! The idea!" Ssu-min was suddenly furious. "Am I a woman, pray?"

Hsueh-cheng recoiled two steps, and stood straighter than ever. Though his father's gait sometimes reminded him of the way old men walked in Peking opera, he had never considered Ssu-min as a woman. His answer, he saw now, had been a great mistake.

"As if I didn't know o-du-fu means a very fierce woman. Would I have to ask you that? — This isn't Chinese, it's foreign devils' language, I'm telling you. What does it mean, do you know?"

"I . . . I don't know." Hsueh-cheng felt even more uneasy.

"Pah! Why do I spend all that money to send you to school if you don't even understand a little thing like this? Your school boasts that it lays equal stress on speech and comprehension, yet it hasn't taught you anything. The ones speaking this devils' language couldn't have been more than fourteen or fifteen, actually a little younger than you, yet they were chattering away in it, while you can't even tell me the meaning. And you have the face to answer 'I don't know.' Go and look it up for me at once!"

"Yes," answered Hsueh-cheng deep down in his throat, then respectfully withdrew.

"I don't know what students today are coming to," declared Ssu-min with emotion after a pause. "As a matter of fact, in the time of Kuang Hsu,† I was all in favor of opening schools; but I never foresaw how great the evils would be. What 'emancipation' and 'freedom' have we had? There is no true learning, nothing but absurdities. I've spent quite a bit of money on Hsueh-cheng, all to no purpose. It wasn't easy to get him into this half-Western, half-Chinese school, where they claim they lay equal stress on 'speaking and comprehend-

---

* In Chinese this means "vicious wife."

† i.e. 1875–1908.

ing English.'* You'd think all should be well. But — bah! —
after one whole year of study he can't even understand *o-du-fu!*
He must still be studying dead books. What use is such a
school, I ask you? What I say is: Close the whole lot of them!"

"Yes, really, better close the whole lot of them," chimed in
his wife sympathetically, pasting away at the paper money.

"There's no need for Hsiu-erh and her sister to attend any
school. As Ninth Grandpa said, What's the good of girls
studying?' When he opposed girls' schools I attacked him for
it; but now I see the old folk were right after all. Just think,
it's already in very poor taste the way women wander up and
down the streets, and now they want to cut their hair as well.
Nothing disgusts me so much as these short-haired school-
girls. What I say is: There's some excuse for soldiers and
bandits, but these girls are the ones who turn everything
upside down. They ought to be very severely dealt with
indeed. . . ."

"Yes, as if it wasn't enough for all men to look like monks,
the women are imitating nuns."†

"Hsueh-cheng!"

Hsueh-cheng hurried in holding a small, fat, gilt-edged
book, which he handed to his father.

"This looks like it," he said, pointing to one place.
"Here. . . ."

Ssu-min took it and looked at it. He knew it was a dictionary, but the characters were very small and horizontally
printed too. Frowning, he turned towards the window and
screwed up his eyes to read the passage Hsueh-cheng had
pointed out.

"'A society founded in the eighteenth century for mutual
relief.' — No, that can't be it. — How do you pronounce this?"
He pointed to the devils' word in front.

"Oddfellows."

"No, no, that wasn't it." Ssu-min suddenly lost his temper
again. "I told you it was bad language, a swear-word of some

---

* English was taught in nearly all the new schools at that time, and
   learning to speak was considered as important as learning to read.

† Monks and nuns in China shaved their heads. Hence, at the end of
   the Ching dynasty and later, conservatives laughed at the men who
   cut their queues, claiming they looked like monks.

sort, to abuse someone of my type. Understand? Go and look it up!"

Hsueh-cheng glanced at him several times, but did not move.

"This is too puzzling. How can he make head or tail of it? You must explain things clearly to him first, before he can look it up properly." Seeing Hsueh-cheng in a quandary, his mother felt sorry for him and intervened rather indignantly on his behalf.

"It was when I was buying soap at Kuang Jun Hsiang on the main street," sighed Ssu-min, turning to her. "There were three students shopping there too. Of course, to them I must have seemed a little pernickety. I looked at five or six kinds of soap all over forty cents, and turned them down. Then I looked at some priced ten cents a cake, but it was too poor, with no scent at all. Since I thought it best to strike a happy mean, I chose that green soap at twenty-four cents a cake. The assistant was one of those supercilious young fellows with eyes on the top of his head, so he pulled a long dog's face. At that those impudent students started winking at each other and talking devils' language. I wanted to unwrap the soap and look at it before paying — for with all that foreign paper round it, how could I tell whether it was good or bad? But that supercilious young fellow not only refused, but was very unreasonable and passed some offensive remarks, at which those whipper-snappers laughed. It was the youngest of the lot who said that, looking straight at me, and the rest of them started laughing. So it must have been some bad word." He turned back to Hsueh-cheng. "Look for it in the section headed Bad Language!"

"Yes," answered Hsueh-cheng deep down in his throat, then respectfully withdrew.

"Yet they still shout 'New Culture! New Culture!' when the world's in such a state! Isn't this bad enough?" His eyes on the rafters, Ssu-min continued. "The students have no morals, society has no morals. Unless we find some panacea, China will really be finished. How pathetic she was. . . ."

"Who?" asked his wife casually, not really curious.

"A filial daughter. . . ." His eyes came round to her, and there was respect in his voice. "There were two beggars on the main street. One was a girl who looked eighteen or nineteen. Actually, it's most improper to beg at that age, but beg she did. She was with an old woman of about seventy, who had white hair and was blind. They were begging under the eaves of that clothes shop, and everybody said how filial she was. The old one was her grandmother. Whatever trifle the girl received, she gave it to her grandmother, choosing to go hungry herself. But do you think people would give alms even to such a filial daughter?"

He fixed her with his eye, as if to test her intelligence.

She made no answer, but fixed him with her eye, as if waiting for him to elucidate.

"Bah — no!" At last he supplied the answer himself. "I watched for a long time, and saw one person only give her a copper. Plenty of others gathered round, but only to jeer at them. There were two low types as well, one of whom had the impertinence to say:

"'Ah-fa! Don't be put off by the dirt on this piece of goods. If you buy two cakes of soap, and give her a good scrubbing, the result won't be bad at all!' Think, what a way to talk!"

She snorted and lowered her head. After quite a time, she asked rather casually: "Did *you* give her any money?"

"Did I? — No. I'd have felt ashamed to give just one or two coins. She wasn't an ordinary beggar, you know. . . ."

"Mm." Without waiting for him to finish she stood up slowly and walked to the kitchen. Dusk was gathering, and it was time for supper.

Ssu-min stood up too, and walked into the courtyard. It was lighter out than in. Hsueh-cheng was practicing Hexagram Boxing in a corner by the wall. This constituted his "home education," and he used the economical method of employing the hour between day and night for this purpose. Hsueh-cheng had been boxing now for about half a year. Ssu-min nodded very slightly, as if in approval, then began to pace the courtyard with his hands behind his back. Before long, the broad leaves of the evergreen which was the only potted plant they had were swallowed up in the darkness, and stars twinkled between white clouds which looked like torn cotton. Night had fallen. Ssu-min could not repress his growing indignation. He felt called on to do great deeds, to declare war on all bad students about and on this wicked society. By degrees he grew bolder and bolder, his steps became longer and longer, and the thud of his cloth soles grew louder and louder, waking the hen and her chicks in the coop so that they cheeped in alarm.

A light appeared in the hall — the signal that supper was ready — and the whole household gathered round the table in the middle. The lamp stood at the lower end of the table, while Ssu-min sat alone at the head. His plump, round face was like Hsueh-cheng's, with the addition of two sparse whiskers. Seen through the hot vapor from the vegetable soup, he looked like the God of Wealth you find in temples. On the left sat Mrs. Ssu-min and Chao-erh, on the right Hsueh-cheng and Hsiu-erh. Chopsticks pattered like rain against the bowls. Though no one said a word, their supper table was very animated.

Chao-erh upset her bowl, spilling soup over half the table. Ssu-min opened his narrow eyes as wide as he could. Only when he saw she was going to cry did he stop glaring at her and reach out with his chopsticks for a tender morsel of cabbage he had spotted. But the tender morsel had disappeared. He looked right and left, and discovered Hsueh-cheng on the point of stuffing it into his wide-open mouth. Disappointed, Ssu-min ate a mouthful of yellowish leaves instead.

"Hsueh-cheng!" He looked at his son. "Have you found that phrase or not?"

"Which phrase? — No, not yet!"

"Pah! Look at you, not a good student and with no sense either — all you can do is eat! You should learn from that filial daughter: although she's a beggar, she still treats her grandmother very respectfully, even if it means going hungry herself. But what do you impudent students know of such things? You'll grow up like those low types. . . ."

"I've thought of one possibility, but I don't know if it's right . . . . I think, perhaps, they may have said *o-du-fu-la* (Chinese transliteration of 'old fool' — *Translator*)."

"That's right! That's it exactly! That's exactly the sound it was: *o-du-fu-la*. What does that mean? You belong to the same group: you must know."

"Mean? — I'm not sure what it means."

"Nonsense. Don't try to deceive me. You're all a bad lot."

"'Even thunder won't strike folk at meat,'" burst out Mrs. Ssu-min suddenly. "Why do you keep losing your temper today? Even at supper you can't stop hitting the hen while pointing at the dog. What do boys that age understand?"

"What?" Ssu-min was on the point of answering back when he saw her sunken cheeks were quivering with anger, her color had changed, and a fearful glint had come into her eyes. He hastily changed his tune. "I'm not losing my temper. I'm just telling Hsueh-cheng to learn a little sense."

"How can he understand what's in *your* mind?" She looked angrier than ever. "If he had any sense, he'd long since have lit a lantern or a torch and gone out to fetch that filial daughter. You've already bought her one cake of soap: all you have to do is buy another. . . ."

"Nonsense! That's what that low type said."

"I'm not so sure. If you buy another cake and give her a good scrubbing, then worship her, the whole world will be at peace."

"How can you say such a thing? What connection is there? Because I remembered you'd no soap. . . . . ."

"There's a connection all right. You bought it specially for the filial daughter; so go and give her a good scrubbing. I don't deserve it. I don't want it. I don't want to share her glory."

"Really, how can you talk like that?" mumbled Ssu-min. "You women. . . ." His face was perspiring like Hsueh-cheng's after Hexagram Boxing, probably mostly because the food had been so hot.

"What about us women? We women are much better than you men. If you men aren't cursing eighteen or nineteen-year-old girl students, you're praising eighteen or nineteen-year-old girl beggars: such dirty minds you have! Scrubbing, indeed! — Disgusting!"

"Didn't you hear? That's what one of those low types said."

"Ssu-min!" A thundering voice was heard from the darkness outside.

"Tao-tung? I'm coming!"

Ssu-min knew this was Ho Tao-tung, famed for his power-ful voice, and he shouted back as joyfully as a criminal newly reprieved.

"Hsueh-cheng, hurry up and light the lamp and show Uncle Ho into the library!"

Hsueh-cheng lit a candle, and ushered Tao-tong into the west room. They were followed by Pu Wei-yuan.

"I'm sorry I didn't welcome you. Excuse me." With his mouth still full of rice, Ssu-min went in and bowed with clasped hands in greeting. "Won't you join us at our simple meal. . . ?"

"We've already eaten," Wei-yuan stepped forward and greeted him. "We've hurried here at this time of night because of the eighteenth essay and poem contest of the Moral Rear-mament Literary League. Isn't tomorrow the seventeenth?"

"What? Is it the sixteenth today?" asked Ssu-min in sur-prise.

"See how absent-minded you are!" boomed Tao-tung.

"So we'll have to send something in tonight to the news-paper office, to make sure they print it tomorrow."

"I've already drafted the title of the essay. See whether you think it will do or not." As he was speaking, Tao-tung pro-duced a slip of paper from his handkerchief and handed it to Ssu-min.

Ssu-min stepped up to the candle, unfolded the paper, and read it word by word: " We humbly suggest an essay in the name of the whole nation to beg the President to issue an order for the promotion of the Confucian classics and the worship of the mother of Mencius,* in order to revive this moribund world and preserve our national character.' Very good. Very good. Isn't it a little long, though?"

"That doesn't matter," answered Tao-tung loudly. "I've worked it out, and it won't cost more to advertise. But what about the title for the poem?"

"The title for the poem?" Ssu-min suddenly looked most respectful. "I've thought of one. How about The Filial Daugh-ter? It's a true story, and she deserves to be eulogized. On the main street today. . . ."

---

* A woman famous for her virtue. According to tradition, she moved house three times to avoid undesirable companions for her son.

"Oh, no, that won't do," put in Wei-yuan hastily, waving his hand to stop Ssu-min. "I saw her too. She isn't from these parts, and I couldn't understand her dialect, nor she mine. I don't know where she's from. Everyone says she's filial; but when I asked her if she could write poems, she shook her head. If she could, that would be fine."*

"But since loyalty and filial piety are so important, it doesn't matter too much if she can't write poems. . . ."

"That isn't true. Quite otherwise." Wei-yuan raised his hands and rushed towards Ssu-min, to shake and push him. "She'd only be interesting if she could write poems."

"Let's use this title." Ssu-min pushed him aside. "Add an explanation and print it. In the first place, it will serve to eulogize her; in the second, we can use this to criticize society. What is the world coming to anyway? I watched for some time, and didn't see anybody give her a cent — people are utterly heartless. . . !"

"Aiya, Ssu-min!" Wei-yuan rushed over again. "You're cursing baldheads to a monk. I didn't give her anything because I didn't happen to have any money on me."

"Don't be so sensitive, Wei-yuan." Ssu-min pushed him aside again. "Of course you're an exception. Let me finish. There was quite a crowd around them, showing no respect, just jeering. There were two low types as well, who were even more impertinent. One of them said: 'Ah-fa! If you buy two cakes of soap and give her a good scrubbing, the result won't be bad at all!' Just think. . . ."

"Ha, ha! Two cakes of soap!" Tao-tong suddenly bellowed with laughter, nearly splitting their ear-drums. "Buy soap! Ho, ho, ho!"

"Tao-tung! Tao-tung! Don't make such a noise!" Ssu-min gave a start, panic-stricken.

"A good scrubbing! Ho, ho, ho!"

"Tao-tung!" Ssu-min looked stern. "We're discussing serious matters. Why should you make such a noise, nearly deafening everyone? Listen to me: we'll use both these titles, and send them straight to the newspaper office so that they

---

* In old China, it was considered romantic for women to exchange ideas with men through the medium of poems. The fashionable courtesans could write poetry.

come out without fail tomorrow. I'll have to trouble you both to take them there."

"All right, all right. Of course," agreed Wei-yuan readily.

"Ha, ha! A good scrubbing! Ho, ho!"

"Tao-tung!" shouted Ssu-min furiously.

This shout made Tao-rung stop laughing. After they had drawn up the explanation, Wei-yuan copied it on the paper and left with Tao-tung for the newspaper office. Ssu-min carried the candle to see them out, then walked back to the door of the hall feeling rather apprehensive. After some hesitation, though, he finally crossed the threshold. As he went in, his eyes fell on the small, green, oblong package of soap in the middle of the central table, the gold characters with fine designs around them glittering in the lamplight.

Hsiu-erh and Chao-erh were playing on the floor at the lower end of the table, while Hsueh-cheng sat on the right side looking up something in his dictionary. Last of all, on the high-backed chair in the shadows far from the lamp, Ssu-min discovered his wife. Her impassive face showed neither joy nor anger, and she was staring at nothing.

"A good scrubbing indeed! Disgusting!"

Faintly, Ssu-min heard Hsiu-erh's voice behind him. He turned, but she was not moving. Only Chao-erh put both small hands to her face as if to shame somebody.

This was no place for him. He blew out the candle, and went into the yard to pace up and down. Because he forgot to be quiet, the hen and her chicks started cheeping again. At once he walked more lightly, moving further away. After a long time, the lamp in the hall was transferred to the bedroom. The moonlight on the ground was like seamless white gauze, and the moon — quite full — seemed a jade disc among the bright clouds.

He felt not a little depressed, as if he, like the filial daughter. were "utterly forlorn and alone." That night he did not sleep till very late.

By the next morning, however, the soap was being honored by being used. Getting up later than usual, he saw his wife leaning over the wash-stand rubbing her neck, with bubbles heaped up over both her ears like those emitted by great crabs The difference between these and the small white bubbles produced by honey locust pods was like that between heaven and earth. After this, an indefinable fragrance rather reminiscent of olives always emanated from Mrs. Ssu-min. Not for neatly half a year did this suddenly give place to another scent, which all who smelt it averred was like sandalwood.

March 22, 1924

The Misanthrope

I

My friendship with Wei Lien-shu, now that I come to think of it, was certainly a strange one. It began and ended with a funeral.

When I lived in S———, I often heard him mentioned as an odd fellow: after studying zoology, he had become a history teacher in a middle school. He treated others in cavalier fashion, yet liked to concern himself with their affairs; and while maintaining that the family system should be abolished, he sent his salary to his grandmother the same day that he drew it. He had many other strange ways, enough to set tongues wagging in the town. One autumn I stayed at Hanshihshan with some relatives also named Wei, who were distantly related to him. However, they understood him even less, looking on him as if he were a foreigner. "He's not like us!" they said.

This was not strange, for although China had had modern schools for some twenty years, there was not even a primary school in Hanshihshan. He was the only one who had left that mountain village to study; hence in the villagers' eyes he was an undoubted freak. They also envied him, though, saying he had made much money.

Towards the end of autumn, there was an epidemic of dysentery in the village, and in alarm I thought of returning to the town. I heard his grandmother had contracted the disease too, and because of her age her case was serious. Moreover there was not a single doctor in the village. Wei had no other relative but this grandmother, who with one maid-servant led a simple life. As he had lost both parents in his childhood, she had brought him up. She was said to have known much hardship earlier, but was now leading a comfortable life. Since he had neither wife nor children, however, his family was very quiet, and this presumably was one of the things about him considered freakish.

The village was more than thirty miles from the town by land, and more than twenty miles by water; so that it would take four days to fetch Wei back. In this out-of-the-way village such matters were considered momentous news, eagerly canvassed by all. The next day the old woman was reported to be in a critical state, and the messenger on his way. However, before dawn she died, her last words being:

"Why won't you let me see my grandson?"

Elders of the clan, close relatives, members of his grand-mother's family and others, crowded the room anticipating Wei's return, which would be in time for the funeral. The coffin and shroud had long been ready, but the immediate problem was how to cope with this grandson, for they expected he would insist on changing the funeral rites. After a conference, they decided on three terms which he must accept. First, he must wear deep mourning; secondly, he must kowtow to the coffin; and, thirdly, he must let Buddhist monks and Taoist priests say mass. In short, all must be done in the traditional manner.

This decision once reached, they decided to gather there in full force when Wei arrived home, to assist each other in this negotiation which could admit of no compromise. Licking their lips, the villagers eagerly awaited developments. Wei, as a "modern," "a follower of foreign creeds," had always proved unreasonable. A struggle would certainly ensue, which might even result in some novel spectacle.

He arrived home, I heard, in the afternoon, and only bowed to his grandmother's shrine as he entered. The elders proceeded at once according to plan. They summoned him to the hall, and after a lengthy preamble led up to the subject. Then, speaking in unison and at length, they gave him no chance to argue. At last, however, they dried up, and a deep silence fell in the hall. All eyes fastened fearfully on his lips. But without changing countenance, he answered simply:

"All right."

This was totally unexpected. A weight had been lifted from their minds, yet their hearts felt heavier than ever, for this was so "freakish" as to give rise to anxiety. The villagers looking for news were also disappointed, and said to each other, "Strange. He said, 'All right.' Let's go and watch." Wei's "all right" meant that all would be in accordance with tradition, in which case it was not worth watching; still, they wanted to look on, and after dusk the hall filled with light-hearted spectators.

I was one of those who went, having first sent along my gift of incense and candles. As I arrived he was already putting the shroud on the dead. He was a thin man with an angular face, hidden to a certain extent by his disheveled hair, dark eyebrows and moustache. His eyes gleamed darkly. He laid out the body very well, as deftly as an expert, so that the spectators were impressed. According to the local custom, at a married woman's funeral members of the dead woman's family found fault even when everything was well done; however, he remained silent, complying with their wishes with a face devoid of all expression. An old, grey-haired woman standing before me gave a sigh of envy and respect.

People kowtowed; then they wailed, all the women chanting as they wailed. When the body was put in the coffin, all kowtowed again, then wailed again, until the lid of the coffin was nailed down. Silence reigned for a moment, and then there was a stir of surprise and dissatisfaction. I too suddenly realized that from beginning to end Wei had not shed a single tear. He was simply sitting on the mourner's mat, his two eyes gleaming darkly.

In this atmosphere of surprise and dissatisfaction, the ceremony ended. The disgruntled mourners seemed about to leave, but Wei was still sitting on the mat, lost in thought. Suddenly, tears fell from his eyes, then he burst into a long wail like a wounded wolf howling in the wilderness in the dead of night, anger and sorrow mingled with his agony. This was not in accordance with tradition and, taken by surprise, we were at a loss. After a little hesitation, some went to try to persuade him to stop, and these were joined by more and more people until finally there was a crowd round him. But he sat there wailing, motionless as an iron statue.

Feeling awkward, the crowd dispersed. Wei continued to cry for about half an hour, then suddenly stopped, and without a word to the mourners went straight inside. Later it was reported by spies that he had gone into his grandmother's room, lain down on the bed and, to all appearances, fallen sound asleep.

Two days later, on the eve of my return to town, I heard the villagers discussing eagerly, as if they were possessed, how Wei intended to burn most of his dead grandmother's furniture and possessions, giving the rest to the maidservant who had served her during her life and attended her on her deathbed. Even the house was to be lent to the maid for an indefinite period. Wei's relatives argued themselves hoarse, but could not shake his resolution.

On my way back, largely out of curiosity perhaps, I passed his house and went in to express condolence. He received me wearing a hemless white mourning dress, and his expression was as cold as ever. I urged him not to take it so to heart, but apart from grunting noncommittally all he said was:

"Thanks for your concern."

II

*E*arly that winter we met for the third time. It was in a bookshop in S——, where we nodded simultaneously, showing at least that we were acquainted. But it was at the end of that year, after I lost my job, that we became friends. Thenceforward I paid Wei many visits. In the first place, of course, I had nothing to do; in the second place, despite his habitual reserve, he was said to sympathize with lame dogs. However, fortune being fickle, lame dogs do not remain lame forever, hence he had few steady friends. Report proved true, for as soon as I sent in my card, he received me. His sitting room consisted of two rooms thrown into one, quite bare of ornament, with nothing in it apart from table and chairs, but some bookcases. Although he was reputed to be terribly "modern," there were few modern books on the shelves. He knew that I had lost my job; but after the usual polite remarks had been exchanged, host and guest sat silent, with nothing to say to each other. I noticed he very quickly finished his cigarette, only dropping it to the ground when it nearly burned his fingers.

"Have a cigarette," he said suddenly, reaching for another.

I took one and, between puffs, spoke of teaching and books, still finding very little to say. I was just thinking of leaving when I heard shouts and footsteps outside the door, and four children rushed in. The eldest was about eight or nine, the smallest four or five. Their hands, faces and clothes were very dirty, and they were thoroughly unprepossessing; yet Wei's face lit up with pleasure, and getting up at once he walked to the other room, saying:

"Come, Ta-liang, Erh-liang, all of you! I have bought the mouth-organs you wanted yesterday."

The children rushed in after him, to return immediately with a mouth-organ apiece; but once outside they started fighting, and one of them cried.

"There's one each; they're exactly the same. Don't squabble!" he said as he followed them.

"Whose children are they?" I asked.

"The landlord's. They have no mother, only a grandmother."

"Your landlord is a widower?"

"Yes. His wife died three or four years ago, and he has not remarried. Otherwise, he would not rent his spare rooms to a bachelor like me." He said this with a cold smile.

I wanted very much to ask why he had remained single so long, but I did not know him well enough.

Once you knew him well, he was a good talker. He was full of ideas, many of them quite remarkable. What exasperated me were some of his guests. As a result, probably, of reading Yu Ta-fu's romantic stories,* they constantly referred to themselves as "the young unfortunate" or "the outcast"; and, sprawling on the big chairs like lazy and arrogant crabs, they would sigh, smoke and frown all at the same time.

Then there were the landlord's children, who always fought among themselves, knocked over bowls and plates, begged for cakes and kept up an ear-splitting din. Yet the sight of them invariably dispelled Wei's customary coldness, and they seemed to be the most precious thing in his life. Once the third child was said to have measles. He was so worried that his dark face took on an even darker hue. The attack proved a light one, however, and thereafter the children's grandmother made a joke of his anxiety.

Apparently sensing my impatience, he seized an opening one day to say, "Children are always good. They are all so innocent. . . . . "

"Not always," I answered casually.

"Always. Children have none of the faults of grown-ups. If they turn out badly later, as you contend, it is because they have been molded by their environment. Originally they are nor bad, but innocent. . . . I think China's only hope lies in this."

"I don't agree. Without the root of evil, how could they bear evil fruit in later life? Take a seed, for example. It is because it contains the embryo leaves, flowers and fruits, that later it grows into these things. There must be a cause. . . . ." Since my unemployment, just like those great officials who resigned from office and took up Buddhism, I had been reading the Buddhist sutras. I did not understand Buddhist philosophy though, and was just talking at random.

However, Wei was annoyed. He gave me a look, then said no more. I could nor tell whether he had no more to say, or whether he felt it not worth arguing with me. But he looked cold again, as he had nor done for a long time, and smoked two cigarettes one after the other in silence. By the time he reached for the third cigarette, I beat a retreat.

Our estrangement lasted three months. Then, owing in part to forgetfulness, in part to the fact that he fell out with those "innocent" children, he came to consider my slighting

---

§ A contemporary of Lu Hsun's, who wrote about repressed young men.

remarks on children as excusable. Or so I surmised. This happened in my house after drinking one day, when, with a rather melancholy look, he cocked his head and said:

"Come to think of it, it's really curious. On my way here I met a small child with a reed in his hand, which he pointed at me, shouting, 'Kill!' He was just a toddler. . . ."

"He must have been molded by his environment."

As soon as I had said this, I wanted to take it back. However, he did not seem to care, just went on drinking heavily, smoking furiously in between.

"I meant to ask you," I said, trying to change the subject. "You don't usually call on people, what made you come out today? I've known you for more than a year, yet this is the first time you've been here."

"I was just going to tell you: don't call on me for the time being. There are a father and son in my place who are perfect pests. They are scarcely human!"

"Father and son? Who are they?" I was surprised.

"My cousin and his son. Well, the son resembles the father."

"I suppose they came to town to see you and have a good time?"

"No. They came to talk me into adopting the boy."

"What, to adopt the boy?" I exclaimed in amazement. "But you are not married."

"They know I won't marry. But that's nothing to them. Actually they want to inherit that tumbledown house of mine in the village. I have no other property, you know; as soon as I get money I spend it. I've only that house. Their purpose in life is to drive out the old maidservant who is living in the place for the time being."

The cynicism of his remark took me aback. However I tried to soothe him, by saying:

"I don't think your relatives can be so bad. They are only rather old-fashioned. For instance, that year when you cried bitterly, they came forward eagerly to plead with you

"When I was a child and my father died, I cried bitterly because they wanted to take the house from me and make me put my mark on the document. They came forward eagerly then to plead with me. . . ." He looked up, as if searching the air for that bygone scene.

"The crux of the matter is — you have no children. Why don't you get married?" I had found a way to change the subject, and this was something I had been wanting to ask for a long time. It seemed an excellent opportunity.

He looked at me in surprise, then dropped his gaze to his knees, and started smoking. I received no answer to my question.

III

*Y*et he was not allowed to enjoy even this inane existence in peace. Gradually anonymous attacks appeared in the less reputable papers, and rumors concerning him were spread in the schools. This was not the simple gossip of the old days, but deliberately damaging. I knew this was the outcome of articles he had taken to writing for magazines, so I paid no attention. The citizens of S—— disliked nothing more than fearless argument, and anyone guilty of it indubitably became the object of secret attacks. This was the rule, and Wei knew it too. However, in spring, when I heard he had been asked by the school authorities to resign, I confessed it surprised me. Of course, this was only to be expected, and it surprised me simply because I had hoped my friend would escape. The citizens of S—— were not proving more vicious than usual.

I was occupied then with my own problems, negotiating to go to a school in Shanyang that autumn, so I had no time to call on him. Some three months passed before I was at leisure, and even then it had not occurred to me to visit him. One day, passing the main street, I happened to pause before a secondhand bookstall, where I was startled to see an early edition of the *Commentaries on Ssuma Chien's "Historical Records"*[*] from Wei's collection on display. He was no connois-

* By Ssuma Chen of the Tang dynasty (618-907).

seur, but he loved books, and I knew he prized this particular one. He must be very hard pressed to have sold it. It seemed scarcely possible he could have become so poor only two or three months after losing his job; yet he spent money as soon as he had it, and had never saved. I decided to call on him. On the same street I bought a bottle of liquor, two packages of peanuts and two smoked fish-heads.

His door was closed. I called out twice, but there was no reply. Thinking he was asleep, I called louder, at the same time hammering on the door.

"He's probably out." The children's grandmother, a fat woman with small eyes, thrust her grey head our from the opposite window, and spoke impatiently.

"Where has he gone?" I asked.

"Where? Who knows — where could he go? You can wait, he will be back soon."

I pushed open the door and went into his sitting room. It was greatly changed, looking desolate in its emptiness. There was little furniture left, while all that remained of his library were those foreign books which could not be sold. The middle of the room was still occupied by the table around which those woeful and gallant young men, unrecognized geniuses, and dirty, noisy children had formerly gathered. Now it all seemed very quiet, and there was a thin layer of dust on the table. I put the bottle and packages down, pulled over a chair, and sat down by the table facing the door.

Very soon, sure enough, the door opened, and someone stepped in as silently as a shadow. It was Wei. It might have been the twilight that made his face look dark; but his expression was unchanged.

"Ah, it's you? How long have you been here?" He seemed pleased.

"Not very long," I said. "Where have you been?"

"Nowhere in particular. Just taking a stroll."

He pulled up a chair too and sat by the table. We started drinking, and spoke of his losing his job. However, he did not care to talk much about it, considering it only to be expected. He had come across many similar cases. It was not strange at all, and nor worth discussing. As usual, he drank heavily, and discoursed on society and the study of history.

Something made me glance at the empty bookshelves, and, remembering the *Commentaries on Ssuma Chien's "Historical Records,"* I was conscious of a slight loneliness and sadness.

"Your sitting room has a deserted look Have you had fewer visitors recently?"

"None at all. They don't find it much fun when I'm not in a good mood. A bad mood certainly makes people uncomfortable Just as no one goes to the park in winter. . . ."

He took two sips of liquor in succession, then fell silent. Suddenly, looking up, he asked, "I suppose you have had no luck either in finding work?"

Although I knew he was only venting his feelings as a result of drinking, I felt indignant at the way people treated him. Just as I was about to say something, he pricked up his ears, then, scooping up some peanuts, went our. Outside, I could hear the laughter and shouts of the children.

But as soon as he went out, the children became quiet. It sounded as if they had left. He went after them, and said something, but I could hear no reply. Then, as silent as a shadow, he came back and put the handful of peanuts back in the package.

"They don't even want to eat anything I give them," he said sarcastically, in a low voice.

"Old Wei," I said, forcing a smile, although I was sick at heart, "I think you are tormenting yourself unnecessarily. Why think so poorly of your fellow men?"

He only smiled cynically.

"I haven't finished yet. I suppose you consider people like me, who come here occasionally, do so in order to kill time or amuse themselves at your expense?"

"No, I don't. Well, sometimes I do. Perhaps they come to find something to talk about."

"Then you are wrong. People are not like that. You are really wrapping yourself up in a cocoon. You should take a more cheerful view." I sighed.

"Maybe. But tell me, where does the thread for the cocoon come from? Of course, there are plenty of people like that; take my grandmother, for example. Although I have none of her blood in my veins, I may inherit her fate. But that doesn't matter, I have already bewailed my fate together with hers. . . ."

Then I remembered what had happened at his grandmother's funeral. I could almost see it before my eyes.

"I still don't understand why you cried so bitterly," I said bluntly.

"You mean at my grandmother's funeral? No, you wouldn't." He lit the lamp. "I suppose it was because of that that we became friends," he said quietly. "You know, this grandmother was my grandfather's second wife. My father's own mother died when he was three." Growing thoughtful, he drank silently, and finished a smoked fish-head.

"I didn't know it to begin with. Only, from my childhood I was puzzled. At that time my father was still alive, and our family was well off. During the lunar New Year we would hang up the ancestral images and hold a grand sacrifice. It was one of my rare pleasures to look at those splendidly dressed images. At that time a maidservant would always carry me to an image, and point at it, saying: 'This is your own grandmother. Bow to her so that she will protect you and make you grow up strong and healthy.' I could not understand how I came to have another grandmother, in addition to the one beside me. But I liked this grandmother who was 'my own.' She was not as old as the granny at home. Young and beautiful, wearing a red costume with golden embroidery and a headdress decked with pearls, she resembled my mother. When I looked at her, her eyes seemed to gaze down on me, and a faint smile appeared on her lips. I knew she was very fond of me too.

"But I liked the granny at home too, who sat all day under the window slowly plying her needle. However, no matter how merrily I laughed and played in front of her, or called to her, I could not make her laugh; and that made me feel she was cold, unlike other children's grandmothers. Still, I liked her. Later on, though, I gradually cooled towards her, nor because I grew older and learned she was not my own grandmother, but rather because I was exasperated by the way she kept on sewing mechanically, day in, day our. She was unchanged, however. She sewed, looked after me, loved and protected me as before; and though she seldom smiled, she never scolded me. It was the same after my father died. Later on, we lived almost entirely on her sewing, so it was still the same, until I went to school. . . ."

The light flickered as the paraffin gave out, and he stood up to refill the lamp from a small tin kettle under the bookcase.

"The price of paraffin has gone up twice this month," he said slowly, after turning up the wick. "Life becomes harder every day. She remained the same until I graduated from school and had a job, when our life became more secure. She didn't change, I suppose, until she was sick, couldn't carry on, and had to take to her bed. . . .

"Since her later days, I think, were not too unhappy on the whole, and she lived to a great age, I need not have mourned. Besides, weren't there a lot of others there eager to wail? Even those who had tried their hardest to rob her, wailed, or appeared bowed down with grief." He laughed. "However, at that moment her whole life rose to my mind — the life of one who created loneliness for herself and tasted its bitterness. I felt there were many people like that. I wanted to weep for them; but perhaps it was largely because I was too sentimental. . . .

"Your present advice to me is what I felt with regard to her. But actually my ideas at that time were wrong. As for myself, since I grew up my feelings for her cooled. . . ."

He paused, with a cigarette between his fingers; and bending his head lost himself in thought. The lamplight flickered.

"Well, it is hard to live so that no one will mourn for your death," he said, as if to himself. After a pause he looked up at me, and said, "I suppose you can't help? I shall have to find something to do very soon."

"Have you no other friends you could ask?" I was in no position to help myself then, let alone others.

"I have a few, but they are all in the same boat. . . ."

When I left him, the full moon was high in the sky and the night was very still.

IV

*T*he teaching profession in Shanyang was no bed of roses. I taught for two months without receiving a cent of salary, until I had to cut down on cigarettes. But the school staff, even those earning only fifteen or sixteen dollars a month, were easily contented. They all had iron constitutions steeled by hardship, and, although lean and haggard, they worked from morning till night; while if interrupted at work by their superiors, they stood up respectfully. Thus they all practiced plain living and high thinking. This reminded me, somehow, of Wei's parting words. He was then even more hard up, and often looked embarrassed, having apparently lost his former cynicism. When he heard that I was leaving, he came late at night to see me off, and, after hesitating for some rime, he stuttered:

"Would there be anything for me there? Even copying work, at twenty to thirty dollars a month, would do. I . . . ."

I was surprised. I had not thought he would consider anything so low, and did nor know how to answer.

"I . . . I have to live a little longer. . . ."

"I'll look out when I get there. I'll do my best."

This was what I had promised at the rime, and the words often rang in my ears later, as if Wei were still before me, stuttering: "I have to live a little longer." I tried to interest various people in his case, but to no avail. Since there were few vacancies, and many unemployed, these people always ended by apologizing for being unable to help, and I would write him an apologetic letter. By the end of the term, things had gone from bad to worse. The magazine Reason, edited by some of the local gentry, began to attack me. Naturally no names were mentioned, but it cleverly insinuated that I was stirring up trouble in the school, even my recommendation of Wei being interpreted as a maneuver to gather a clique about me.

So I had to keep quiet. Apart from attending class, I lay low in my room, sometimes when cigarette smoke escaped from my window, I even feared they might consider I was stirring up trouble. For Wei, naturally, I could do nothing. This state of affairs prevailed till midwinter.

It had been snowing all day, and the snow had not stopped by evening. Outside was so still, you could almost hear the sound of stillness. I closed my eyes and sat there in the dim lamplight doing nothing, imagining the snow-flakes falling, creating boundless drifts of snow. It would be nearly New Year at home too, and everybody would be busy. I saw myself a child again, making a snow man with a group of children on the level ground in the back yard. The eyes of the snow man, made of jet-black fragments of coal, suddenly turned into Wei's eyes.

"I have to live a little longer." The same voice again.

"What for?" I asked inadvertently, aware immediately of the ineptitude of my remark.

This reply woke me up. I sat up, lit a cigarette and opened the window, only to find the snow' falling even faster. I heard a knock at the door, and a moment later it opened to admit the servant, whose step I knew. He handed me a big envelope, more than six inches in length. The address was scrawled, but I saw Wei's name on it.

This was the first letter he had written me since I left S———. Knowing he was a bad correspondent, I had not wondered at his silence, only sometimes I had felt he should have given me some news of himself. The receipt of this letter was quite a surprise. I tore it open. The letter had been hastily scrawled, and said:

"...Shen-fei,

"How should I address you? I am leaving a blank for you to fill in as you please. It will be all the same to me.

"I have received three letters from you altogether. I did nor reply for one simple reason: I had no money even to buy stamps.

"Perhaps you would like to know what has happened to me. To put it simply: I have failed. I thought I had failed before, but I was wrong then; now, however, I am really a failure. Formerly there was someone who wanted me to live a little longer, and I wished it too, but found it difficult. Now, there is no need, yet I must go on living. . . .

"Shall I live on?

"The one who wanted me to live a little longer could not live himself. He was trapped and killed by the enemy. Who killed him? No one knows.

"Changes take place so swiftly! During the last half year I have virtually been a beggar; it's true, I could be considered a beggar. However, I had my purpose: I was willing to beg for the cause, to go cold and hungry for it, to be lonely for it, to suffer hardship for it. But I did not want to destroy myself. So you see, the fact that one person wanted me to live on, proved extremely potent. Now there is no one, nor one. At the same time I feel I do nor deserve to live, nor, in my opinion, do some other people. Yet, I am conscious of wanting to live on to spite those who wish me dead; for at least there is no one left who wants me to live decently, and so no one will be hurt. I don't want to hurt such people. But now there is no one, not one. What a joy! Wonderful! I am now doing what I formerly detested and opposed. I am now giving up all I formerly believed in and upheld. I have really failed — but I have won.

"Do you think I am mad? Do you think I have become a hero or a great man? No, it is not that. It is very simple; I have become adviser to General Tu, hence I have eighty dollars salary a month.

". . . Shen-fei,

"What will you think of me? You decide; it is all the same to me.

"Perhaps you still remember my former sitting room, the one in which we had our first and last talks. I am still using it. There are new guests, new bribes, new flattery, new seeking for promotion, new kowtows and bows, new mahjong and drinking games, new haughtiness and disgust, new sleeplessness and vomiting of blood. . . .

"You said in your last letter that your teaching was nor going well. Would you like to be an adviser? Say the word, and I will arrange it for you. Actually, work in the gatehouse would be the same. There would be the same guests, bribes and flattery. . . .

"It is snowing heavily here. How is it where you are? It is now midnight, and having just vomited some blood has sobered me. I recall that you have actually written three times in succession to me since autumn — amazing! I give you this news of myself, hoping you will not be shocked.

"I probably shall nor write again; you know my ways of old. When will you be back? If you come soon, we may meet again. Still, I suppose we have taken different roads; you had better forget me. I thank you from the bottom of my heart for trying to find work for me. Now please forget me; I am doing 'well.'

"*Wei Lien-shu*
"December 14th."

Though this letter did not "shock" me, when, after a hasty perusal, I read it carefully again, I felt both uneasy and relieved. At least his livelihood was secure, and I need not worry about that anymore. At any rate, I could do nothing here. I thought of writing to him, but felt there was nothing to say.

In fact, I gradually forgot him. His face no longer sprang so often to my mind's eye. However, less than ten days after hearing from him, the office of the S—— *Weekly* started sending me its paper. I did not read such papers as a rule, but since it was sent to me I glanced at some of the contents. This reminded me of Wei, for the paper frequently carried poems and essays about him, such as "Calling on scholar Wei at night during a snowstorm," "A poetic gathering at the scholarly abode of Adviser Wei," and so forth. Once, indeed, under the heading "Table Talk," they retailed with gusto certain stories which had previously been considered material for ridicule, but which had now become "Tales of an Eccentric Genius." Only an exceptional man, it was implied, could have done such unusual things.

Although this recalled him to me, my impression of him grew fainter. Yet all the time he seemed to gain a closer hold on me, which often filled me with an inexplicable sense of uneasiness and a shadowy apprehension. However, by autumn the newspaper stopped coming, while the Shanyang magazine began to publish the first installment of a long essay called "The element of truth in rumors," which asserted that rumors about certain gentlemen had reached the ears of the mighty. My name was among those attacked. I had to be very careful then. I had to take care that my cigarette smoke did not get in other people's way. All these precautions took so much time I could attend to nothing else, and naturally had no leisure to think of Wei. I actually forgot him.

I could nor hold my job till summer. By the end of May I had to leave Shanyang.

V

I wandered between Shanyang, Licheng and Taiku for more than half a year, but could find no work, so I decided to go back to S———. I arrived one afternoon in early spring. It was a cloudy day with everything wrapped in mist. Since there were vacant rooms in my old hostel, I stayed there. On the road I started to think of Wei, and after my arrival I made up my mind to call on him after dinner. Taking two packages of the well-known Wenhsi cakes, I threaded my way through several damp streets, stepping cautiously past many sleeping dogs, until I reached his door. It seemed very bright inside. I thought even his rooms were better lit since he had become an adviser, and smiled to myself. However, when I looked up, I saw a strip of white paper* stuck on the door. It occurred to me, as I stepped inside, that the children's grandmother might be dead; but I went straight in.

---

* White is the mourning color in China. White paper on the door indicated that there had been a death in the house.

In the dimly lit courtyard there was a coffin, by which some soldier or orderly in uniform was standing, talking to the children's grandmother. A few workers in short coats were loitering there too. My heart began to beat faster. Just then she turned to look at me.

"Ah, you're back?" she exclaimed. "Why didn't you come earlier?"

"Who . . . who has passed away?" Actually by now I knew, yet I asked all the same.

"Adviser Wei died the day before yesterday."

I looked around. The sitting room was dimly lit, probably by one lamp only; the front room, however, was decked with white funeral curtains, and the woman's grandchildren had gathered outside that room.

"His body is there," she said, coming forward and pointing to the front room. "After Mr. Wei was promoted, I let him my front room too; that is where he is now."

There was no writing on the funeral curtain. In front stood a long table, then a square table, spread with some dozen dishes. As I went in, two men in long white gowns suddenly appeared to bar the way, their eyes, like those of a dead fish, fixed in surprise and mistrust on my face. I hastily explained my relationship with Wei, and the landlady came up to confirm my statement. Then their hands and eyes dropped, and they allowed me to go forward to bow to the dead.

As I bowed, a wail sounded beside me from the floor. Looking down I saw a child of about ten, also dressed in white, kneeling on a mat. His hair had been cut short, and had some hemp attached to it.

Later I found out one of these men was Wei's cousin, his nearest in kin, while the other was a distant nephew. I asked to be allowed to see Wei, but they tried their best to dissuade me, saying I was too "polite." Finally they gave in, and lifted the curtain.

This time I saw Wei in death. But, strangely enough, though he was wearing a crumpled shirt, stained in front with blood, and his face was very lean, his expression was unchanged. He was sleeping so placidly, with closed mouth and eyes, that I was tempted to put my finger before his nostrils to see if he were still breathing.

Everything was deathly still, both the living and the dead. As I withdrew, his cousin accosted me to state that Wei's untimely death, just when he was in the prime of life and had a great future before him, was not only a calamity for his humble family but a cause of sorrow for his friends. He seemed to be apologizing for Wei for dying. Such eloquence is rare among villagers. However, after that he fell silent again and everything was deathly still, both the living and the dead.

Feeling cheerless, but by no means sad, I withdrew to the courtyard to chat with the old woman. She told me the funeral would soon take place. They were waiting for the shroud, she said, and when the coffin was nailed down, people born under certain stars should nor be near. She rattled on, her words pouring out like a flood. She spoke of Wei's illness, incidents during his life, and even voiced certain criticisms.

"You know, after Mr. Wei came into luck, he was a different man. He held his head high and looked very haughty. He stopped treating people in his old formal way. Did you know, he used to act like an idiot, and call me madam? Later on," she chuckled, "he called me 'old bitch'; it was too funny for words. When people sent him rare herbs like atractylis, instead of eating them himself, he would throw them into the courtyard, just here, and call out, 'You take this, old bitch!' After he came into luck, he had scores of visitors; so I vacated my front room for him, and moved into a side one. As we have always said jokingly, he became a different man after his good luck. If you had come one month earlier, you could have seen all the fun here: drinking games practically every day, talking, laughing, singing, poetry writing and mah-jong games. . . .

"He used to be more afraid of children than they are of their own father, practically groveling to them. But recently that changed too, and he was a good one for jokes. My grandchildren liked to play with him, and would go to his rooms whenever they could. He would think up all sorts of practical jokes. For instance, when they wanted him to buy things for them, he would make them bark like dogs or make a thumping kowtow. Ah, that was fun. Two months ago, my second grandchild asked Mr. Wei to buy him a pair of shoes, and had to make three thumping kowtows. He's still wearing them; they aren't worn out yet."

When one of the men in white came out, she stopped talking. I asked about Wei's illness, but there was little she could tell me. She knew only that he had been losing weight for a long time, but they had thought nothing of it because he always looked so cheerful. About a month before, they heard he had been coughing blood, but it seemed he had not seen a doctor. Then he had to stay in bed, and three days before he died he seemed to have lost the power of speech. His cousin had come all the way from the village to ask him if he had any savings, but he said not a word. His cousin thought he was shamming, but some people say those dying of consumption do lose the power of speech. . . .

"But Mr. Wei was a queer man," she suddenly whispered. "He never saved money, always spent it like water. His cousin still suspects we got something out of him. Heaven knows, we got nothing. He just spent it in his haphazard way. Buying something today, selling it tomorrow, or breaking it up — God knows what happened. When he died there was nothing left, all spent! Otherwise it would not be so dismal today. . . .

"He just fooled about, not wanting to do the proper thing. At his age, he should have got married; I had thought of that, and spoken to him. It would have been easy for him then. And if no suitable family could be found, at least he could have bought a few concubines to go on with. People should keep up appearances. But he would laugh whenever I brought it up. 'Old bitch, you are always worrying about such things for other people,' he would say. He was never serious, you see; he wouldn't listen to good advice. If he had listened to me, he wouldn't be wandering lonely in the nether world now; at least his dear ones would be wailing. . . . ."

A shop assistant arrived, bringing some clothes with him. The three relatives of the dead picked out the underwear, then disappeared behind the curtain. Soon, the curtain was lifted; the new underwear had been put on the corpse, and they proceeded to put on his outer garments. I was surprised to see them dress him in a pair of khaki military trousers with broad red stripes, and a tunic with glittering epaulettes. I did not know what rank these indicated, or how he had acquired it. The body was placed in the coffin. Wei lay there awkwardly, a pair of brown leather shoes beside his feet, a paper sword at his waist, and beside his lean and ashen face a military cap with a gilt band.

The three relatives wailed beside the coffin, then stopped and wiped away their tears. The boy with hemp attached to his hair withdrew, as did the old woman's third grandchild — no doubt they were born under the wrong stars.

As the laborers lifted the coffin lid, I stepped forward to see Wei for the last time.

In his awkward costume he lay placidly, with closed mouth and eyes. There seemed to be an ironical smile on his lips, mocking the ridiculous corpse.

When they began to hammer in the nails, the wailing started afresh. I could not stand it very long, so I withdrew to the courtyard; then, somehow, I was out of the gate. The damp road glistened, and I looked up at the sky where the cloud banks had scattered and a full moon hung, shedding a cold light.

I walked with quickened steps, as if eager to break through some heavy barrier, but finding it impossible. Something struggled in my ears, and, after a long, long time, burst out. It was like a long howl, the howl of a wounded wolf crying in the wilderness in the depth of night, anger and sorrow mingled in its agony.

Then my heart felt lighter, and I paced calmly on under the moon along the damp cobbled road.

October 17, 1925

Regret for the Past

Chuan-sheng's Notes

I want, if I can, to describe my remorse and grief for Tzuchun's sake as well as for my own. This shabby room, rucked away in a forgotten corner of the hostel, is so quiet and empty. Time really flies. A whole year has passed since I fell in love with Tzu-chun, and, thanks to her, escaped from this dead quiet and emptiness. On my return, as ill luck would have it, this was the only room vacant. The broken window with the half dead locust tree and old wisteria outside and square table inside are the same as before. The same too are the moldering wall and wooden bed beside it. At night I lie in bed alone just as I did before I started living with Tzu-chun. The past year has been blotted out as if it had never been — as if I had never moved out of this shabby room so hopefully to set up a small home in Chichao Street.

Nor is that all. A year ago this silence and emptiness were different — there was often an expectancy about them. I was expecting Tzu-chun's arrival. As I waited long and impatiently, the tapping of high heels on the brick pavement would galvanize me into life. Then I would see her pale round face dimpling in a smile, her thin white arms, striped cotton blouse and black skirt. She would bring in a new leaf from the half withered locust tree outside the window for me to look at, or clusters of the mauve flowers that hung from the old wisteria tree, the trunk of which looked as if made of iron.

Now there is only the old silence and emptiness. Tzu-chun will not come again — never, never again.

*I*n Tzu-chun's absence, I saw nothing in this shabby room. Out of sheer boredom I would pick up a book — science or literature, it was all the same to me — and read on and on, till I realized I had turned a dozen pages without taking in a word I had read. Only my ears were so sensitive, I seemed able to hear all the footsteps outside the gate, those of Tzu-chun among the rest. Her steps often sounded as if they were drawing nearer and nearer — only to grow fainter again, until they were lost in the tramping of other feet. I hated the servant's son who wore cloth-soled shoes which sounded quite different from Tzu-chun's. I hated the pansy next door who used face cream, who often wore new leather shoes, and whose steps sounded all too like Tzu-chun's.

Had her rickshaw been upset? Had she been knocked over by a tram. . . ?

I would be on the point of putting on my hat to go and see her, then remember her uncle had cursed me to my face.

Suddenly I would hear her coming nearer step by step, and by the time I was out to meet her she would already have passed the wisteria trellis, her face dimpling in a smile. Probably she wasn't badly treated after all in her uncle's home. I would calm down and, after we had gazed at each other in silence for a moment, the shabby room would be filled with the sound of my voice as I held forth on the tyranny of the home, the need to break with tradition, the equality of men and women, Ibsen, Tagore and Shelley. . . . She would nod her head, smiling, her eyes filled with a childlike look of wonder. On the wall was nailed a copperplate bust of Shelley, cut out from a magazine. It was one of the best likenesses of him, but when I pointed it out to her she only gave it a hasty glance, then hung her head as if embarrassed. In matters like this, Tzuchun probably hadn't yet freed herself entirely from old ideas. It occurred to me later it might be better to substitute a picture of Shelley being drowned at sea, or a portrait of Ibsen. But I never got round to it. Now even this picture has vanished.

"*I*'m my own mistress. None of them has any right to interfere with me."

She came out with this statement clearly, firmly and gravely, after a thoughtful silence — we had been talking about her uncle who was here and her father who was at home. We had then known each other for half a year. I had already told her all my views, all that had happened to me, and what my failings were. I had hidden very little, and she understood me completely. These few words of hers stirred me to the bottom of my heart, and rang in my ears for many days after. I was unspeakably happy to know that Chinese women were not as hopeless as the pessimists made out, and that we should see them in the not too distant future in all their glory.

Each time I saw her out, I always kept several paces behind her. The old man's face with its whiskers like fishy tentacles was always pressed hard against the dirty windowpane, so that even the tip of his nose was flattened. When we reached the outer courtyard, against the bright glass window there was that little fellow's face, plastered with face cream. But walking out proudly, without looking right or left, Tzu-chun did not see them. And I walked proudly back.

"I'm my own mistress. None of them has any right to interfere with me." Her mind was completely made up on this point. She was by far the more thoroughgoing and resolute of the two of us. What did she care about the half pot of face cream or the flattened nose tip?

I can't remember clearly now how I expressed my true, passionate love for her. Nor only now — even just after it happened, my impression was very blurred. When I thought back at night, I could only remember snatches of what I had said; while during the month or two after we started living together, even these fragments vanished like a dream without a trace. I only remember how for about a fortnight before-hand I had reflected very carefully what attitude to adopt, prepared what to say, and decided what to do if I were refused. But when the time came it was all no use. In my nervousness,

I unconsciously did what I had seen in the movies. The memory of this makes me thoroughly ashamed, yet this is the one thing I remember clearly. Even today it is like a solitary lamp in a dark room, lighting me up. I clasped her hand with tears in my eyes, and went down on one knee. . . .

I did not even see clearly how Tzu-chun reacted at the time. All I know was that she accepted me. However, I seem to remember her face first turned pale then gradually flushed red — redder than I have ever seen it before or since. Sadness and joy flashed from her childlike eyes, mingled with apprehension, although she struggled to avoid my gaze, looking, in her confusion, as if she would like to fly out of the window. Then I knew she consented, although I didn't know what she said, or whether she said anything at all.

She, however, remembered everything. She could recite all that I said non-stop, as if she had learned it by heart. She described all my actions in detail, to the life, like a film unfolding itself before my eyes, which included, naturally, that shallow scene from the movies which I was anxious to forget. At night, when all was still, it was our time for review. I was often questioned and examined, or ordered to retell all that had been said on that occasion; but she often had to fill up gaps and correct my mistakes, as if I were a Grade D student.

Gradually these reviews became few and far between. But whenever I saw her gazing raptly into space with a tender look and dimpling, I knew she was going over that old lesson again, and would be afraid she was seeing my ridiculous act from the movies. I knew, though, that she did see it, and that she insisted on seeing it.

But she didn't find it ridiculous. Though I thought it laughable, even contemptible, she didn't find it so at all. And I knew this was because she loved me so truly and passionately.

*L*ate spring last year was our happiest and busiest time. I was calmer then, although one part of my mind became as active as my body. This was when we started going out together. We went several times to the park, but more often to look for lodgings. On the road I was conscious of searching looks, sarcastic smiles or lewd and contemptuous glances which tended, if I was not careful, to make me shiver. Every instant I had to summon all my pride and defiance to my support. She was quite fearless, however, and completely impervious to all this. She proceeded slowly, as calmly as if there were nobody in sight.

To find lodgings was no easy matter. In most cases we were refused on some pretext, while some places we turned down as unsuitable. In the beginning we were very particular — and yet not too particular either, because most of these lodgings were not places where we could live. Later on, all we asked was to be tolerated. We looked at over twenty places before we found one we could make do — two rooms facing north in a small house on Chichao Street. The owner of the house was a petty official, but an intelligent man, who only occupied the central and side rooms. His household consisted simply of a wife, a baby a few months old, and a maid from the country. As long as the child didn't cry, it would be very quiet.

Our furniture, simple as it was, had already taken the greater part of the money I had raised: and Tzu-chun had sold her only gold ring and earrings too. I tried to stop her, but she insisted, so I didn't press the point. I knew, if she hadn't a share in our home, she would feel uncomfortable.

She had already quarreled with her uncle — in fact he was so angry that he had disowned her. I had also broken with several friends who thought they were giving me good advice but were actually either afraid for me, or jealous. Still, this meant we were very quiet. Although it was nearly dark when I left the office, and the rickshaw man went so slowly, the time finally came when we were together again. First we would look at each other in silence, then relax and talk intimately, and finally fall silent again, bowing our heads without thinking of anything in particular. Gradually I was able to read her soberly like a book, body and soul. In a mere three weeks I learned much more about her, and broke down barriers which I had not known existed, but then discovered had been real barriers.

As the days passed, Tzu-chun became more lively. However, she didn't like flowers. I bought two pots of flowers at the fair, but after four days without water they died neglected in a corner. I hadn't the time to see to everything. She had a liking for animals, though, which she may have picked up from the official's wife; and in less than a month our household was greatly increased. Four chicks of ours started picking their way across the courtyard with the landlady's dozen. But the two mistresses could tell them apart, each able to spot her own. Then there was a spotted dog, bought at the fair. I believe he had a name to begin with, but Tzu-chun gave him a new one — Ahsui. I called him Ahsui too, though I didn't like the name.

It is true that love must be constantly renewed, must grow and create. When I spoke of this to Tzu-chun, she nodded understandingly.

Ah, what peaceful, happy evenings those were!

*T*ranquility and happiness must be consolidated, so that they may last forever. When we were in the hostel, we had occasional differences of opinion or misunderstandings; but after we moved into Chichao Street even these slight differences vanished. We just sat opposite each other in the lamplight, reminiscing, savoring again the joy of the new harmony which had followed our disputes.

Tzu-chun grew plumper and her cheeks became rosier; the only pity was she was too busy. Her house-keeping left her no time even to chat, much less to read or go out for walks. We often said we would have to get a maid.

Another thing that upset me when I got back in the evening, was to see her try to hide a look of unhappiness or — and this depressed me even more — force a smile on to her face. Luckily I discovered this was due to her secret feud with the petty official's wife, and the bone of contention was the chicks. But why wouldn't she tell me? People ought to have a home of their own. This was no place to live in.

I had my routine too. Six days of the week I went from home to the office and from the office home. In the office I sat at my desk endlessly copying official documents and letters. At home I kept her company or helped her light the stove, cook rice or steam bread. This was when I learned to cook.

Still, I ate much better than when I was in the hostel. Although cooking was not Tzu-chun's strongest point, she threw herself into it heart and soul. Her ceaseless anxieties on this score made me anxious too, and in this way we shared the sweet and the bitter together. She kept at it so hard all day, perspiration made her short hair stick to her head, and her hands grew rough.

And then she had to feed Ahsui and the chicks . . . nobody else could do this.

I told her, I would rather not eat than see her work herself to the bone like this. She just gazed at me without a word, rather wistfully; and I couldn't very well say anymore. Still she went on working as hard as ever.

*F*inally the blow I had been expecting fell. The evening before the Double Tenth Festival, I was sitting idle while she washed the dishes, when we heard a knock on the door. When I went to open it, I found the messenger from our office who handed me a mimeographed slip of paper. I guessed what it was, and when I took it to the lamp, sure enough, it read:

By order of the commissioner, Shih Chuan-sheng is discharged.

The Secretariat
October 9th.

I had foreseen this while we were still in the hostel. That Face Cream was one of the gambling friends of the commissioner's son. He was bound to spread rumors and try to make trouble. I was only surprised this hadn't happened sooner. In fact this was really no blow, because I had already decided I could work as a clerk somewhere else or teach, or, although it was a little more difficult, do some translation work. I knew the editor of *Freedom's Friend,* and had corresponded with him a couple of months previously. All the same, my heart was thumping. What distressed me most was that even Tzu-chun, fearless as she was, had turned pale. Recently she seemed to have grown weaker.

"What does it matter?" she said. "We'll make a new start, won't we? We'll

She didn't finish, and her voice sounded flat. The lamplight seemed unusually dim. Men are really laughable creatures, so easily upset by trifles. First we gazed at each other in silence, then started discussing what to do. Finally we decided to live as economically as possible on the money we had, to advertise in the paper for a post as clerk or teacher, and to write at the same time to the editor of *Freedom's Friend*, explaining my present situation and asking him to accept a translation to help me out of this difficulty.

"As good said as done! Let's make a fresh start."

I went straight to the table and pushed aside the bottle of vegetable oil and dish of vinegar, while Tzu-chun brought over the dim lamp. First I drew up the advertisement; then I made a selection of books to translate. I hadn't looked at my books since we moved house, and each volume was thick with dust. Finally I wrote the letter.

I hesitated for a long time over the wording of the letter, and when I stopped writing to think, and glanced at her in the dusky lamplight, she was looking very wistful again. I had never imagined a trifle like this could cause such a striking change in someone so firm and fearless as Tzu-chun. She really had grown much weaker lately — it wasn't something that had just started that evening. This made me feel more put out. I had a sudden vision of a peaceful life — the quiet of my shabby room in the hostel flashed before my eyes, and I was just going to take a good look at it when I found myself back in the dusky lamplight again.

After a long time the letter was finished. It was very lengthy, and I was so tired after writing it, I realized I must have grown weaker myself lately too. We decided to send in the advertisement and post the letter the next day. Then with one accord we straightened up, silently, as if conscious of each other's fortitude and strength, and able to see new hope growing from this fresh beginning.

*A*ctually, this blow from outside infused a new spirit into us. In the office I had lived like a wild bird in a cage, given just enough canary-seed by its captor to keep alive, but not to grow fat. As time passed it would lose the use of its wings, so that if ever it were let out of the cage it could no longer fly. Now, at any rate, I had got out of the cage, and must soar anew in the wide sky before it was too late, while I could still flap my wings.

*O*f course we could not expect results from a small advertisement right away. However, translating is not so simple either. You read something and think you understand it, but when you come to translate it difficulties crop up everywhere, and it's very slow going. Still, I determined to do my best. In less than a fortnight, the edge of a fairly new dictionary was black with my fingerprints, which showed how seriously I took my work. The editor of *Freedom's Friend* had said that his magazine would never ignore a good manuscript.

Unfortunately, there was no room where I could be undisturbed, and Tzu-chun was not as quiet or considerate as she had been. Our room was so cluttered up with dishes and bowls and filled with smoke, it was impossible to work steadily there. Of course I had only myself to blame for this — it was my fault for not being able to afford a study. On top of this there was Ahsui and the chicks. The chicks had grown into hens now, and were more of a bone of contention than ever between the two families.

Then there was the never-ending business of eating every day. All Tzu-chun's efforts seemed to be devoted to our meals. One ate to earn, and earned to eat; while Ahsui and the hens had to be fed too. Apparently she had forgotten all she had ever learned, and did not realize that she was interrupting my train of thought when she called me to meals. And although as I sat down I sometimes showed a little displeasure, she paid no attention at all, but just went on munching away quite unconcerned.

It took her five weeks to learn that my work could not be restricted by regular eating hours. When she did realize it she was probably annoyed, but she said nothing. After that my work did go forward faster, and soon I had translated 50,000 words. I had only to polish the manuscript, and it could be sent in with two already completed shorter pieces to *Freedom's Friend.* Those meals were still a headache though. It didn't matter if the dishes were cold, but there weren't enough of them. My appetite was much smaller than before, now that I was sitting at home all day using my brain, but even so there wasn't always even enough rice. It had been given to Ahsui, sometimes along with the mutton which recently, I myself had rarely a chance to eat. She said Ahsui was so thin, it was really pathetic, and it made the landlady sneer at us. She couldn't stand being laughed at.

So there were only the hens to eat my left-overs. It was a long time before I realized this. I was very conscious, however, that my "place in the universe," as Huxley describes it, was only somewhere between the dog and the hens.

*L*ater on, after much argument and insistence, the hens started appearing on our table, and we and Ahsui were able to enjoy them for over ten days. They were very thin, though, because for a long time they had only been fed a few grains of *kaoliang* a day. After that life became much more peaceful. Only Tzu-chun was very dispirited, and seemed so sad and bored without them, she grew rather sulky. How easily people change!

However, Ahsui too would have to be given up. We had stopped hoping for a letter from anywhere, and for a long time Tzu-chun had had no food left to make the dog beg or stand on his hind legs. Besides, winter was coming on very fast, and we didn't know what to do about a stove. His appetite had long been a heavy liability, of which we were all too conscious. So even the dog had to go.

If we had tied a tag on him and taken him to the market to sell, we might have made a few coppers. But neither of us could bring ourselves to do this.

Finally I muffled his head in a cloth and took him outside the West Gate where I let him loose. When he ran after me, I pushed him into a pit that wasn't too deep.

When I got home, I found it more peaceful; but I was quite taken aback by Tzu-chun's tragic expression. I had never seen her so woebegone. Of course, it was because of Ahsui, but why take it so to heart? I didn't tell her about pushing him into the pit.

That night, something icy crept into her expression too.

"Really!" I couldn't help saying. "What's got into you today, Tzu-chun?"

"What?" She didn't even look at me.

"You look so. . . ."

"It's nothing — nothing at all."

Eventually I realized she must consider me callous. Actually, when I was on my own I had got along very well, although I was too proud to mix much with family acquaintances. But since my move I had become estranged from all my old friends. Still, if I could only get away from all this, there were plenty of ways open to me. Now I had to put up with all these hardships mainly because of her — getting rid of Ahsui was a case in point. But Tzu-chun seemed too obtuse now even to understand that.

When I took an opportunity to hint this to her, she nodded as if she understood. But judging by her behavior later, she either didn't take it in or else didn't believe me.

*T*he cold weather and her cold looks made it impossible for me to be comfortable at home. But where could I go? I could get away from her icy looks in the street and parks, but the cold wind outside whistled through me. Finally I found a haven in the public library.

Admission was free, and there were two stoves in the reading room. Although the fire was very low, the mere sight of the stoves made me warm. There were no books worth reading: the old ones were out of date, and there were practically no new ones.

But I didn't go there to read. There were usually a few other people there, sometimes as many as a dozen, all thinly clad like me. We kept up a pretence of reading, in order to keep out of the cold. This suited me down to the ground. You were liable to meet people you knew on the road who would glance at you contemptuously, but here there was no trouble of that kind, because my acquaintances were all gathered round other stoves or warming themselves at the stoves in their own homes.

Although there were no books for me to read there, I found quiet in which to think. As I sat there alone thinking over the past, I felt that during the last half year for love — blind love — I had neglected all the important things in life. First and foremost, livelihood. A man must make a living before there can be anyplace for love. There must be a way out for those who struggle, and I hadn't yet forgotten how to flap my wings, though I was much weaker than before. . . .

The room and readers gradually faded. I saw fishermen in the angry sea, soldiers in the trenches, dignitaries in their ears, speculators at the stock exchange, heroes in mountain forests, teachers on their platforms, night prowlers, thieves in the dark. . . . Tzu-chun was far away. She had lost all her courage in her resentment over Ahsui and absorption in her cooking. The strange thing was that she didn't look particularly thin. . . .

It grew colder. The few lumps of slow-burning hard coal in the stove had at last burned out, and it was closing time. I had to go back to Chichao Street, to expose myself to that icy look. Of late I had sometimes been met with warmth, but this only upset me more. I remember one evening, the child-like look I had not seen for so long flashed from Tzu-chun's eyes as she reminded me with a smile of something that had happened at the hostel. But there was a constant look of fear in her eyes too. The fact that I had treated her more coldly recently than she had me worried her. Sometimes I forced myself to talk and laugh to comfort her. But the emptiness of my laughter and speech, and the way it immediately re-echoed in my ears like a hateful sneer, was more than I could bear.

Tzu-chun might have felt it too, for after this she lost her wooden calm and, though she tried her best to hide it, often showed anxiety. She treated me, however, much more tenderly.

I wanted to speak to her plainly, but hadn't the courage. Whenever I made up my mind to speak, the sight of those childlike eyes compelled me, for the time being, to smile. But my smile turned straightway into a sneer at myself, and made me lose my cold composure.

*A*fter that she revived the old questions and started new tests, forcing me to give all sorts of hypocritical answers to show my affection for her. Hypocrisy became branded on my heart, so filling it with falseness it was hard to breathe. I often felt, in my depression, that really great courage was needed to tell the truth; for a man who lacked courage and reconciled himself to hypocrisy would never find a new path. What's more, he just could not exist.

Then Tzu-chun started looking resentful. This happened for the first time one morning, one bitterly cold morning, or so I imagined. I smiled secretly to myself, cold with indignation. All the ideas and intelligent, fearless phrases she had learned were empty after all. Yet she did not know this. She had given up reading long ago, and did not realize the first thing in life is to make a living, that to do this people must advance hand in hand, or go forward singly. All she could do was cling to someone else's clothing, making it difficult even for a fighter to struggle, and bringing ruin on both.

I felt that our only hope lay in parting. She ought to make a clean break. Suddenly I thought of her death, but immediately was ashamed and reproached myself. Happily it was morning, and there was plenty of time for me to tell her the truth. Whether or not we could make a fresh start depended on this.

I deliberately brought up the past. I spoke of literature, then of foreign authors and their works, of Ibsen's *A Doll's House* and *The Lady from the Sea*. I praised Nora for being strong-minded, . . . All this had been said the previous year in the shabby room in the hostel, but now it rang hollow. As the words left my mouth I could not free myself from the suspicion that there was an unseen urchin behind me maliciously parroting all I said.

She listened, nodding in agreement, then was silent. I finished what I had to say abruptly, and my voice died away in the emptiness.

"Yes," she said after another silence, "but . . . Chuansheng, I feel you've changed a lot lately. Is it true? Tell me!"

This was a blow, but I took a grip on myself, and explained my views and proposals: to make a fresh start and turn over a new leaf, to avoid being ruined together.

To clinch the matter, I said firmly:

". . . Besides, you need have no more scruples but go boldly ahead. You asked me to tell the truth. Yes, we shouldn't be hypocritical. Well, to tell the truth — it's because I don't love you anymore! Actually, this makes it better for you, because it'll be easier for you to work without any regret. . . ."

I was expecting a scene, but all that followed was silence. Her face turned ashy pale, like a corpse; but in a moment her color came back, and that childlike look darted from her eyes. She looked all round, like a hungry child searching for its kind mother, but only looked into space. Fearfully she avoided my eyes.

The sight was more than I could stand. Fortunately it was still early. I braved the cold wind to hurry to the library.

There I saw *Freedom's Friend*, with all my short articles in it. This took me by surprise, and seemed to bring me new life. "There are plenty of ways open to me," I thought. "But things can't go on like this."

I started calling on old friends with whom I had had nothing to do for a long time, but didn't go more than once or twice. Naturally, their rooms were warm, but I felt chilled to the marrow there. In the evenings I huddled in a room colder than ice.

An icy needle pierced my heart, making me suffer continually from numb wretchedness. "There are plenty of ways open

to me," I thought. "I haven't forgotten how to flap my wings."
Suddenly I thought of her death, but immediately was
ashamed and reproached myself.

In the library I often saw like a flash a new path ahead of
me. I imagined she had faced up bravely to the facts and
boldly left this icy home. Left it, what was more, without any
malice towards me. Then I felt light as a cloud floating in the
void, with the blue sky above and high mountains and great
oceans below, big buildings and skyscrapers, battlefields, mo-
torcars, thoroughfares, rich men's houses, bright, bustling
markets, and the dark night. . . .

What's more, I really felt this new life was just round the
corner.

Somehow we managed to live through the bitter Peking
winter. But we were like dragonflies that had fallen into the
hands of mischievous imps, been tied with threads, played
with and tormented at will. Although we had come through
alive, we were prostrate, and the end was only a matter of
time.

Three letters were sent to the editor of *Freedom's Friend*
before he replied. The envelope contained two book tokens,
one for twenty cents, one for thirty cents. But I had spent
nine cents on postage to press for payment, and gone hungry
for a whole day, all for nothing.

However, I felt that at last I had got what I expected.

Winter was giving place to spring, and the wind was not
quite so icy now. I spent more time wandering outside, and
generally did not reach home till dusk. One dark evening, I
came home listlessly as usual and, as usual, grew so depressed
at the sight of our gate that I slowed down. Eventually,
however, I reached my room. It was dark inside, and as I
groped for the matches to strike a light, the place seemed
extraordinarily quiet and empty.

I was standing there in bewilderment, when the official's wife called to me through the window.

"Tzu-chun's father came today," she said simply, "and took her away."

This was not what I had expected. I felt as if hit on the back of the head, and stood speechless.

"She went?" I finally managed to ask.

"Yes."

"Did — did she say anything?"

"No. Just asked me to tell you when you came back that she had gone."

I couldn't believe it; yet the room was so extraordinarily quiet and empty. I looked everywhere for Tzu-chun, but all I could see was the old, discolored furniture which appeared very scattered, to show that it was incapable of hiding anyone or anything. It occurred to me she might have left a letter or at least jotted down a few words, but no. Only salt, dried paprika, flour and half a cabbage had been placed together, with a few dozen coppers at the side. These were all our worldly goods, and now she had carefully left all this to me, bidding me without words to use this to eke our my existence a little longer.

Feeling my surroundings pressing in on me, I hurried out to the middle of the courtyard, where all around was dark. Bright lamplight showed on the window paper of the central rooms, where they were teasing the baby to make her laugh. My heart grew calmer, and I began to glimpse a way out of this heavy oppression: high mountains and great marshlands, thoroughfares, brightly lit feasts, trenches, pitch-black night, the thrust of a sharp knife, noiseless footsteps. . . .

I relaxed, thought about traveling expenses, and sighed.

I conjured up a picture of my future as I lay with closed eyes, but before the night was half over it had vanished. In the gloom I suddenly seemed to see a pile of groceries, then Tzu-chun's ashen face appeared to gaze at me beseechingly with childlike eyes. But as soon as I took a grip on myself, there was nothing there.

However, my heart still felt heavy. Why couldn't I have waited a few days instead of blurting out the truth like that to her? Now she knew all that was left to her was the passionate sternness of her father — who was as heartless as a creditor with his children — and the icy cold looks of bystanders. Apart from this there was only emptiness. How terrible to bear the heavy burden of emptiness, treading out one's life amid sternness and cold looks! And at the end not even a tombstone to your grave!

I shouldn't have told Tzu-chun the truth. Since we had loved each other, I should have gone on lying to her. If truth is a treasure, it shouldn't have proved such a heavy burden of emptiness to Tzu-chun. Of course, lies are empty too, but at least they wouldn't have proved so crushing a burden in the end.

I thought if I told Tzu-chun the truth, she could go forward boldly without scruples, just as when we started living together. But I was wrong. She was fearless then because of her love.

I hadn't the courage to shoulder the heavy burden of hypocrisy, so I thrust the burden of the truth on to her. Because she had loved me, she had to bear this heavy burden, amid sternness and cold glances to the end of her days.

I had thought of her death. . . . I realized I was a weakling. I deserved to be cast out by the strong, no matter whether they were truthful or hypocritical. Yet she, from first to last, had hoped that I could live longer. . . .

I wanted to leave Chichao Street; it was too empty and lonely here. I thought, if once I could get away, it would be as if Tzu-chun were still at my side. Or at least as if she were still in town, and might drop in on me anytime, as she had when I lived in the hostel.

However, all my letters went unanswered, as did my applications to friends to find me a post. There was nothing for it but to go to see a family acquaintance I hadn't visited for a long time. This was an old classmate of my uncle's, a highly respected senior licentiate, who had lived in Peking for many years and had a wide circle of acquaintances.

The gatekeeper stared at me scornfully — no doubt because my clothes were shabby — and only with difficulty was I admitted. My uncle's friend still remembered me, but treated me very coldly. He knew all about us.

"Obviously, you can't stay here," he said coldly, after I asked him to recommend me to a job somewhere else. "But where will you go? It's extremely difficult. That — er — that friend of yours, Tzu-chun, I suppose you know, is dead."

I was dumbfounded.

"Are you sure?" I finally blurted out.

He gave an artificial laugh. "Of course I am. My servant Wang Sheng comes from the same village as her family."

"But — how did she die?"

"Who knows? At any rate, she's dead."

I have forgotten how I took my leave and went home. I knew he wouldn't lie. Tzu-chun would never be with me again, as she had last year. Although she wanted to bear the burden of emptiness amid sternness and cold glances till the end of her days, it had been too much for her. Fate had decided that she should die knowing the truth I had told her — die unloved!

Obviously, I could not stay there. But where could I go?

All around was a great void, quiet as death. I seemed to see the darkness before the eyes of every single person who had died unloved, and to hear all the bitter and despairing cries of their struggle.

I was waiting for something new, something nameless and unexpected. But day after day passed in the same deadly quiet.

I went out now much less than before, sitting or lying in this great void, allowing this deathly quiet to eat away my soul. Sometimes the silence itself seemed afraid, seemed to recoil. At such times there would flash up nameless, unexpected, new hope.

One overcast morning, when the sun was unable to struggle out from behind the clouds and the very air was tired, the patter of tiny feet and a snuffling sound made me open my eyes. A glance round the room revealed nothing, but when I looked down I saw a small creature pattering around — thin, covered with dust, more dead than alive. . . .

*W*hen I looked harder, my heart missed a beat. I jumped up.

It was Ahsui. He had come back.

I left Chichao Street not just because of the cold glances of my landlord and the maid, but largely on account of Ahsui. But where could I go? I realized, naturally, there were many ways open to me, and sometimes seemed to see them stretching before me. I didn't know, though, how to take the first step.

After much deliberation, I decided the hostel was the only place where I could put up. Here is the same shabby room as before, the same wooden bed, half dead locust tree and wisteria. But what gave me love and life, hope and happiness before has vanished. There is nothing but emptiness, the empty existence I exchanged for the truth.

There are many ways open to me, and I must take one of them because I am still living. I don't know, though, how to take the first step. Sometimes the road seems like a great, grey serpent, writhing and darting at me. I wait and wait and watch it approach, but it always disappears suddenly in the darkness.

The early spring nights are as long as ever. I sit idly for a long time and recall a funeral procession I saw on the street this morning. There were paper figures and paper horses in front, and behind crying that sounded like a lilt. I see how clever they are — this is so simple.

Then Tzu-chun's funeral springs to my mind. She bore the heavy burden of emptiness alone, advancing down the long grey road, only to be swallowed up amid sternness and cold glances.

I wish we really had ghosts and there really were a hell. Then, no matter how the wind of hell roared, I would go to find Tzu-chun, tell her of my remorse and grief, and beg her forgiveness. Otherwise, the poisonous flames of hell would surround me, and fiercely devour my remorse and grief.

In the whirlwind and flames I would put my arms round Tzu-chun, and ask her pardon, or try to make her happy. . . .

*H*owever, this is emptier than the new life. Now there is only the early spring night which is still as long as ever. Since I am living, I must make a fresh start. The first step is just to describe my remorse and grief, for Tzu-chun's sake as well as for my own.

All I can do is to cry. It sounds like a lilt as I mourn for Tzu-chun, burying her in oblivion.

I want to forget. For my own sake I don't want to remember the oblivion I gave Tzu-chun for her burial.

I must make a fresh start in life. I must hide the truth deep in my wounded heart, and advance silently, taking oblivion and falsehood as my guide. . . .

October 21, 1925

The Divorce

"Ah, Uncle Mu! A happy New Year and good luck to you!"

"How are you, Pa-san? Happy New Year. . . !"

"Happy New Year! So Ai-ku's here as well. . . ."

"Well met, Grandad Mu. . . !"

As Chuang Mu-san and his daughter Ai-ku stepped down into the boat from Magnolia Bridge Wharf a hum of voices broke out on board. Some of the passengers clasped their hands and bowed, and four places were vacated on the benches of the cabin. Calling out greetings, Chuang Mu-san sat down, leaning his long pipe against the side of the boat. Ai-ku sat on his left opposite Pa-san, her feet fanning out to form a V.

"Going into town, Grandad Mu?" asked a man with a ruddy face like the shell of a crab.

"Not to town." Grandad Mu sounded rather dispirited. His dark red face was so wrinkled in any case that he looked much the same as usual. "We're making a trip to Pang Village."

All on board stopped talking to stare at them.

"Is it Ai-ku's business again?" asked Pa-san at last.

"It is. . . . This affair will be the death of me. It's dragged on now for three years. We've quarreled and patched it up time after time; yet still the thing isn't settled. . . ."

"Will you be going to Mr. Wei's house again?"

"That's right. This won't be the first time he's acted as peace-maker; but I've never agreed to his terms. Not that it matters. Their family's having their New Year reunion now. Even Seventh Master from the city will be there. . . ."

"Seventh Master?" Pa-san opened his eyes very wide. "So he'll be there to put his word in too, eh. . . ? Well. . . . As a matter of fact, since we pulled down their kitchen range last year we've had our revenge more or less. Besides, there's really no point in Ai-ku going back there. . . ." He lowered his eyes again.

"I'm not set on going back there, brother Pa-san!" Ai-ku looked up indignantly. "I'm doing this to spite them. Just think! Young Beast carried on with that little widow and decided he didn't want me. But is it as simple as that? Old Beast just egged on his son and tried to get rid of me too — as if it were all that easy! What about Seventh Master? Just because he exchanges cards with the magistrate, does that mean he can't talk our language? He can't be such a blockhead as Mr. Wei, who says nothing but: 'Separate, better separate.' I'll tell him what I've had to put up with all these years, and we'll see who he says is right!"

Pa-san was convinced, and kept his mouth shut.

The boat was very quiet, with no sound but the plash of water against the bow. Chuang Mu-san reached for his pipe and filled it.

A fat man sitting opposite, next to Pa-san, rummaged in his girdle for a flint and struck a light, which he held to Chuang Mu-san's pipe.

"Thank you, thank you," said Chuang Mu-san, nodding to him.

"Though this is the first time we've met," said the fat man respectfully, "I heard of you long ago. Yes, who is there in all the eighteen villages by the coast who doesn't know of Uncle Mu? We've known too for some time that Young Shih was carrying on with a little widow. When you took your six sons to tear down their kitchen range last year, who didn't say you were right. . . ? All the big gates open for you, you have plenty of face. . . . Why be afraid of *them*. . . ."

"This uncle is a truly discerning man," said Ai-ku approvingly. "I don't know who he is, though."

"My name is Wang Te-kuei," replied the fat man promptly.

"They can't just push me out! I don't care whether it's Seventh Master or Eighth Master. I'll go on making trouble till their family's ruined and all of them are dead! Mr. Wei has been at me four times, hasn't he? Even dad's been thrown off his balance by the sight of that settlement money. . . . ." Chuang Mu-san swore softly to himself.

"But, Grandad Mu, didn't the Shih family send Mr. Wei a whole feast at the end of last year?" asked Crabface.

"Makes no difference," said Wang Te-kuei. "Can a feast blind a man completely? If so, what happens when you send him a foreign banquet? Those scholars who know the truth will always stick up for justice. If anyone's bullied by everyone else, for instance, they will up and speak for him no matter whether there's wine to be had or not. At the end of last year, Mr. Yung of our humble village came back from Peking. He's not like us villagers, he's seen the great world. He said that a Madame Kuang there, who's the best. . . ."

"Wang Jetty!" shouted the boatman, preparing to moor. "Any passengers for Wang Jetty?"

"Here, me!" Fatty grabbed his pipe, and darted out of the cabin, jumping ashore just as the boat drew in.

"Excuse me!" he called back with a nod to the passengers.

The boat rowed on in fresh silence, broken only by the plash of water. Pa-san began to doze off, facing Ai-ku's shoes, and by degrees his mouth fell open. The two old women in the front cabin began softly chanting Buddhist prayers and telling their beads. They looked at Ai-ku and exchanged significant glances, pursing their lips and nodding.

Ai-ku was staring at the awning above her, probably considering how best to raise such trouble that Old Beast's family would be ruined and he and Young Beast would have no way to turn. She was not afraid of Mr. Wei. She had seen him twice and he was nothing but a squat, round-headed fellow — there were plenty like him in her own village, only a little darker.

Chuang Mu-san had come to the end of his tobacco, and the oil in the pipe was sputtering, but still he went on puffing. He knew that after Wang Jetty came Pang Village. Already, in fact, you could see Literary Star Pavilion at the entrance to the village. He had been here so often it was not worth talking about, anymore than Mr. Wei. He remembered how his daughter had come home crying, how badly her husband and father-in-law had behaved, and how he had worsted them.

The past unfolded again before his eyes. Usually when he recalled how he had punished evil-doers, he gave a bleak smile — but nor this time. The fat form of Seventh Master had somehow intervened, and was squeezing his thoughts out of any semblance of order.

The boat went on in continued silence. Only the Buddhist prayers swelled in volume. Everyone else seemed sunk in thought like Ai-ku and her father.

"Here you are, Uncle Mu. Pang Village."

Roused by the boatman's voice, they looked up to see Literary Star Pavilion before them.

Chuang jumped ashore, and Ai-ku followed him. They passed the pavilion and headed for Mr. Wei's house. After passing thirty houses on their way south, they turned a corner and reached their destination. Four boats with black awnings were moored in a row at the gate.

As they stepped through the great, black-lacquered gate, they were asked into the gatehouse. It was full of boatmen and farm-hands, who were seated at two tables. Ai-ku dared not stare at them, but she took one hasty look round, and saw there was no sign of Old Beast and Young Beast.

When a servant brought in soup containing sweet New Year cakes, without knowing why, she felt even more uncomfortable and uneasy. "Just because he exchanges cards with the magistrate doesn't mean he can't talk our language, does it?" she thought. "These scholars who know the truth will always stick up for justice. I must tell Seventh Master the whole story, beginning from the time I married at the age of fifteen. . . ."

When she finished the soup, she knew the time was at hand. Sure enough, before long she found herself following one of the farm-hands, who ushered her and her father across the great hall, and round a corner into the reception room.

The room was so crammed with things she could not take in all it contained. There were many guests as well, whose short jackets of red and blue satin were shimmering all around her. In the midst of them was a man who she knew at once must be Seventh Master. Though he had a round head and a round face too, he was a great deal bigger than Mr. Wei and the others. He had narrow slits of eyes in his great round face, a wispy black moustache, and though he was bald his head and face were ruddy and glistening. Ai-ku was quite puzzled for a moment, then concluded he must have rubbed his skin with lard.

"*T*his is an anus-stop,* which the ancients used in burials."

Seventh Master was holding something which looked like a corroded stone, and, as he spoke, he rubbed his nose twice with this object. "Unfortunately, it comes from a recent digging. Still, it's worth having: it can't be later than Han.† Look at this 'mercury stain'. . . ."‡

The "mercury stain" was at once surrounded by several heads, one of which, of course, was Mr. Wei's. There were several sons of the house as well, whom Ai-ku had not yet noticed, for so awed were they by Seventh Master that they looked like flattened bed-bugs.

She did not understand all he had just said; she was not interested in this "mercury stain," nor did she dare investigate it. Instead she took this chance to look round. Standing behind her by the wall, close to the door, were both Old Beast and Young Beast. She saw at a glance that they looked older than when she had met them by chance half a year before.

People drifted away from the "mercury stain." Mr. Wei took the anus-stop and sat down to stroke it, turning to ask Chuang Mu-san:

"Did just the two of you come?"

"Just the two of us."

"Why have none of your sons come?"

"They hadn't time.

"We wouldn't have troubled you to come at New Year, if not for this business . . . I'm sure you've had enough of it yourself. It's over two years now, isn't it? Better to remove enmity than keep it, I say. Since Ai-ku's husband didn't get

---

* It was the custom for small pieces of jade to be inserted in a dead person's orifices, for people believed this prevented the corpse from decaying.

† The Han dynasty (206 B.C.-220 AD.).

‡ The jade and metal objects found in tombs are often stained with mercury, which was placed in corpses to prevent them from decaying too rapidly.

on with her, and his parents didn't like her . . . better take the advice I gave you before and let them separate. I haven't enough face to convince you, but Seventh Master, as you know, is a champion of justice. And Seventh Master's view is the same as mine. However, he says both sides must make some concessions, and he's told the Shih family to add another ten dollars to the settlement, making it ninety dollars!"

"............"

"Ninety dollars! If you took the case right up to the emperor, you couldn't get such favorable terms. Nobody but Seventh Master would make such a handsome offer!"

Seventh Master widened his slits of eyes to nod at Chuang Mu-san.

Ai-ku saw that the situation was critical and marveled that her father, of whom all the coastal families stood in awe, should have not a word to say for himself here. This was quite uncalled for, she thought. Although she could not follow all Seventh Master said, he somehow struck her as a kindly old soul, not nearly as frightening as she had imagined.

"Seventh Master's a scholar who knows the truth," she said boldly. "He's nor like us country folk. I had no one to complain to of all the wrong that's been done me; but now I'll tell Seventh Master. All the time I was married I tried to be a good wife — I bowed my head as I went in and out, and I didn't fail in a single wifely duty. But they kept finding fault with me — each one was a regular bully. That year the weasel killed the big cock, why did they blame me for not closing the coop? It was that mangy cur — curse it — who pushed open the door of the coop to steal some rice mixed with husks. But that Young Beast wouldn't distinguish black from white. He gave me a slap on the cheek. . . ."

Seventh Master looked at her.

"I knew there must be a reason. This is something Seventh Master will not fail to notice, for scholars .who know the truth know everything. He was bewitched by that bitch, and wanted to drive me away! I married him with the proper ceremonies — three lots of tea and six presents — and was carried to his house in a bridal sedan! Is it so easy for him to toss me aside. . . ? I mean to show them, I don't mind going to court. If it can't be settled at the district court, we'll go to the prefecture. . . ."

"Seventh Master knows all this," said Mr. Wei, looking up. "If you persist in this attitude, Ai-ku, it won't be to your advantage. You haven't changed in the least. Look, how sensible your father is! It's a pity you and your brothers aren't like him. Suppose you do take this matter to the prefect, won't he consult Seventh Master? But then the case will be dealt with publicly, and nobody's feelings will be spared. . . . That being so. . . ."

"I'll stake my life if need be, even if it ruins both families!"

"There's no need for such desperate measures," put in Seventh Master slowly. "You're still young. We should all keep the peace. 'Peace breeds wealth.' Isn't that true? I've added a whole ten dollars: that's more than generous. If your father-in-law and mother-in-law say 'Go!', then go you must. Don't talk about the prefecture, this would be the same in Shanghai, Peking or even abroad. If you don't believe me, ask him! He's just come back from the foreign school in Peking." He turned towards a sharp-chinned son of the house. "Isn't that so?" he asked.

Sharp-chin hastily straightened up to answer in low, respectful tones, "Ab — so — lutely."

Ai-ku felt completely isolated. Her father refused to speak, her brothers had not dared come, Mr. Wei had always been on the other side, and now Seventh Master had failed her, while even this young sharp-chin, with his soft talk and air of a flattened bug, was simply saying what was expected of him. But confused as she was, she resolved to make a last stand.

"What, does even Seventh Master" Her eyes showed surprise and disappointment. "Yes . . . I know, we rough folk are ignorant. My father's to blame for nor even understanding how to deal with people — he's lost his old wits completely. He let Old Beast and Young Beast have their way in everything. They stoop to every means, however foul, to fawn on those above them. . . ."

"Look at her, Seventh Master!" Young Beast, who had been standing silently behind her, suddenly spoke up now. "She dares act like this even in Seventh Master's presence. At home she gave us no peace at all. She calls my father Old Beast and me Young Beast or Bastard."

"Who the devil is calling you a bastard?" Ai-ku rounded on him fiercely, then turned back to Seventh Master. "I've something else I'd like to say in public. He was always mean to me. It was 'slut' and 'bitch' all the time. After he started carrying on with that whore, he even cursed my ancestors. Judge between us, Seventh Master. . . ."

She gave a start, and the words died on her lips, for suddenly Seventh Master rolled his eyes and lifted his round face. From the mouth framed by that wispy moustache issued a shrill, trailing cry:

"Come here. . . !"

Her heart, which had-missed a heat, suddenly started pounding. The battle was lost, the tables were turned it seemed. She had taken a false step and fallen into the water, and she knew it was all her own fault.

A man in a blue gown and black jacket promptly came in, and stood like a stick with his arms at his sides in front of Seventh Master.

There was not a cheep in the room. Seventh Master moved his lips, but nobody could hear what he was saying. Only his servant heard, and the force of this order entered his very marrows, for twice he twitched as if overcome by awe. And he answered:

"Very good, sir." Then he backed away several paces, turned and went out.

Ai-ku knew that something unexpected and completely unforeseen was about to happen — something which she was powerless to prevent. Only now did she realize the full power of Seventh Master. She had been mistaken before, and acted too rashly and rudely. She repented bitterly, and found herself saying:

"I always meant to accept Seventh Master's decision. . . . ."

There was not a cheep in the room. Although her words were as soft as strands of silk, they carried like a thunder-clap to Mr. Wei.

"Good!" he exclaimed approvingly, leaping up. "Seventh Master is truly just, and Ai-ku is truly reasonable. In that case, Mu-san, you can't have any objection, since your daughter's consented herself. I'm sure you've brought the wedding certificates as I asked you. So let both sides produce them now. . . . ."

Ai-ku saw her father fumble in his girdle for something. The sticklike servant came in again to hand Seventh Master a small, flat, jet-black object shaped like a tortoise. Ai-ku was afraid something dreadful was going to happen. She darted a look at her father; but he was opening a blue cloth package at the table, and taking out silver dollars.

Seventh Master removed the tortoise's head, poured something from its body into his palm, then returned the flat-looking object to the sticklike servant. He rubbed one finger in his palm, then stuffed it up each nostril, staining his nose and upper lip a bright yellow. Then he wrinkled his nose as if about to sneeze.

Chuang Mu-san was counting the silver dollars. Mr. Wei extracted a few from a pile which had not been counted, and handed them to Old Beast. He also changed the position of the red and green certificates, restoring them to their original owners.

"Put them away," he said. "You must see if the amount is correct, Mu-san. This is no joking matter — all this silver. . . . ."

"Ah-tchew!"

Though Ai-ku knew it was only Seventh Master sneezing, she could not help turning to look at him. His mouth was wide open and his nose was twitching. In two fingers he was still clutchng the small object "used by the ancients in burials." Indeed, he was rubbing the side of his nose with it.

With some difficulty Chuang Mu-san finished counting the money, and both sides put away the red and green certificates. They all seemed to draw themselves up, and their tense expressions relaxed. Complete harmony prevailed.

"Good! This business has been settled satisfactorily," said Mr. Wei. Seeing that they seemed to be on the point of leaving, he breathed a sigh of relief. "Well, there's nothing more to be done now. Congratulations on unraveling this knot! Must you be going? Won't you stay to share our New Year feast? This is a rare occasion."

"We mustn't stay," said Ai-ku. "We'll come to drink with you next year.

"Thank you, Mr. Wei. We won't drink just now. We have other business. . . ." Chuang Mu-san, Old Beast and Young Beast withdrew most respectfully.

"What? Not a drop before you go?" Mr. Wei looked at Ai-ku who brought up the rear.

"Really we mustn't. Thank you, Mr. Wei."

November 6, 1925

The Flight to the Moon

I

*I*t is a fact that intelligent beasts can divine the wishes of men. As soon as their gate came in sight the horse slowed down and, hanging its head at the same moment as its rider, let it jog with each step like a pestle pounding rice.

The great house was overhung with evening mist, while thick black smoke rose from the neighbors' chimneys. It was time for supper. At the sound of hoofs, retainers had come out and were standing erect with their arms at their sides before the entrance. As Yi* dismounted listlessly beside the rubbish heap, they stepped forward to relieve him of his reins and whip. At the moment of crossing the threshold, he looked down at the quiverful of brand-new arrows at his waist and the three crows and one shattered sparrow in his bag, and his heart sank within him. But he strode in, putting a bold face on things, the arrows rattling in his quiver.

Reaching the inner courtyard, he saw Chang-ngo† looking out from the round window. He knew her sharp eyes must have seen the crows, and in dismay he came to a sudden stop — but he had to go on in. Serving-maids came out to greet him, unfastened his bow and quiver and took his game bag. He noticed that their smiles were rather forced.

---

* Yi or Hon Yi was a heroic archer in ancient Chinese legends.
† A goddess in ancient Chinese mythology, supposed to be Yi's wife. She took some drug of immortality and flew to the moon to become a goddess there.

After wiping his face and hands he entered the inner apartment, calling: "Madam. . . ."

Chang-ngo had been watching the sunset from the round window. She turned slowly and threw him an indifferent glance without returning his greeting.

He had been used to this treatment for some time, for over a year at least. But as usual he went on in and sat down on the old, worn leopard skin over the wooden couch opposite. Scratching his head, he muttered:

"I was out of luck again today. Nothing but crows. . . . ."

"Pah!"

Raising her willowy eyebrows, Chang-ngo sprang up and swept from the room, grumbling as she went: "Noodles with crow sauce again! Noodles with crow sauce again! I'd like to know who else eats nothing but noodles with crow sauce from one year to the next? How ill-fated I was to marry you and eat noodles with crow sauce the whole year round!"

"Madam!" Yi leaped to his feet and followed her. "It wasn't so bad today," he continued softly. "I shot a sparrow too, which can be dressed for you. . . . Nu-hsin!" he called to the maid. "Bring that sparrow to show your mistress."

The game had been taken to the kitchen, but Nu-hsin ran to fetch the sparrow and held it out in both hands to Chang-ngo.

"That!" With a disdainful glance she reached slowly out to touch it. "How disgusting!" she said crossly. "You've smashed it to pieces! Where's the meat?"

"I know," admitted Yi, discomfited. "My bow is too powerful, my arrow-heads are too large."

"Can't you use smaller arrows?"

"I haven't any. When I shot the giant boar and the huge python. . . ."

"Is this a giant boar or a huge python?" She turned to Nu-hsin and ordered: "Use it for soup!" Then she went back to her room.

Left alone at a loss, Yi sat down with his back to the wall to listen to the crackling of firewood in the kitchen. He remembered the bulk of the giant boar which had loomed like a small hillock in the distance. If he hadn't shot it then but left it till now, it would have kept them in meat for half a year and spared them this daily worry about food. And the huge python! What soups it could have made!

Nu-yi lit the lamp. The vermilion bow and arrows, the black bow and arrows, the crossbow, the sword and the dagger glimmered on the opposite wall in its faint rays. After one look, Yi lowered his head and sighed. Nu-hsin brought supper in and set it on the table in the middle: five large bowls of noodles on the left, two large bowls of noodles and one of soup on the right, in the center one large bowl of crow sauce.

While eating, Yi had to admit that this was not an appetizing meal. He stole a glance at Chang-ngo. Without so much as looking at the crow sauce, she had steeped her noodles in soup, and she set down her bowl half finished. Her face struck him as paler and thinner than before — suppose she were to fall ill?

By the second watch, in a slightly better mood, she sat without a word on the edge of the bed to drink some water. Yi sat on the wooden couch next to her, stroking the old leopard skin which was losing its fur.

"Ah," he said in a conciliatory tone. "I bagged this spotted leopard on the Western Hill before we married. It was a beauty — one glossy mass of gold."

That reminded him of how they had lived in the old days. Of bears they ate nothing but the paws, of camels nothing but the hump, giving all the rest to the serving-maids and retainers. When the big game was finished they ate wild boars, rabbits and pheasants. He was such a fine archer, he could shoot as much as he pleased.

A sigh escaped him.

"The fact is I'm too good a shot," he said. "That's why the whole place is cleaned out. Who could have guessed we'd be left with nothing but crows?"

Chang-ngo gave the ghost of a smile.

"Today I was luckier than usual." Yi's spirits were rising. "At least I caught a sparrow. I had to go an extra thirty *li* to find it."

"Can't you go a little further still?"

"Yes, madam. That's what I mean to do. I'll get up earlier tomorrow morning. If you wake first, call me. I mean to go fifty *li* further to see if I can't find some roebucks or rabbits. . . . It won't be easy, though. Remember all the game there was when I shot the giant boar and the huge python? Black bears used to pass in front of your mother's door, and she asked me several times to shoot them. . . ."

"Really?" It seemed to have slipped Chang-ngo's memory.

"Who could have foreseen they would all disappear like this? Come to think of it, I don't know how we're going to manage. *I'm* all right. I've only to eat that elixir the priest gave me, and I can fly up to heaven. But first I must think of you . . . that's why I've decided to go a little further tomorrow. . . ."

"Um."

Chang-ngo finished the water. She lay down slowly and closed her eyes.

The lamp, burning low, lit up her fading make-up. Much of her powder had rubbed off, there were dark circles beneath her eyes and one of her eyebrows was blacker than the other; yet her mouth was as red as fire, and though she wasn't smiling you could see faint dimples on her cheeks.

"Ah, no! How can I feed a woman like this on nothing but noodles and crow sauce!"

Overcome by shame, Yi flushed up to his ears.

II

*N*ight passed, a new day dawned.

In a flash Yi opened his eyes. A sunbeam aslant the western wall told him it could not be early. He looked at Chang-ngo, who was lying stretched out fast asleep. Without a sound he threw on his clothes, slipped down from his leopard skin couch and tiptoed into the hall. As he washed his face he told Nu-keng to order Wang Sheng to saddle his horse.

Having so much to do, he had long since given up breakfast. Nu-yi put five baked cakes, five stalks of leek and a package of paprika in his game bag, fastening this firmly to his waist with his bow and arrows. He tightened his belt and strode lightly out of the hall, telling Nu-keng whom he met:

"I mean to go further today to look for game. I may be a little late getting back. When your mistress has had her breakfast and is in good spirits, give her my apologies and ask her to wait for me for supper. Don't forget — my apologies!"

He walked swiftly out, swung into the saddle and flashed past the retainers ranged on either side. Very soon he was out of the village. In front were the *kaoliang* fields through which he passed every day. These he ignored, having learned long ago that there was nothing here. With two cracks of his whip he galloped forward, covering sixty *li* without a pause. In front was a dense forest, and since his horse was winded and in a lather it naturally slowed down. Another ten li and they were in the forest, yet Yi could see nothing but wasps, butterflies, ants and locusts — not a trace of birds or beasts. The first sight of this unexplored territory had raised hopes of catching at least a couple of foxes or rabbits but now he knew that had been an idle dream. He made his way out and saw another stretch of green *kaoliang* fields ahead, with one or two mud cottages in the distance. The breeze was balmy, the sun warm; neither crow nor sparrow could be heard.

"Confound it!" he bellowed to relieve his feelings.

A dozen paces further on, however, and his heart leaped with joy. On the flat ground outside a mud hut in the distance there was actually a fowl. Stopping to peck at every step, it looked like a large pigeon. He seized his bow and fitted an arrow to it, drew it to its full extent and then let go. His shaft sped through the air like a shooting star.

With no hesitation, for he never missed his quarry, he spurred after the arrow to retrieve the game. But as he approached it an old woman hurried towards the horse. She had picked up the large pigeon transfixed by his arrow and was shouting:

"Who are you? Why have you shot my best black laying hen? Have you nothing better to do. . . ?"

Yi's heart missed a beat. He pulled up short.

"What! A hen?" he echoed nervously. "I thought it was a wood pigeon."

"Are you blind? You must be over forty too."

"Yes, ma'am. Forty-five last year."

"No fool like an old fool, they say. Imagine mistaking a hen for a wood pigeon! Who are you anyway?"

"I am Yi." While saying this he saw that his arrow had pierced the hen's heart, killing it outright. So his voice trailed away on his name as he dismounted.

"Never heard of him!" She peered into his face.

"There are those who know my name. In the days of good King Yao I shot wild boars and serpents. . . ."

"Oh, you liar! Those were shot by *Lord Feng Meng** and some others. Maybe you helped. But how can you boast of doing it all yourself? For shame!"

"Why, ma'am, that fellow Feng Meng has just taken to calling on me during the last few years. We never worked together. He had no part in it."

"Liar! Everybody says so. I hear it four or five times a month."

"All right. Let's come down to business. What about this hen?"

"You must make it up! She was my best: she laid me an egg every day. You'll have to give me two hoes and three spindles in exchange."

"Look at me, ma'am — I neither farm nor spin. Where would I get hoes or spindles? I've no money on me either, only five baked cakes — but they're made of white flour. I'll give you these for your hen with five stalks of leek and a package of paprika into the bargain. What do you say. . . ?"

Taking the cakes from his bag with one hand, he picked up the hen with the other.

The old woman was not averse to taking cakes of white flour, but insisted on having fifteen. After haggling for some time they agreed on ten, and Yi promised to bring the rest over by noon the next day at the latest, leaving the arrow there as security. Then, his mind at rest, he stuffed the dead hen in his bag, sprang into his saddle and headed home. Though

---

* Yi's pupil and another good archer. This is a thrust at Kan Chang-hung, a young writer who was Lu Hsun's pupil but later attacked him in his articles. The story of Feng Meng shooting Yi suggests Kan's attack on Lu Hsun.

famished, he was happy. It was over a year since they had last tasted chicken soup.

It was afternoon when he emerged from the forest, and he plied his whip hard in his eagerness to get home. His horse was exhausted, though, and they did not reach the familiar *kaoliang* fields till dusk. He glimpsed a shadowy figure some way off, and almost at once an arrow sang through the air towards him.

Without reining in his horse, which was trotting along, Yi fitted an arrow to his bow and let fly. Zing! Two arrowheads collided, sparks flew into the air and the two shafts thrust up to form an inverted V before toppling over and falling to the ground. No sooner had the first two met than both men loosed their second, which again collided in mid-air. They did this nine times, till Yi's supply was exhausted; and now he could see Feng Meng opposite, gloating as he aimed another arrow at his throat.

"Well, well!" thought Yi. "I imagined he was fishing at the seaside, but he's been hanging about to play dirty tricks like this. Now I understand the old woman talking as she did. . . ."

In a flash, his enemy's bow arched like a full moon and the arrow whistled through the air towards Yi's throat. Perhaps the aim was at fault, for it struck him full in the mouth. He tumbled over, transfixed, and fell to the ground. His horse stood motionless.

Seeing Yi was dead, Feng Meng tiptoed slowly over. Smiling as if drinking to his victory, he gazed at the face of the corpse.

As he stared long and hard, Yi opened his eyes and sat up.

"You've learned nothing in a hundred visits or more to me." He spat out the arrow and laughed. "Don't you know my skill in 'biting the arrow'? That's too bad! These tricks of yours won't get you anywhere. You can't kill your boxing master with blows learned from him. You must work out something of your own."

"I was trying to 'pay you out in your own coin' . . ." mumbled the victor.

Yi stood up, laughing heartily. "You're always quoting some adage. Maybe you can impress old women that way, but you can't impose on *me*. I've always stuck to hunting, never taken to highway robbery like you. . . ."

Relieved to see that the hen in his bag was not crushed, he remounted and rode away.

"Curse you . . . ." An oath carried after him.

"To think he should stoop so low . . . . Such a young fellow, and yet he's picked up swearing. No wonder that old woman was taken in."

Yi shook his head sadly as he rode along.

III

*B*efore he came to the end of the *kaoliang* fields, night had fallen. Stars appeared in the dark blue sky, and in the west the evening star shone with unusual brilliance. The horse picked its way along the white ridges between the fields, so weary that its pace was slower than ever. Fortunately, at the horizon the moon began to shed its silver light.

"Confound it!" Yi, whose belly was rumbling now, lost patience. "The harder I try to make a living, the more tiresome things happen to waste my time." He spurred his horse, but it simply twitched its rump and jogged on as slowly as before.

"It's so late, Chang-ngo is sure to be angry," he thought. "She may fly into a temper. Thank goodness I've this little hen to make her happy. I'll tell her: 'Madam, I went two hundred *li* there and back to find you this.' No, that's no good: sounds too boastful."

Now to his joy he saw lights ahead and stopped worrying. And without any urging the horse broke into a canter. A round, snow-white moon lit up the path before him and a cool wind soothed his cheeks — this was better than coming home from a great hunt!

The horse stopped of its own accord beside the rubbish heap. Yi saw at a glance that something was amiss. The whole house was in confusion. Chao Fu alone came out to meet him.

"What's happened? Where's Wang Sheng?" he demanded.

"He's gone to the Yao family to look for our mistress."

"What? Has your mistress gone to the Yao family?" Yi was too taken aback to dismount.

"Yes, sir." Chao took the reins and whip.

Then Yi got down from his horse and crossed the threshold. After a moment's thought he turned to ask:

"Are you sure she didn't grow tired of waiting and go to a restaurant?"

"No, sir. I've asked in all three restaurants. She isn't there."

His head lowered in thought, Yi entered the house. The three maids were standing nervously in front of the hall. He cried out in amazement:

"What! All of you here? Your mistress never goes alone to the Yao family."

They looked at him in silence, then took off his bow, the quiver and the bag holding the small hen. Yi had a moment of panic. Suppose, in anger, Chang-ngo had killed herself? He sent Nu-keng for Chao Fu, and told him to search the pond in the back and the trees. Once in their room, though, he knew his guess had been wrong. The place was in utter disorder, all the chests were open and one glance behind the bed showed that the jewel-case was missing. He felt as if doused with cold water. Gold and pearls meant nothing to him, but the elixir given him by the priest had been in that case too.

After walking twice round the room, he noticed Wang Sheng at the door.

"Please, sir, our mistress isn't with the Yaos. They're not playing mah-jong today."

Yi looked at him and said nothing. Wang Sheng withdrew.

"Did you call me, sir?" asked Chao Fu, coming in.

Yi shook his head and waved him away.

He walked round and round the room, then went to the hall and sat down. Looking up he could see on the opposite wall the vermilion bow and arrows, the black bow and arrows, the crossbow, the sword and the dagger. After some reflection, he asked the maids who were standing there woodenly:

"What time did your mistress disappear?"

"She wasn't here when I brought in the lamp," said Nu-yi. "But no one saw her go out."

"Did you see her take the medicine in that case?"

"No, sir. But she did ask me for some water this afternoon."

Yi stood up in consternation. He suspected that he had been left alone on earth!

"Did you see anything flying to heaven?" he asked.

"Oh!" Nu-hsin was struck by a thought. "When I came out after lighting the lamp, I did see a black shadow flying this way. I never dreamed it was our mistress. . . ." Her face turned pale.

"It must have been!" Yi clapped his knee and sprang up. He started out, turning back to ask Nu-hsin: "Which way did the shadow go?"

Nu-hsin pointed with one finger. But all he could see in that direction was the round, snow-white moon, with its hazy pavilions and trees, suspended in the sky. When he was a child his grandmother had told him of the lovely landscape of the moon; he still had a vague recollection of her description. As he watched the moon floating in a sapphire sea, his own limbs seemed very heavy.

Fury took possession of him. And in his fury he felt the urge to kill. With eyes starting from his head, he roared at the maids:

"Bring my bow! The one with which I shot the suns! And three arrows!"

Nu-yi and Nu-keng took down the huge bow in the middle of the hall and dusted it. Together with three long arrows they handed it to him.

Holding the bow in one hand, with the other he fitted the three arrows to the string. He drew the bow to the full, aiming straight at the moon. Standing there firm as a rock, his eyes darting lightning, his beard and hair flying in the wind like black tongues of flame, for one instant he looked again the hero who, long ago, had shot the suns.

There was a whistle, one only. The three shafts left the string, one after the other, too fast for eye to see or ear to hear. They should have struck the moon in the same place, for they followed each other without a hair's breadth between them. But to be sure of reaching his mark he had given each a slightly different direction, so that the arrows struck three different points, inflicting three wounds.

The maids gave a cry. They saw the moon quiver and thought it must surely fall — but still it hung there peacefully, shedding a calm, even brighter light, as if completely unscathed.

Yi threw back his head to hurl an oath at the sky. He watched and waited. But the moon paid no attention. He took three paces forward, and the moon fell back three paces. He took three paces back, and the moon moved forward.

They looked at each other in silence.

Listlessly, he leaned his bow against the door of the ball. He went inside. The maids followed him.

He sat down and sighed. "Well, your mistress will be happy on her own forever after. How could she have the heart to leave me and fly up there alone? Did she find me too old? But only last month she said: 'You're not old. It's a sign of mental weakness to think of yourself as old. . . .'"

"That couldn't be it," said Nu-yi. "Folk still describe you as a warrior, sir."

"Sometimes you seem like an artist," put in Nu-hsin.

"Nonsense! The fact is, those noodles with crow sauce were uneatable. I can't blame her for not being able to stomach them. . . ."

"That leopard skin is worn out on one side. I'll cut a piece of the leg facing the wall to mend it. That will look better." Nu-hsin walked inside.

"Wait a bit!" said Yi and reflected. "There's no hurry for that. I'm famished. Make haste and cook me a dish of chicken with paprika, and make five catties of flapjacks. After that I can go to bed. Tomorrow I'm going to ask that priest for another elixir, so that I can follow her. Tell Wang Sheng, Nu-keng, to give my horse four measures of beans!"

December 1926

Forging the Swords

I

Mei Chien Chih had no sooner lain down beside his mother than rats came out to gnaw the wooden lid of the pan. The sound got on his nerves. The soft hoots he gave had some effect at first, but presently the rats ignored him, crunching and munching as they pleased. He dared not make a loud noise to drive them away, for fear of waking his mother, so tired by her labors during the day that as soon as her head touched the pillow she had fallen asleep.

After a long time silence fell. He was dozing off when a sudden splash made him open his eyes with a start. He heard the rasping of claws against earthenware.

"Good! I hope you drown!" he thought gleefully and sat up quietly.

Getting out of bed, he picked his way by the light of the moon to the door. He groped for the fire stick behind it, lit a chip of pine wood and lighted up the water vat. Sure enough, a huge rat had fallen in. There was too little water inside for it to get out. It was just swimming round, scrabbling at the side of the vat.

"Serves you right!" the boy exulted. This was one of the creatures that kept him awake every night by gnawing the furniture. He stuck the torch into a small hole in the mud wall to gloat over the sight, till the creature's beady eyes revolted him and reaching for a dried reed he pushed it under the water. After a time he removed the reed and the rat, coming to the surface, went on swimming round and scrabbling at the side of the vat, but less powerfully than before. Its eyes were under water — all that could be seen was the red rip of a small pointed nose, snuffling desperately.

For some time he had had an aversion to red-nosed people. Yet now this small pointed red nose struck him as pathetic. He thrust his reed under the creature's belly. The rat clutched at it, and after catching its breath clambered upon it. But the sight of its whole body — sopping black fur, bloated belly, wormlike tail — struck him again as so revolting that he hastily shook the reed. The rat dropped back with a splash into the vat. Then he hit it several times over the head to make it sink.

Now the pine chip had been changed six times. The rat, exhausted, was floating submerged in the middle of the jar, from time to time straining slightly towards the surface. Once more the boy was seized with pity. He broke the reed in two and, with considerable difficulty, fished the creature up and put it on the floor. To begin with, it didn't budge; then it rook a breath; after a long time its feet twitched and it turned over, as if meaning to make off. This gave Mei Chien Chih a jolt. He raised his left foot instinctively and brought it heavily down. He heard a small cry. When he squatted down to look, there was blood on the rat's muzzle — it was probably dead.

He felt sorry again, as remorseful as if he had committed a crime. He squatted there, staring, unable to get up.

By this time his mother was awake.

"What are you doing, son?" she asked from the bed.

"A rat

He rose hastily and turned to her answering briefly.

"I know it's a rat. But what are you doing? Killing it or saving it?"

*H*e made no answer. The torch had burned out. He stood there silently in the darkness, accustoming his eyes to the pale light of the moon.

His mother sighed.

"After midnight you'll be sixteen, but you're still the same — so lukewarm. You never change. It looks as if your father will have no one to avenge him."

Seated in the grey moonlight, his mother seemed to be trembling from head to foot. The infinite grief in her low tones made him shiver. The next moment, though, hot blood raced through his veins.

"Avenge my father? Does he need avenging?" He stepped. forward in amazement.

"He does. And the task falls to you. I have long wanted to tell you, but while you were small I said nothing. Now you're not a child any longer though you still act like one. I just don't know what to do. Can a boy like you carry through a real man's job?"

"I can. Tell me, mother. I'm going to change. . . ."

"Of course. I can only tell you. And you'll have to change. . . . Well, come over here."

He walked over. His mother sat upright in bed, her eyes flashing in the shadowy white moonlight.

"Listen!" she said gravely. "Your father was famed as a forger of swords, the best in all the land. I sold his tools to keep us from starving, so there's nothing left for you to see. But he was the best sword-maker in the whole world. Twenty years ago, the king's concubine gave birth to a piece of iron which they said she conceived after embracing an iron pillar. It was pure, transparent iron. The king, realizing that this was a rare treasure, decided to have it made into a sword with which to defend his kingdom, kill his enemies and ensure his own safety. As ill luck would have it, your father was chosen for the task, and in both hands he brought the iron home. He tempered it day and night for three whole years, until he had forged two swords.

"What a fearful sight when he finally opened his furnace! A jet of white vapor billowed up into the sky, while the earth shook. The white vapor became a white cloud above this spot; by degrees it turned a deep scarlet and cast a peach blossom tint over everything. In our pitch-black furnace lay two red-hot swords. As your father sprinkled them drop by drop with clear well water, the swords hissed and spat and little by little turned blue. So seven days and seven nights passed, till the swords disappeared from sight. But if you looked hard, they were still in the furnace, pure blue and as transparent as two icicles.

"Great happiness flashed from your father's eyes. Picking up the swords, he stroked and fondled them. Then lines of sadness appeared on his forehead and at the corners of his mouth. He put the swords in two caskets.

"'You've only to look at the portents of the last few days to realize that everybody must know the swords are forged,' he told me softly. 'Tomorrow I must go to present one to the king. But the day that I present it will be the last day of my life. I am afraid we shall never meet again.'

"Horrified, uncertain what he meant, I didn't know what to reply. All I could say was: 'But you've done such fine work.'

"'Ah, you don't understand! The king is suspicious and cruel. Now I've forged two swords the like of which have never been seen, he is bound to kill me to prevent my forging swords for any of his rivals who might oppose or surpass him.'

"I shed tears.

"'Don't grieve,' he said. 'There's no way out. Tears can't wash away fate. I've been prepared for this for some time. His eyes seemed to dart lightning as he placed a sheath on my knee. 'This is the male sword,' he told me. 'Keep it. Tomorrow I shall take the female to the king. If I don't come back, you'll know I'm dead. Won't you be brought to bed in four or five months? Don't grieve, but bear our child and bring him up well. As soon as he's grown, give him this sword and tell him to cut off the king's head to avenge me!'"

"Did my father come back that day?" demanded the boy.

"He did not," she replied calmly. "I asked everywhere, but there was no news of him. Later someone told me that the first to stain with his blood the sword forged by your father was your father himself. For fear his ghost should haunt the palace, they buried his body at the front gate, his head in the park at the back."

Mei Chien Chih felt as if he were on fire and sparks were flashing from every hair of his head. He clenched his fists in the dark till the knuckles cracked.

His mother stood up and lifted aside the board at the head of the bed. Then she lit a torch, took a hoe from behind the door and handed it to her son with the order:

"Dig!"

Though the lad's heart was pounding, he dug calmly, stroke after stroke. He scooped out yellow earth to a depth of over five feet, when the color changed to that of rotten wood.

"Look! Be careful now!" cried his mother.

Lying flat beside the hole he had made, he reached down gingerly to shift the rotted wood till the tips of his fingers touched something as cold as ice. It was the pure, transparent sword. He made out where the hilt was, grasped it, and lifted it out.

The moon and stars outside the window and the pine torch inside the room abruptly lost their brightness. The world was filled with a blue, steely light. And in this steely light the sword appeared to melt away and vanish from sight. But when the lad looked hard he saw something over three feet long which didn't seem particularly sharp — in fact the blade was rounded like a leek.

"You must stop being soft now," said his mother. "Take this sword to avenge your father!"

"I've already stopped being soft. With this sword I'll avenge him!"

"I hope so. Put on a blue coat and strap the sword to your back. No one will see it if they are the same color. I've got the coat ready here." His mother pointed to the shabby chest behind the bed. "You'll set out tomorrow. Don't worry about me.

Mei Chien Chih tried on the new coat and found that it fitted him perfectly. He wrapped it around the sword which he placed by his pillow, and calmly lay down again. He believed he had already stopped being soft. He determined to act as if nothing were on his mind, to fall straight asleep, to wake the next morning as usual, and then to set out confidently in search of his mortal foe.

However, he couldn't sleep. He tossed and turned, eager all the time to sit up. He heard his mother's long, soft, hopeless sighs. Then he heard the first crow of the cock and knew that a new day had dawned, that he was sixteen.

II

Mei Chien Chih, his eyelids swollen, left the house without once looking back. In the blue coat with the sword on his back, he strode swiftly towards the city. There was as yet no light in the east. The vapors of night still hid in the dew that clung to the tip of each fir leaf. But by the time he reached the far end of the forest, the dew drops were sparkling with lights which little by little took on the tints of dawn. Far ahead he could just see the outline of the dark grey, crenellated city walls.

Mingling with the vegetable vendors, he entered the city. The streets were already full of noise and bustle. Men stood about idly in groups. Every now and then women put their heads out from their doors. Most of their eyelids were swollen from sleep too, their hair was uncombed and their faces were pale because they had had no time to put on rouge.

Mei Chien Chih sensed that some great event was about to take place, something eagerly yet patiently awaited by all these people.

As he advanced, a child darted past, almost knocking into the point of the sword on his back. He broke into a cold sweat. Turning north not far from the palace, he found a press of people craning their necks towards the road. He heard the cries of women and children in the crowd. Afraid his invisible sword might hurt one of them, he dared not push his way forward; but new arrivals pressed him from behind. He had to move out of their way, till all he could see was the backs of those in front and their craning necks.

All of a sudden, the people in front fell one by one to their knees. In the distance appeared two riders galloping forward side by side. They were followed by warriors carrying batons, spears, swords, bows and flags, who raised a cloud of yellow dust. After them came a large cart drawn by four horses, bearing musicians sounding gongs and drums and blowing strange wind instruments. Behind were carriages with courtiers in bright clothes, old men or short, plump fellows, their faces glistening with sweat. These were followed by outriders armed with swords, spears and halberds. Then the kneeling people prostrated themselves and Mei Chien Chih saw a great carriage with a yellow canopy drive up. In the middle of this was seated a fat man in brightly colored clothes with a grizzled moustache and small head. He was wearing a sword like the one on the boy's back.

Mei Chien Chih gave an instinctive shudder, but at once he felt burning hot. Reaching out for the hilt of the sword on his back, he picked his way forward between the necks of the kneeling crowd.

But he had taken no more than five or six steps when someone tripped him and he fell headlong on top of a young fellow with a wizened face. He was getting up nervously to see whether the point of his sword had done any damage, when he received two hard punches in the ribs. Without stopping to protest he looked at the road. But the carriage with the yellow canopy had passed. Even the mounted attendants behind it were already some distance away.

On both sides of the road everyone got up again. The young man with the wizened face had seized Mei Chien Chih by the collar and would not let go. He accused him of crushing his solar plexus, and ordered the boy to pay with his own life if he died before the age of eighty. Idlers crowded round to gape but said nothing, till a few taking the side of the wizened youth let fall some jokes and curses. Mei Chien Chih could neither laugh at such adversaries nor lose his temper. Annoying as they were, he could not get rid of them. This went on for about the time it takes to cook a pan of millet. He was afire with impatience. Still the onlookers, watching as avidly as ever, refused to disperse.

Then through the throng pushed a dark man, lean as an iron rake, with a black beard and black eyes. Without a word, he smiled coldly at Mei Chien Chih, then raised his hand to flick the jaw of the youngster with the wizened face and looked steadily into his eyes. For a moment the youth returned his stare, then let go of the boy's collar and went off. The dark man went off too, and the disappointed spectators drifted away. A few came up to ask Mei Chien Chih his age and address, and whether he had sisters at home. But he ignored them.

He walked south, reflecting that in the bustling city it would be easy to wound someone by accident. He had better wait outside the South Gate for the king's return, to avenge his father. That open, deserted space was the best place for his purpose. By now the whole city was discussing the king's trip to the mountain. What a retinue! What majesty! What an honor to have seen the king! They had prostrated themselves so low that they should be considered as examples to all the nation! They buzzed like a swarm of bees. Near the South Gate, however, it became quieter.

Having left the city, he sat down under a big mulberry tree to eat two rolls of steamed bread. As he ate, the thought of his mother brought a lump to his throat, but presently that passed. All around grew quieter and quieter, until he could hear his own breathing quite distinctly.

As dusk fell, he grew more and more uneasy. He strained his eyes ahead, but there was not a sign of the king. The villagers who had taken vegetables to the city to sell were going home one by one with empty baskets.

Long after all these had gone, the dark man came darting out from the city.

"Run, Mei Chien Chih! The king is after you!" His voice was like the hoot of an owl.

Mei Chien Chih trembled from head to foot. Spellbound, he followed the dark man, running as if he had wings. At last, stopping to catch breath, he realized they had reached the edge of the fir wood. Far behind were the silver rays of the rising moon; but in front all he could see were the dark man's eyes gleaming like will-o'-the-wisps.

"How did you know me. . . ?" asked the lad in fearful amazement.

"I've always known you." The man laughed. "I know you carry the male sword on your back to avenge your father. And I know you will fail. Not only so, but today someone has informed against you. Your enemy went back to the palace by the East Gate and has issued an order for your arrest."

Mei Chien Chih began to despair.

"Oh, no wonder mother sighed," he muttered.

"But she knows only half. She doesn't know that I'm going to take vengeance for you."

"You? Are you willing to take vengeance for me, champion of justice?"

"Ah, don't insult me by giving me that title."

"Well, then, is it out of sympathy for widows and orphans?"

"Don't use words that have been sullied, child," he replied sternly. "Justice, sympathy and such terms, which once were clean, have now become capital for fiendish usurers. I have no place for these in my heart. I want only to avenge you!"

"Good. But how will you do it?"

"I want two things only from you." His voice sounded from beneath two burning eyes. "What two things? First your sword, then your head!"

Mei Chien Chih thought the request a strange one. But though he hesitated, he was not afraid. For a moment he was speechless.

"Don't be afraid that I want to trick you out of your life and your treasure," continued the implacable voice in the dark. "It's entirely up to you. If you trust me, I'll go; if not, I won't."

"But why are you going to take vengeance for me? Did you know my father?"

"I knew him from the start, just as I've always known you. But that's not the reason. You don't understand, my clever lad, how I excel at revenge. What's yours is mine, what concerns him concerns me too. I bear on my soul so many wounds inflicted by others as well as by myself, that now I hate myself."

The voice in the darkness was silent. Mei Chien Chih raised his hand to draw the blue sword from his back and with the same movement swung it forward from the nape of his neck. As his head fell on the green moss at his feet, he handed the sword to the dark man.

"Aha!" The man took the sword with one hand, with the other he picked up Mei Chien Chih's head by the hair. He kissed the warm dead lips twice and burst into cold, shrill laughter.

His laughter spread through the fir wood. At once, deep in the forest, flashed blazing eyes like the light of the will-o'the-wisp which the next instant came so close that you could hear the snuffling of famished wolves. With one bite, Mei Chien Chih's blue coat was torn to shreds; the next disposed of his whole body, while the blood was instantaneously licked clean. The only sound was the soft crunching of bones.

The huge wolf at the head of the pack hurled itself at the dark man. But with one sweep of the blue sword, its head fell on the green moss at his feet. With one bite the other wolves tore its skin to shreds, then next disposed of its whole body, while the blood was instantaneously licked clean. The only sound was the soft crunching of bones.

The dark man picked up the blue coat from the ground to wrap up Mei Chien Chih's head. Having fastened this and the blue sword on his back, he turned on his heel and swung off through the darkness towards the capital.

The wolves stood stock-still, hunched up, tongues lolling, panting. They watched him with green eyes as he strode away.

He swung through the darkness towards the capital, singing in a shrill voice as he went:

Sing hey, sing ho!
The single one who loved the sword
Has taken death as his reward.
Those who go single are galore,
Who love the sword are alone no more!
Foe for foe, ha! Head for head!
Two men by their own hands are dead.

III

*T*he king had taken no pleasure in his trip to the mountain, and the secret report of an assassin lying in wait on the road sent him back even more depressed. He was in a bad temper that night. He complained that not even the ninth concubine's hair was as black and glossy as the day before. Fortunately, perched kittenishly on the royal knee, she wriggled over seventy times till at last the wrinkles on the kingly brow were smoothed out.

But on rising after noon the next day the king was in a bad mood again. By the time lunch was over, he was furious.

"I'm bored!" he cried with a great yawn.

From the queen down to the court jester, all were thrown into a panic. The king had long since tired of his old ministers' sermons and the clowning of his plump dwarfs; recently he had even been finding insipid the marvelous tricks of rope-walkers, pole-climbers, jugglers, somersaulters, sword-swallowers and fire-spitters. He was given to bursts of rage, during which he would draw his sword to kill men on the slightest pretext.

Two eunuchs just back after playing truant from the palace, observing the gloom which reigned over the court, knew that dire trouble was impending again. One of them turned pale with fear. The other, however, quite confident, made his way unhurriedly to the king's presence to prostrate himself and announce:

"Your slave begs to inform you that he has just met a remarkable man with rare skill, who should be able to amuse Your Majesty."

"What?" The king was not one to waste words.

"He's a lean, dark fellow who looks like a beggar. He's dressed in blue, has a round blue bundle on his back and sings snatches of strange doggerel. When questioned, he says he can do a wonderful trick the like of which has never been seen, unique in the world and absolutely new. The sight will end all care and bring peace to the world. But when we asked for a demonstration, he wouldn't give one. He says he needs a golden dragon* and a golden cauldron. . . ."

"A golden dragon? That's me. A golden cauldron? I have one."

"That's just what your slave thought. . . ."

---

* The ancient Chinese emperors, to bolster their prestige, often called themselves dragons. The dragon in Chinese legend was divine.

"Bring him in!"

Before the king's voice had died away, four guards hurried out with the eunuch. From the queen down to the court jester, all beamed with delight, hoping this conjuror would end all care and bring peace to the world. Even if the show fell flat, there would be the lean, dark, beggarly-looking fellow to bear the brunt of the royal displeasure. If they could last till he was brought in, all would be well.

They did not have long to wait. Six men came hurrying towards the golden throne. The eunuch led the way, the four guards brought up the rear, and in the middle was a dark man. On nearer inspection they could see his blue coat, black beard, eyebrows and hair. He was so thin that his cheekbones stood out and his eyes were sunken. As he knelt respectfully to prostrate himself, they saw a small round bundle, wrapped in blue cloth patterned in a dark red, on his back.

"Well!" shouted the king impatiently. The simplicity of this fellow's paraphernalia did not augur well for his tricks.

"Your subject's name is Yen-chih-ao-che, born in Wenwen Village. I wasn't bred to any trade, but when I was grown I met a sage who taught me how to conjure with a boy's head. I can't do this alone, though. It must be in the presence of a golden dragon, and I must have a golden cauldron filled with clear water and heated with charcoal. Then when the boy's head is put in and the water boils, the head will rise and fall and dance all manner of figures. It will laugh and sing too in a marvelous voice. Whoever hears its song and sees its dance will know an end to care. When all men see it, the whole world will be at peace."

"Go ahead!" the king ordered loudly.

They did not have long to wait. A great golden cauldron, big enough to boil an ox, was set outside the court. It was filled with clear water, and charcoal was lit beneath it. The dark man stood at one side. When the charcoal was red he put down his bundle and undid it. Then with both hands he held up a boy's head with fine eyebrows, large eyes, white teeth and red lips. A smile was on its face. Its tangled hair was like faint blue smoke. The dark man raised it high, turning round to display it to the whole assembly. He held it over the cauldron while he muttered something unintelligible, and finally dropped it with a splash into the water. Foam flew up at least five feet high. Then all was still.

For a long time nothing happened. The king lost patience, the queen, concubines, ministers and eunuchs began to feel alarmed, while the plump dwarfs started to sneer. These sneers made the king suspect that he was being made to look a fool. He turned to the guards to order them to have this oaf, who dared deceive his monarch, thrown into the great cauldron and boiled to death.

But that very instant he heard the water bubbling. The fire burning with all its might cast a ruddy glow over the dark man, turning him the dull red of molten iron. The king looked round. The dark man, stretching both hands towards the sky, stared into space and danced, singing in a shrill voice:

Sing hey for love, for love heigh ho!
Ah, love! Ah, blood! Who is not so?
Men grope in the dark, the king laughs loud,
Ten thousand heads in death have bowed.
I only use one single head,
For one man's head let blood be shed!
Blood — let it flow!
Sing hey, sing ho!

As he sang, the water in the cauldron seethed up like a small cone-shaped mountain, flowing and eddying from tip to base. The head bobbed up and down with the water, skimming round and round, turning nimble somersaults as it went. They could just make out the smile of pleasure on its face. Then abruptly it gave this up to start swimming against the stream, circling, weaving to and fro, splashing water in all directions so that hot drops showered the court. One of the dwarfs gave a yelp and rubbed his nose. Scalded, he couldn't suppress a cry of pain.

The dark man stopped singing. The head remained motionless in the middle of the water, a grave expression on its face. After a few seconds, it began to bob up and down slowly again. From bobbing it put on speed to swim up and down, not quickly but with infinite grace. Three times it circled the cauldron, ducking up and down. Then, its eyes wide, the jet-black pupils phenomenally bright, it sang:

> *The sovereign's rule spreads far and wide,*
> *He conquers foes on every side.*
> *The world may end, but not his might,*
> *So here I come all gleaming bright.*
> *Bright gleams the sword — forget me not!*
> *A royal sight, but sad my lot.*
> *Sing hey, sing ho, a royal sight!*
> *Come back, where gleams the bright blue light.*

The head stopped suddenly at the crest of the water. After several somersaults, it started plying up and down again, casting bewitching glances to right and to left as it sang once more:

> *Heigh ho, for the love we know!*
> *I cut one head, one head, heigh ho!*
> *I use one single head, not more,*
> *The heads he uses are galore. . . !*

By the last line of the song the head was submerged, and since it did not reappear the singing became indistinct. As the song grew fainter, the seething water subsided little by little like an ebbing tide, until it was below the rim of the cauldron. From a distance nothing could be seen.

"Well?" demanded the king impatiently, tired of waiting.

"Your Majesty!" The dark man went down on one knee. "It's dancing the most miraculous Dance of Union at the bottom of the cauldron. You can't see this unless you come close. I can't make it come up, because this Dance of Union has to be performed at the bottom of the cauldron."

The king stood up and strode down the steps to the cauldron. Regardless of the heat, he bent forward to watch. The water was as smooth as a mirror. The head, lying there motionless, looked up and fixed its eyes on the king. When the king's glance fell on its face, it gave a charming smile. This smile made the king feel that they had met before. Who could this be? While he wondered, the dark man drew the blue sword from his back and swept it forward like lightning from the nape of the king's neck. The king's head fell with a splash into the cauldron.

When enemies meet they know each other at a glance, particularly at close quarters. The moment the king's head touched the water, Mei Chien Chih's head came up to meet it and savagely bit its ear. The water in the cauldron boiled and bubbled as the two heads engaged upon a fight to the death. After about twenty encounters, the king was wounded in five places, Mei Chien Chih in seven. The crafty king contrived to slip behind his enemy, and in an unguarded moment Mei Chien Chih let himself be caught by the back of his neck, so that he could not turn round. The king fastened his teeth into him and would not let go, like a silkworm burrowing into a mulberry leaf. The boy's cries of pain could be heard outside the cauldron.

From the queen down to the court jester, all who had been petrified with fright before were galvanized into life by this sound. They felt as if the sun had been swallowed up in darkness. But even as they trembled, they knew a secret joy. They waited, round-eyed.

The dark man, rather taken aback, did not change color. Effortlessly he raised his arm like a withered branch holding the invisible sword. He stretched forward as if to peer into the cauldron. Of a sudden his arm bent, the blue sword thrust down and his head fell into the cauldron with a plop, sending snow-white foam flying in all directions.

As soon as his head hit the water, it charged at the king's head and took the royal nose between its teeth, nearly biting it off. The king gave a cry of pain and Mei Chien Chih seized this chance to get away, whirling round to cling with a vicelike grip to his jaw. They pulled with all their might in opposite directions, so that the king could not keep his mouth shut. Then they fell on him savagely, like famished hens pecking at rice, till the king's head was mauled and savaged out of all recognition. To begin with he lashed about frantically in the cauldron; then he simply lay there groaning; and finally he fell silent, having breathed his last.

Presently the dark man and Mei Chien Chih stopped biting. They left the king's head and swam once round the edge of the cauldron to see whether their enemy was shamming or not. Assured that the king was indeed dead, they exchanged glances and smiled. Then, closing their eyes, their faces towards the sky, they sank to the bottom of the water.

IV

*T*he smoke drifted away, the fire went out. Not a ripple remained on the water. The extraordinary silence brought high and low to their senses. Someone gave a cry, and at once all called out together in horror. Someone walked over to the golden cauldron, and the others pressed after him. Those crowded at the back could only peer between the necks of those in front.

The heat still scorched their cheeks. The water, now as smooth as a mirror, was coated with oil which reflected a sea of faces: the queen, the concubines, guards, old ministers, dwarfs, eunuchs. . . .

"Heavens! Our king's head is still in there! Oh, horrors!" The sixth concubine suddenly burst into frantic sobbing.

From the queen down to the court jester, all were seized by consternation. They scattered in panic, at a loss, running round in circles. The wisest old councilor went forward alone and put out a hand to touch the side of the cauldron. He winced, snatched back his hand and put two fingers to his mouth to blow on them.

Finally regaining control, they gathered outside the palace to discuss how best to recover the king's head. They consulted for the time it would take to cook three pans of millet. Their conclusion was: collect wire scoops from the big kitchen, and order the guards to do their best to retrieve the royal head.

Soon the implements were ready:

wire scoops, strainers, golden plates and dusters were all placed by the cauldron. The guards rolled up their sleeves. Some with wire scoops, some with strainers, respectfully they set about bringing up the remains. The scoops clashed against each other and scraped the edge of the cauldron, while the water eddied in their wake. After some time, one of the guards, with a grave face, raised his scoop slowly and carefully in both hands. Drops of water like pearls were dripping from the utensil, in which lay a snow-white skull. As the others cried out with astonishment, he deposited the skull on one golden plate.

"Oh, dear! Our king!" The queen, concubines, ministers and even the eunuchs burst out sobbing. They soon stopped, however, when another guard fished out another skull identical with the first.

They watched dully with tear-filled eyes as the sweating guards went on with their salvaging. They retrieved a tangled mass of white hair and black hair, and several spoonfuls of some shorter hair no doubt from white and black moustaches. Then another skull. Then three hairpins.

They stopped only when nothing but clear soup was left in the cauldron, and divided what they had on to three golden plates: one of skulls, one of hair, one of hairpins.

"His Majesty had only one head, Which is his?" demanded the ninth concubine frantically.

"Quite so. . . ." The ministers looked at each other in dismay.

"If the skin and flesh hadn't boiled away, it would be easy to tell," remarked one kneeling dwarf.

They forced themselves to examine the skulls carefully, but the size and color were about the same. They could not even distinguish which was the boy's. The queen said the king had a scar on his right temple as the result of a fall while still crown prince, and this might have left a trace on the skull. Sure enough, a dwarf discovered such a mark on one skull, and there was general rejoicing until another dwarf discovered a similar mark on the right temple of a slightly yellower skull.

"I know!" exclaimed the third concubine happily. "Our king had a very high nose."

The eunuchs hastened to examine the noses. To be sure, one of them was relatively high, though there wasn't much to choose between them; but unfortunately that particular skull had no mark on the right temple.

"Besides," said the ministers to the eunuchs, "was the back of His Majesty's skull so protuberant?"

"We never paid any attention to the back of His Majesty's skull. . . ."

The queen and the concubines searched their memories. Some said it had been protuberant, some flat. When they questioned the eunuch who had combed the royal hair, he would not commit himself to an answer.

That evening a council of princes and ministers was held to determine which head was the king's, but with no better result than during the day. In fact, even the hair and moustaches presented a problem. The white was of course the king's, but since he had been grizzled it was very hard to decide about the black. After half a night's discussion, they had just eliminated a few red hairs when the ninth concubine protested. She was sure she had seen a few brown hairs in the king's moustache; in which case how could they be sure there was not a single red one? They had to put them all together again and leave the case unsettled.

By the early hours of the morning they had reached no solution. They prolonged the discussion yawning, till the cock crowed a second time, before fixing on a safe and satisfactory solution: All three heads should be placed in the golden coffin beside the king's body for interment.

The funeral took place a week later. The whole city was agog. Citizens of the capital and spectators from far away flocked to the royal funeral. As soon as it was light, the road was thronged with men and women. Sandwiched in between were tables bearing sacrificial offerings. Shortly before midday horsemen cantered out to clear the roads. Some time later came a procession of flags, batons, spears, bows, halberds and the like, followed by four cartloads of musicians. Then, rising and falling with the uneven ground, a yellow canopy drew near. It was possible to make out the hearse with the golden coffin in which lay three heads and one body.

The people knelt down, revealing rows of tables with offerings. Some loyal subjects gulped back tears of rage to think that the spirits of the two regicides were enjoying the sacrifice now together with the king. But there was nothing they could do about it.

Then followed the carriages of the queen and concubines. The crowd stared at them and they stared at the crowd, not stopping their wailing. After them came the ministers, eunuchs and dwarfs, all of whom assumed a mournful air. But no one paid the least attention to them, and their ranks were squeezed out of all semblance of order.

October 1926

Printed in the United States
57898LVS00008B/85

9 780809 594092